IN DEEP WATER

INSPECTOR JIM CARRUTHERS - BOOK 5

TANA COLLINS

BLOODHOUND
— BOOKS —

Print ISBN 978-1-913419-74-5

ALSO BY TANA COLLINS

This book is dedicated to two wonderful women. Jackie McLean, who originally came up with the idea of a day trip to the Isle of May. Without you, this book would never have been written. You have become a great friend and your support has been invaluable. And Jacky Collins whose encouragement and enthusiasm for this series, and for the work of all crime fiction writers, has been and continues to be incredible. Love you both.

PROLOGUE

Tom Ramsey lies on his back on a grassy verge. As he stares up at the blue sky, frothy bubbles of blood run down the side of his mouth. The noise of the seabirds all around him are deafening as the deep guttural grunts of the cormorants compete with the cooing of the guillemots. The sky is a swirling black mass of birds, the hysterical cries growing louder and louder as they constantly launch themselves from the rocks.

He feels the sharp painful cuts of his wounds. His body is cold, so cold, and he shivers. The slim yellow bill and the dark eye of a kittiwake come into view as it flies low over his body and lands on a rock. The high nasal sound of the gull mocks him as he lies, body battered; clothes ripped to shreds.

Above the cry of the seabirds Tom hears the boat being dragged to the water's edge. He tries to call out as the chug of the motorboat roars into life but he knows that with every passing second his assailant is putting more and more distance between them until the boat will be so far out in the Firth of Forth that the small island will be no more than a distant speck. At that moment Tom realises he has been left to die alone with only the company of 150,000 birds. His last thought is the hope that the engine revs from the boat won't frighten the nesting seabirds.

1

D I Jim Carruthers sighed as he switched on his computer. Unless something more interesting came in, it was going to be another day of organising role profiles and training courses. Not his favourite type of work. His phone rang. He placed his glasses on top of his greying head and took the call.

'Jim.' The voice was that of DC Willie Brown. Carruthers wondered what the older balding police officer with the comb-over wanted. 'We've just had a call from a woman in Anstruther. She wants to report her husband missing.'

Carruthers picked up a pen and a piece of paper. It crossed his mind that, living in the same wee coastal village, he might know the man. 'Name?'

'Robert Paterson. He's sixty-two and is a local fisherman.'

Carruthers' heart lurched. He did know the man. 'How long's he been missing?'

'About three hours. He took his boat out at first light. He was expected back about seven this morning but hasn't turned up. His wife has been trying to raise him but there's been no contact. She's worried sick.'

Carruthers didn't know Paterson well, admittedly, but he'd

3

shared a few pints with some of the fishermen, including Robbie, from time to time, in the newly reopened Dreel Tavern. Alarm bells were already ringing as they would for any missing fisherman. 'Okay, we'd better notify the coastguard and let's get an appeal out. We'll need to circulate a description. Any idea what he was wearing?'

'His wife said what he always wears. Orange oilskins and yellow wellington boots.'

Carruthers put the phone down and sat in pensive thought for a few moments. The last time he had seen Robert Paterson the man had been mending his creels down by the harbour.

DS Andrea Fletcher walked into the office carrying two coffees. She placed one on Carruthers' desk. She must have seen his anxious look. 'What's up? Everything okay?'

Carruthers glanced up at his younger colleague, frown still in evidence. 'I'm not sure. Call's just come through. Fisherman's gone missing. Robert Paterson. He went out in his boat at first light and hasn't come home. I know him. He lives in Anstruther.'

Fletcher put one hand on Carruthers' desk and leant into him as she talked. 'If he's had an accident it won't be due to bad weather. There hasn't been a breath of air. No fog either, although I've got to say, I think the weather's on the turn.'

'That's not what's worrying me.'

Fletcher raised an eyebrow.

Carruthers picked up his coffee while he made eye contact with Fletcher. 'I want to know what he was doing taking his boat out at first light. That's about half four at the moment.'

'How do you mean?'

'The local fishermen go after lobster and you don't fish for lobster at night.' He stood up, gathering his paperwork and the coffee Fletcher had given him and sighed. 'I'd better let Sandra know.'

Carruthers knocked on DCI Sandra McTavish's door. He hesitated for a moment before walking in.

The attractive black-haired woman in her mid-forties looked up at her DI over the reading glasses perched on the end of her nose. As ever she was smartly dressed wearing a cream silk shirt tucked into a navy blue skirt. 'What is it, Jim?'

'Local fisherman's gone missing from Anstruther, Sandra. Thought you should know.'

McTavish put down the report she had been reading. 'Give me the details.'

'Robert Paterson, sixty-two. He should have been back at about seven, according to his wife, but his boat's not returned to harbour. She called it in. She's very worried about him.' As he spoke he couldn't help but notice his DCI's paperwork was stacked away in various trays; her desk bare except for her phone, computer, a family photograph and the report. When he'd been a DCI using that same office it had never looked like that. His paperwork had been so overflowing that quite often he'd had to put piles on the floor, much to the disgust of their superintendent.

McTavish steepled her hands. 'I pity the wife. More than likely she's keeping a quayside vigil. How long did you say he's been missing?'

'About three hours.'

McTavish was unsmiling. Clearly she was as worried as Carruthers. 'And there's been no sightings of his boat?'

'None so far.'

'There's still hope. He's only been missing three hours.'

Carruthers frowned. 'I know Robert Paterson and I'm wondering what he was doing taking the boat out at night at all. He fishes for lobster.'

McTavish made an exasperated noise. 'Jim, I'm not a fisherman. What's your point?'

'They wouldn't take their boats out at night. They would go out during the day.'

'Could he not have gone fishing for something else?'

Could he? Carruthers usually switched off when the boys in the pub talked about fishing.

McTavish looked at her watch. 'Jim, can I leave this to you? I've got a meeting with Superintendent Bingham in five.' Her face lightened. 'Try not to worry.'

But Carruthers *was* worried. DCI Sandra McTavish was a townie, originally from Glasgow, like himself. He calculated that at this time of year the water's temperature was about ten or eleven degrees. Someone in the water, if they had gone overboard, could only survive for a couple of hours. Mind you, it would also depend on how many layers of clothing they were wearing and the state of their general health. He dragged his mind back to what his DCI was saying.

She tucked a stray tendril of dark hair behind an ear. 'You'll need to liaise with the coastguard.'

'Right, will do.' Carruthers turned to go. The voice of his DCI called him back.

'Oh, Jim, I thought you'd want to know. Superintendent Bingham is taking early retirement. We need to get something organised for his send-off.'

He couldn't help himself. 'You want me to get the party hats and streamers?' It was good to get his mind off the fisherman for a moment.

McTavish gave the most unladylike snort of laughter before her face broke into a smile that made her look ten years younger. Carruthers grinned back. Neither of them had much time for Bingham who, it seemed, had been marking time until his retirement for a good few years now.

'Do you know who's replacing him?'

'Not yet.' McTavish's face suddenly became serious. 'Before you go, Jim, how's Gayle? I'm sure the death will hit her hard. Funeral's tomorrow, isn't it?'

Carruthers nodded, visualising one of their newer recruits, DS Gayle Watson. She had become such a fixture around the police station and had a dress style all of her own, favouring men's suits and colourful ties, which she pulled off beautifully. It had come as a shock to the whole station when she told them that her niece had died from a drug overdose.

'Keep an eye on her, will you?'

Carruthers did a mock salute and closed the door quietly behind him. He sighed. Last week Gayle Watson's seventeen-year-old niece had been busy looking forward to her beauty therapy course at Fife College. Now she was dead. He thought of her grieving family and wondered if there would be yet more grief still to come in the East Neuk of Fife. More than likely Robert Paterson's wife would be keeping a lonely vigil down at the quayside for her fisherman husband. He could visualise the woman in her sixties dressed in her purple coat and headscarf muffled up against the morning cold. He hoped, wherever the fisherman was and whatever had happened to him, that Paterson was still alive.

Caroline Young positioned her petite frame at the back of the boat next to a young couple. She looked up over the sea of faces. *There must be close to a hundred on board.* She had deliberately chosen a seat open to the elements despite the light drizzle. Her curly auburn hair was tied up in a ponytail away from her heart-shaped face. She wasn't a great traveller and had heard that seasickness could be prevented by being out in the fresh sea air.

I'd rather be wet than sick, she thought, watching the colour drain from some of the other passengers as they turned the unflattering colour of putty.

She had been looking forward to her first day trip to the Isle of May, the tiny island that was six miles off Anstruther out in the Firth of Forth, but now, as she gripped the sides of the boat tighter and took some deep breaths, she was just trying to focus on not throwing up. The swell on the sea surprised her. The sea had been calm when they had boarded with no more than a light breeze. The night before she had been strolling down by the picturesque harbour, looking out at the clear sky and the stars, thankful that the sea was calm for their trip the day after. However, as soon as they were out of the harbour the swell became apparent and there was a collective gasp as it hit the boat full on and a combination of sea spray and light rain soon soaked the passengers who chose to sit outdoors.

'Try no' to look down. Keep yer heid up. You'll feel better.' The weather-beaten skipper who had introduced himself as Scott Gardner deftly navigated his way between rows of passengers to get to Caroline.

'Focus on something on the horizon,' he shouted, encouragingly. Another swell hit the boat and even he lurched towards a Japanese family; a fellow passenger grabbing his arm and steadying him before he lost his balance completely and crashed into them. The good-natured skipper with the ruddy face looked up and smiled at Caroline. She felt reassured by his presence. 'Try no' to look doon,' he repeated. His voice was louder as he drew close, the concern in it obvious. 'Have ye been sick yet?'

Caroline could only shake her head in response as the skipper thrust a blue sick bag in her direction. Caroline lifted her head and glanced around her. Several of the passengers were now clutching sick bags, which had been distributed by the crew. She stared into the bottom of her own. Something told her the crew were well used to handing them out. Perhaps this crossing was known to be rough? She chastised herself for not doing more research before making the booking.

The skipper looked around him, making conversation with some of the passengers well enough to talk. 'If you dinnae use your sick bag for being sick in, you have a 5p bag for nothing. You could put your sandwiches in there.' He beamed. Caroline had the feeling it wasn't the first time he had cracked that particular joke.

At the mention of food another wave of nausea came over her. Caroline raised her head just as the skipper had suggested and tried to focus on a point on the horizon where the sea met the sky.

'Would it help to have a seasickness tablet? I brought extra.' The accented voice came from the female passenger to her left who was offering her a packet of Kwells. Caroline glanced over and tried to smile at the younger woman who was dressed from head to toe in waterproof trousers and bright pink Gore-Tex jacket. German perhaps? *She's come prepared.* She felt a moment of irritation with herself as she glanced down at her jeans, the flared bottoms of which were already wet from water that was running up and down the boat. *Why the heck didn't I bring my waterproof trousers? Or seasickness tablets?*

'Oh yes, thank you.' Caroline tasted salt on her lips as she took a tablet out of the blister pack, fumbled around in her rucksack for a bottle of water, which was on the seat next to her, unscrewed the lid while all the time trying to focus ahead of her. She took a long gulp of the ice-cold liquid, glad it had been refrigerated in preparation for her trip. As soon as she gave the packet of Kwells back to the kind woman the German lady resumed speaking in her native tongue to her partner.

Once more Caroline focused ahead on the horizon taking in

deep breaths of salty air as she did so. She tried to ignore the rising swell of the waves and focused her mind on the puffins she was looking forward to seeing on the island instead. She zoned out the passengers who were still being sick and daydreamed about the birds on the island. This seemed to help and Caroline lost track of time as they cut through the water. Before she knew it forty-odd minutes had gone by.

Suddenly a shout went up. 'There it is. The Isle of May.'

Out of nowhere the dark silhouette of the tiny island rose from the sea like a fortress. Caroline felt her heart pounding with excitement. Another wave hit the boat and her nostrils were filled with salty sea spray. As it was buffeted once more, Caroline held on to the side with wet hands for dear life. She was grateful they would soon disembark.

'As you know, the Isle of May, which is coming into view, is just short of six miles off Anstruther.' The voice of the skipper, who had been making his way through the passengers distributing seasickness bags earlier, was now resuming his guiding skills using his megaphone. 'You've chosen the perfect time to visit the island as you're going to see the cliffs heaving with nesting birds.

'And for those who haven't visited the island before you may be interested to know that it also has a rich and interesting history with monks, Vikings and smugglers all having been visitors. And, for those especially interested in Scottish history in 1715, a group of 300 Jacobite soldiers were marooned here for a week without food or drink. They were finally rescued in a flotilla of small boats.'

Caroline imagined the flotilla of small boats rescuing the stranded soldiers. She thought of what sort of shape they would be in after a week with no food or water. Bloody desperate, she suspected. She got the shakes after a few hours with no food. As if to echo her thoughts the skipper started to talk about food.

'We'll be on the island for about three hours. Hopefully you'll have brought something to eat, as there are no facilities other than toilets on the May. If not, we have snacks and drinks on board the boat for you to purchase but we don't extend to fresh sandwiches I'm afraid.' He looked across at the island.

'The island, which is now a nature reserve, is looked after by Scottish Natural Heritage so if you want to make a complaint about the lack of amenities on the island make it to them.' Caroline suspected this was another joke as a few of the passengers smiled.

As another wave broke over the boat Caroline pulled her rucksack closer to her. It was wet; she only hoped her lunch within it was dry. At least she'd brought some food with her. She'd forgotten to bring just about everything else. She was starting to feel cold and wished she had put on another layer. The German couple pointed out to something at sea and Caroline, glad to have a distraction, focused on the object they were looking at. At first she thought they had spotted the huge tapered body of a gannet, which was flying over the boat but the bird passed and they kept pointing. Caroline frowned and against her better judgement turned her head further sideways so she too could see what had captured their attention. When she saw what was bobbing in the water she gasped. There in the swell of the sea was a small green and white fishing boat. She could just make out the words, *Maid of the Mist*. In alarm she looked into the churning water for any sign of life but there was nothing else there.

The skipper also caught sight of it. He shouted out an instruction. The boat's engine was killed.

'Ahoy there! Robbie!'

There was no response. The skipper bellowed into the megaphone once more, 'Robbie, this is the skipper of the *May Princess*.'

Nothing but silence.

The skipper of the *May Princess* turned to his crewmate. 'Lofty.' The yell was deafening. A lanky, dark-haired youth who had earlier been talking to an attractive blonde-haired woman carrying a backpack, binoculars slung lazily round her neck, stopped staring into the churning water and snapped his head up. 'Lofty!' The yell almost split Caroline's eardrum.

'Skipper?'

'Get on to the coastguard. I've just come across the *Maid of the Mist*. No sign of Robbie.'

Lofty didn't need to be told twice. He said something brief to his female companion then scuttled into the cabin, presumably to put the call through.

Caroline stared at the small empty fishing boat as it bobbed up and down. Her alarm turned to fear as she stared at the choppy water. Caroline looked up at the skipper; his earlier smile replaced with a frown and a look of unease. *Of course they would all know each other,* she thought. *The community will be small and close-knit.* Knowing the name of the fisherman, whose empty boat they had discovered somehow made it more personal. She wondered how long Robbie could survive in the water. She felt sick again but this time for a completely different reason.

Lofty made his way to the skipper who was in hearing distance of Caroline. Even the boy now looked worried. 'Skip, just spoke with the coastguard. Robbie's been reported missing.'

'Aw shit.' There was a hurried conversation between the members of the crew.

The German woman, who had earlier handed Caroline the seasickness pills, leant into her. 'Are you feeling a bit better?' She pointed at the boat. 'Isn't it awful? I wonder what's happened.'

Caroline nodded. Her focus was still on the bobbing boat, which was now being forced by the waves further away from the

May Princess. There was something eerie about its abandonment. She tried to focus on her breathing and not feel fear. Her hands felt wet and numb and she was losing feeling in her fingers. She rubbed them. She started to shake, wondering if it was the cold or whether it was a reaction to the real-life drama being played out in front of them.

The skipper talked to the coastguard on his two-way radio. 'Right you are,' he said.

The German woman leant in closer. 'I wonder if our boat will turn back?' Her partner talked to her in rapid German. She leant in closer to Caroline. 'Detlef doesn't think so. He thinks we'll continue with the journey. The fisherman might have swum ashore. We may be the closest boat to the island and we can get there much faster than the coastguard.'

Caroline nodded.

'My name is Bettina by the way.'

Caroline muttered her own name thinking how absurd it was to be exchanging pleasantries while there could be a man drowning or already dead somewhere close. However, it was reassuring having the chatty Germans sitting next to her.

They might be first to find the battered body of the unfortunate fisherman if he'd been washed up on the island. Her vision turned once more to the choppy water. She couldn't imagine anyone staying alive for long in that sea.

She had been looking forward to a day of adventure but, what with the seasickness and the find of the empty fishing boat, she was getting more than she bargained for and was starting to wish she hadn't booked to come on this trip at all.

2

Middle-aged DS Dougie Harris leant over Carruthers' desk, his paunch resting on the DI's paperwork. 'Aberdeen coastguard's been alerted. If Paterson's still alive we'll find him.' He clamped a large hand awkwardly on Carruthers' shoulder. News must have already gone round the station that the DI knew the fisherman.

Carruthers nodded. He thought of the rugged, bearded man with his brightly coloured sixteen-foot creel boat. He knew Paterson usually went out fishing alone, although his boat could crew two. His thoughts turned to Scott Gardner, the skipper of the *May Princess*, whose job it was to radio into the Aberdeen coastguard on a daily basis. Gardner had been a fisherman up in Aberdeen before he'd become skipper of the *May Princess*. The man's skill and experience with the Scottish fishing community reassured the policeman.

'He's a popular figure in the community. Reckon there'll be several fishermen wanting to assist.' Carruthers realised Harris wasn't talking about Scott Gardner but Robbie Paterson and as Harris spoke Carruthers thought of the flotilla of bright little fishing vessels that would, very soon, be leaving the various harbours in the picturesque East Neuk of Fife in their desperate search for the missing fisherman.

The sound of his phone ringing brought him back to the present. He picked it up. It was the voice of his DCI. 'Jim, I want you to assist in a drugs bust at a property in Glenrothes. Liaise with the NCA as soon as you can, will you? I now gather the raid's being brought forward and is going to be carried out the day after tomorrow.'

The DI scratched his clean-shaven chin. Drugs were an ever-present problem in Scotland, like the rest of the UK, and where there were drugs there was always crime. Carruthers sighed. Every time they put away a major drugs gang another one moved into their patch. They worked closely with the NCA or National Crime Agency, but drug enforcement was an ongoing battle.

His DCI's voice was curt. Carruthers sensed the frustration. He didn't blame her.

'I don't like the way these gangs are starting to get a stranglehold in this area. At the very least it makes us look bad.' She sighed again. 'For God's sake it's now quicker to get class A drugs delivered than a pizza. And as for that used needle found in the kiddie's playground in Anstruther...' She swore.

Carruthers had hardly ever heard her swear before but then McTavish had children of her own and could clearly empathise with the anger and worry of local parents. He was starting to see their new DCI was every bit as passionate about the job as he was. He knew she stayed late after everyone else had gone home. He'd seen her light on under the door. He just worried about what effect that was having on her home life.

As someone who lived in Anstruther he knew how concerned the local community was about the spiralling drug problem. As well as finding used needles there'd also been a spate of drug-related deaths recently in Fife. Carruthers still couldn't believe that Gayle Watson's niece had been one of them.

A few weeks ago he'd sent their newest recruit, Helen Lennox, to a meeting to talk to residents and advise them on what to do if they discovered used needles. Little had he known that three weeks later he'd be consoling one of the station's own officers. A sadness coursed through him that cut his heart like a knife.

He wondered what it was going to take to stop the flood of cocaine, heroin and the other illegal drugs that were coming into Fife and triggering violence on Scotland's streets, not to mention giving birth to a whole new generation of addicts.

Carruthers dragged his mind back to the phone call.

'Anyway, as I said, you're going to need to liaise with the NCA. I'd like you to get on to that straight away.'

Carruthers stared at the paperwork on his desk. Having been the station's DCI before his demotion he still found it difficult taking instruction, even though he was making a concerted effort. His demotion still hurt and the fact it had been all his own fault just made it worse.

He forced the words out. 'What about the training courses and the role profiles you wanted?'

'That still needs to be done, Jim.'

Carruthers let out a puff of air, which McTavish clearly heard.

'It's not ideal.' She clearly knew what he was thinking. 'These cuts are affecting us all. We're all under pressure. We just have to do the best we can. Delegate if you must. Any news on the missing fisherman?'

'Not yet.'

Carruthers heard the warning in her voice. 'Don't get overly involved, although I know it's hard. You're needed here. Let the coastguard and RNLI deal with it. That's their job and they do it well.'

Don't get overly involved? Easy to say. Not easy to do when you know the missing person.

Carruthers tried to push the disappearance of Robert Paterson out of his mind and phoned the National Crime Agency to get more information about the forthcoming raid. They were still finalising the details.

There'd been a good deal of intelligence amassed and following this, surveillance on several properties across Fife for a while. Intelligence from the NCA had it that a significant amount of drugs were in two particular properties in Glenrothes, owned by the same people. The suspicion was that they were no two-bit players but rather a powerful drugs gang who had moved into the area.

He started tapping his pen on the table. If the haul of class A drugs could be recovered before they were distributed then it would be a massive feather in the cap for all involved, not to mention making the streets a safer place. And it would do his career no harm at all.

His eyes settled on Watson who was making a call from her desk. His heart went out to her. He could see the effort she had made to carry on as normal. Today she sported a sky blue shirt, dark grey waistcoat and black tie with blue embroidered flowers. However, he could also see the tiredness etched in her flat eyes in a face unusually pale. He wondered which scumbag had supplied her niece with the fatal dose of the drug that had killed her. For every drug death in Scotland there were family and friends out there who would be devastated. The ripple effect was huge. He hoped Gayle's family was coping.

The bulky form of Harris approached Carruthers' desk. The DS was red-faced as if he'd been hurrying and he looked troubled. 'We've just had a call come in from the *May Princess*.'

Carruthers put down his pen. His heart lurched. *Had the May Princess come across the body of Robert Paterson?*

He saw the look of sympathy in the older man's eyes and even before the DS spoke further he already knew the news wasn't going to be good.

'I'm sorry, Jim. They've come across an empty fishing boat.'

'Empty?' With a sinking heart Carruthers took a swig of his now cold coffee. He grimaced at its bitter taste. He felt he needed something to fortify himself before Harris imparted any more bad news but he could do with something stronger than coffee. Today was shaping up to be a bad one. 'Any further details?' It was most likely Robert Paterson's boat. *Was the body of the man already lying on the seabed?*

Harris flicked open his little black notebook. 'Boat called the *Maid of the Mist*.' He flicked it shut.

'It's the boat belonging to Paterson,' said Carruthers. Once again he pictured the little boat with the green hull and white roof flying the Saltire flag. *Shit*, Carruthers thought quickly. 'Where's it been found?'

'Less than a half-mile off the Isle of May.'

Carruthers glanced at his watch. He knew at this time of year the *May Princess* would be packed with passengers all eager for their day trip to see the birds on the uninhabited island. *So the fishing vessel had been discovered but not the skipper. Where was the missing fisherman?*

Once more his thoughts turned to what DS Andrea Fletcher had said about how still the wind had been the night before.

And she'd been right. There'd also been no fog. And early morning had been beautiful. Not a cloud in the sky until this weather front had come in. He stared out of the window at the streaks of rain coursing down the glass. He remembered the fog had been a major factor in another fatal fishing accident in Scotland a few months back. Of course it was still possible to have an accident and tumble overboard in good weather but even so...

He couldn't imagine the weather being a factor in the man's disappearance and he knew Robert Paterson was a seasoned fisherman of forty years' experience. His first thought was that the old boy must have had an accident. He could have tripped over some of his fishing gear or slipped and fallen overboard. It happened. But Carruthers kept coming back to the same question. If lobster fishermen fished during the day, why had Robert Paterson taken his boat out at night? He needed to speak with the fishing community to see if they could shed any light on this anomaly.

He looked at Fletcher. 'Okay, so what have the coastguard said?'

'The *May Princess* has been told to continue with their journey. The body might have washed up on the island. It's not ideal, with a boatload of sightseers, especially if there are kids on board, but they're the closest. They're sending the lifeboat out, but the *May Princess* will still get there first.'

Carruthers thought quickly. 'He might still be alive. The crew of the *May Princess* can do a sweep of the shore. And half the passengers will have binoculars.' *Sometimes it was useful having a boat full of anoraks.* He could imagine the boat packed with earnest eagle-eyed birdwatchers some of whom would have the latest high-tech gear and top-of-the-range binoculars. 'I–'

'You talking about that missing fisherman?' The young

spiky-haired Helen Lennox, who was passing by, stopped. She leant into Carruthers' desk putting her hands on his table. 'He may be nowhere near the island. Aren't they sending a helicopter?'

Carruthers felt a stab of irritation. *She doesn't behave like a young detective constable, more like an overbearing DCI, and the way she just butted into the conversation is really annoying.* But, he conceded, *you can't fault her keenness.*

'I mean, the wind could have taken him further out to sea. He could be in the North Sea by now,' Lennox continued.

The steel-haired cop glanced at the younger woman's lively face. 'It's possible he's not on the shoreline of the island, Helen, but the truth is that if there's any chance Robbie Paterson is still alive and has been washed up on the rocks there, someone needs to get to him as soon as possible. We don't know what sort of state he'll be in.' Carruthers knew that with anybody in the water, especially the water in the cold Firth of Forth, time was very much of the essence. However, he also knew that the Isle of May lay just where the Firth of Forth began to turn into the North Sea. Lennox was right. Paterson could easily have ended up out in the North Sea. Carruthers' heart sank at the thought.

'How long could he survive if he'd fallen into the sea?'

He was so deep in thought that it was a moment before he realised that Helen Lennox was still talking. *That's what we're all wondering,* he thought. 'It depends on a variety of things – the temperature of the water and what he was wearing for starters,' said Carruthers. 'What do you reckon the temperature is at the moment? About ten or eleven degrees?'

Lennox nodded.

'Reckon he'd survive a couple of hours max,' said DC Willie Brown, who had just appeared behind them. The middle-aged man grasped his wallet.

'We'll just have to hope he reached the shore somewhere,

then. And that he's wearing a lot of layers under his oilskins.' *If the passengers on the* May Princess *did come across the body of the missing fisherman that would definitely be a trip to the Isle of May none of them would ever forget. And all for the wrong reasons.*

'Just heading to the canteen. Anyone want anything?' said Brown, patting his comb-over. They all declined and Brown sauntered off to get his morning bacon sarnie.

Carruthers looked over at Fletcher wondering just what had happened to Robert Paterson, that his boat was floating on its own without its skipper in the middle of the Firth of Forth. Another image came into his head of Paterson propping up the bar in the Dreel Tavern, laughing and joking with friends, his face ruddy and shining with the heat of the pub. The grey-haired cop felt a lump in this throat. He was finding it hard to remain professional. He gave himself a momentary talking to. None of this reminiscing was helping Robbie. What was needed was a plan of action.

'Andie, find out who's on the island just now. There'll be the resident warden staying on site. I can't mind his name. Get him to start a search of the island's beaches before the *May Princess* lands. Perhaps Paterson's had an accident and fallen overboard. You're looking for anywhere he could have drifted in. He might have been washed up on rocks.' As he said it he thought of the many caves, coves and small beaches that were a feature of the island.

Fletcher nodded. 'I've already put a call through to the land-line in the warden's accommodation. There was no answer.' She paused. 'I'll ring Scottish Natural Heritage and see if they have a mobile for him. I'll also look up the sailing times for the *May Princess.* Every day's a different sailing time as they're dictated by the tide. If I get the sailing time I can find out how close they are.'

Carruthers supposed the skipper of the *May Princess* might

have already contacted the warden but there was no harm in the police doing it too. The island was only just under two kilometres long and less than half a kilometre wide and now had no permanent residents, being a nature reserve. He hoped to God the fisherman was still alive.

3

Carruthers then made a call to the National Crime Agency. Perhaps they would now have the details he needed. He was looking forward to getting out from behind his desk and being actively involved in the forthcoming drugs bust. But he also knew that effective policing was more than just about jumping on drug dealers. The operation needed to be part of a much wider strategy. 'Targeted intelligence' is what McTavish called it.

'Gus, what can you tell me about the drugs bust? Have the details been finalised? McTavish has asked me to be part of it.' As Carruthers spoke he visualised the burly, fast-talking officer who worked for the NCA.

'I'm glad you've rung, Jim. Actually, the plan's changed.'

Carruthers was surprised. 'How so?'

'Intel says that there's a haul of heroin currently on a boat, the *Asante Sana*, making its way to the North Sea. We believe it's heading to Fife. The plan is to intercept it over the next few days, if you want to come along? But I warn you it may be as soon as tomorrow. At this point we just don't know.'

Carruthers mind was reeling. 'Fife? That's strange. If a large drugs haul was coming into Scotland it would normally be bound for Aberdeen.'

'Intel says this lot's coming to Fife.'

Carruthers was surprised. He had never heard of a big drugs haul coming into Fife before. He could sense Gus's excitement. It certainly made sense to intercept the vessel before the drugs got to land. The quicker they intercepted the better.

'Where's it come from?'

'Istanbul. We've actually had a tip-off from the French authorities.'

Gus's excitement was infectious. Carruthers could feel his own stomach doing backflips that he was going to be part of such a big operation. 'What else can you tell me?'

'The vessel's Tanzanian registered. This is a massive operation, Jim. We've got a Border Force cutter standing ready to intercept alongside a frigate. We think it might be a bigger drugs seizure than the *MV Hamal* in 2015.'

Carruthers' eyes widened. He remembered that drugs raid. When the vessel had been searched off Aberdeen it had a staggering £512 million of cocaine hidden on board. If his memory served him, that vessel had also been registered in Tanzania. The two Turks who had been on that vessel were now safely in prison for the next twenty years.

He did some quick thinking. 'Where exactly is our boat now?'

'That's it, Jim. We don't know.' Carruthers could hear the frustration in Gus's voice. 'It's turned off its AIS.'

Carruthers knew that under maritime law every vessel was obliged to have an automatic identification system, or AIS, turned on for safety and security. *So they had turned it off. Just like* MV Hamal. *Classic sign it didn't want to be detected.* The vessel could be anywhere and finding it would be like looking for a needle in a haystack. In his mind's eye he imagined Border Force poring over maps plotting various courses that the vessel might be taking.

Carruthers was out of his depth with an operation like this so he knew all he could do was leave it to the experts. 'Okay, so how do we play this?'

'We'll keep in touch with you, Jim. We only have a two- or three-day window in which to operate. The problem is that we are being hampered by the weather. Pretty much every part of the UK is currently experiencing high pressure except for the area of the North Sea where we are hoping to intercept the boat. I'm just about to go into another briefing where we'll be mapping where the boat might be.'

So I was right to imagine them poring over maps and plotting courses.

'We'll be sending out a spotter plane too and we'll have men on the Fife mainland keeping watch on the cliffs. What often happens is that the vessel dumps the drugs in the sea under the cover of darkness for smaller boats to pick up later.' Carruthers could hear Gus talking to a colleague away from the phone. 'Listen, Jim, I've got to go. Meeting's about to start.'

A fleeting thought crossed his mind that Robbie Paterson had taken his boat out at night. As he was thinking about Paterson a shadow fell over his desk. He hoped it wasn't Lennox again and then felt guilty for such an uncharitable thought. He put his phone down and smiled when he saw Fletcher standing over him. His head was still full of his telephone conversation. He needed to fill McTavish in but first he had some questions for Fletcher about the warden on the Isle of May.

'Did you get through to SNH for the warden's mobile number?' He caught the troubled expression on Fletcher's face and knew the news wasn't going to be good.

Her brows furrowed. The thought that came to Carruthers' mind was that his DS was looking perplexed.

I hope today isn't going to be full of bad news, he thought.

'I did. I've been ringing the number but been getting no response.'

'Okay. Keep trying.' He picked up the phone again. He had better phone their DCI to see if she was free for a chat rather than just trot along to her office. Over the last few months he had noticed that their DCI was no longer encouraging an open-door policy. Did she feel swamped by her workload? Or was there something more personal going on?

Carruthers looked up. Fletcher was still looming over him and she didn't appear to be budging. The conversation clearly hadn't finished. Carruthers replaced the phone once more to give his younger DS his full attention.

His junior's brows knitted together. 'I've been trying for the last ten minutes, Jim. Both the landline and the mobile numbers.'

'Well, maybe the poor sod's in the bathroom.'

'Hmmm. The thing is that SNH were expecting an email from the warden first thing this morning. He's expected to email in every Monday morning and give them his findings. They haven't heard from him today.'

'How long ago were they expecting the email?'

She glanced at her watch. 'Nearly two hours ago now. And apparently he's a meticulous timekeeper. He's never missed an email yet.'

Until now. Carruthers could see why Fletcher was looking perplexed. The warden hadn't emailed in and couldn't be reached by phone, either mobile or landline. Perhaps the man had been taken ill. A fleeting thought occurred that the warden could be out looking for the missing fisherman but the timing didn't fit. At the time the warden had been due to send the email to SNH the news hadn't broken of Paterson's disappearance.

'What's the warden's name?'

'Tom Ramsey.'

'Ahh. That's right.' Carruthers racked his memory bank to see if he could remember actually having met him. He drew a blank.

'And before you ask there's currently six people resident on the island, including Ramsey – the others are all volunteers there for the summer, according to SNH.' Fletcher referred to her notebook as she spoke. 'I wonder where the volunteers are? There's also a main phone in the volunteer accommodation block on Fluke Street. I've been trying that number too but nobody's been picking up. I'm guessing they must all be out on the island busy with their duties.'

'I think I know where the volunteers are.' Carruthers suddenly remembered he had seen several of them during his late evening stroll the night before. 'Think there was some sort of celebration on the mainland last night. I saw three of the volunteers at about 11pm while I was down at the harbour.'

Fletcher raised an eyebrow. 'What were you doing down by Anstruther harbour so late at night?'

He spoke quickly trying to ignore the fact the question irritated him, as did the DS's nosiness. 'Just clearing my head from work and taking a bit of a walk.' He was having problems sleeping so he was now in the habit of taking a soothing stroll down by the harbour of an evening but he wasn't going to give Fletcher that piece of information. She was too nosy by half anyway and that would just trigger more questions about his private life that he didn't want to answer.

'Okay, so what's causing your insomnia this time? Is it Mairi? Have you heard from her?'

Damn. She'd already sussed out why he wasn't sleeping. There are no flies on this DS. 'No.'

'I was so sure you would be able to rekindle something after–'

'After I saved her life you mean?'

'I just got the feeling–'

'What?'

'That she still had feelings for you. That's why you're not sleeping, isn't it?'

Carruthers' ex-wife had come close to being murdered by a serial killing maniac, the student slasher, in their last big case. They hadn't met up since he had rescued her, although they had spoken a couple of times on the phone but the conversation had seemed awkward, forced even. And then the phone calls had stopped coming. From both of them.

'Look, Andie, I don't really want to think about my ex-wife, especially when we've got a missing fisherman to worry about.'

'Sorry, course you don't.'

He glanced over at her. Was that a pitying look she just gave him? God, he really didn't want her pity. Now Fletcher was going to get the wrong end of the stick. Carruthers was feeling ambivalent towards his ex-wife. Although part of him still missed her a bigger part of him now wanted to move on and it had only been him coming back into contact with her that had made him realise that.

'Anyway, where were we?'

Fletcher grinned. 'Your stroll by the harbour last night?'

'Ah yes.' He had been on Shore Street looking up at the stars in the sky marvelling at the clearness of the night when the door of the Ship Tavern had burst open as three young people had come out for a smoke. He remembered the happy, carefree-looking girls and tried to recall a time he had last felt that relaxed. Not for a long time and certainly well before he had joined CID. Nostalgia at being that age had meant he had tuned into their conversation. He'd caught the tail end about some girl's PhD and their work on the island as volunteers.

'As I said, it must have been eleven when I saw them. That's pretty late. Don't think they'd be getting back to the Isle of May at that time of night. Maybe they stayed in a B&B in Anstruther?'

'I didn't think they could all leave the island at the same time?' remarked Fletcher.

'I hadn't heard that but if it's true perhaps Ramsey gave the youngsters the night off and he stayed behind. I mean, he wouldn't really be part of the set, would he? He's much older.'

Most likely Ramsey was on his own overnight on the island.

'Keep trying to reach him and keep me posted.' Carruthers hoped the warden hadn't had an accident.

Fletcher looked doubtful. 'I think he's in his late thirties, Jim. And if so he wouldn't be that much older, would he? I mean, if one lass has just finished her PhD that would probably put her in her mid- to late-twenties. I'll give him another call.' Fletcher turned away.

Carruthers had a further thought and called her back. 'Andie, the *May Princess* shouldn't be far off landing.'

Fletcher swivelled round.

Carruthers continued to speak. 'Put a call in to the skipper, will you and ask him which landing site they're using.' If the weather was fair the *May Princess* would ordinarily land at Kirkhaven, a stone's throw away from the new visitor centre and not far from the ruins of the old priory.

The boat would have to expertly navigate the treacherous rocky outlets, which it could only do in fair conditions. Today was becoming a little windy but not as blustery as it might be. But who knew what it was like further out to sea? 'And get him to track down the warden.'

'What do you think's happened?'

Carruthers shook his head. 'No idea.' He knew it was important to keep an open mind but he was having a bad feeling about this one. Robert Paterson's empty boat had been found just off the Isle of May, which, strangely, now appeared to be deserted. *I really don't want to be bothered with organising role profiles*, he thought, *but I'd rather deal with them than with a missing fisherman and an absentee island warden.*

4

Caroline Young took in a deep breath of fresh sea air. The lady next to her touched her arm.

'Do you feel a bit better?'

'Yes, thank you.'

Bettina nodded approvingly. 'You're a better colour.'

Caroline smiled. *I might be a better colour*, she thought, *but I am now absolutely bloody freezing.* The bottoms of her jeans were well and truly soaked through. She noticed that the deck was even more awash with water. With dismay she realised her bottom was also wet. She ran a hand underneath it. It was positively soaking, just like the bench she was sitting on. *How embarrassing.* She hadn't realised when she'd originally sat down that the bench had been wet and her waterproof jacket hadn't been long enough to cover her behind. And she had a sneaky suspicion that her waterproof hillwalking boots had sprung a leak. Her feet felt cold. Her heart sank. *How awful to have to spend the rest of the day with cold, wet feet, not to mention a wet arse.*

She then reminded herself that there was a missing fisherman and gave herself a shake and told herself to get a grip.

What was the expression that now seemed particularly apt? *Worse things happen at sea.*

Bettina leant into her. 'We're nearly there. Look at the birds.'

Caroline turned to look as the boat slowed down and navigated through the rocks. There on the ledges all around her were thousands of seabirds. The passengers, many of whom were seasoned bird spotters, were starting to stand up, keen to disembark, craning their necks to get a better look at the birds on the cliffs and in the sky. Caroline stood up too and gazed in awe at the narrow rocky ledges. There wasn't a square inch that didn't have a bird on it. She counted terns, kittiwakes, cormorants and gannets while she inhaled the fresh sea air. It really was a bird-lover's paradise. How on earth did they all co-exist? Before booking the trip she had found out which month was ideal to visit and early summer seemed to be perfect. The birds were now nesting, yet to return to the sea with their young which would happen towards the end of summer.

There was a squeal from a fellow passenger. 'Puffin. Oh my God, I've just seen a puffin.' The voice was female and American and the high-pitched timbre denoted her excitement. Caroline scrabbled about in her rucksack and brought out her binoculars. She hadn't dared bring them out earlier for fear that looking down and rummaging around in her bag would set off a wave of seasickness. She trained the binoculars on the sky like so many other passengers. There in the air was indeed a puffin. The first one she had ever seen. Its stocky body looked like it couldn't carry its own weight and the short wings were flapping nineteen to the dozen as it flew. It made such a comical but beautiful sight. She watched mesmerised as another two launched themselves in the air from the rocks. Caroline gasped with sheer joy and in that moment forgot all about the missing fisherman.

'The offspring of puffins are called pufflings.' The skipper started up his running commentary again. 'There are estimated to be currently 90,000 on the island. Puffins live in burrows and spend much of the breeding season between April and July underground. We are into the seabird-breeding season now. The first puffin chicks hatched around 22nd May with the guillemot and razorbill chicks hatching early June.

'I just want to talk to you about the importance of the weather for the birds. I know it's a little bit blowy today and unfortunately the outlook is not great for the rest of the week so we've been lucky to land at Kirkhaven. When the wind from the west comes in it whips up the sea creating choppy waves. For most of those birds that nest on the cliff this willnae be a problem but for the lower cliff nesting birds, like the guillemots, it can be disastrous. In the past we've lost over two hundred pairs of guillemots to strong westerly winds within the space of a couple of years. They land only to nest, spending the rest of the time at sea. For this reason they can be vulnerable to oil spills.'

Caroline listened closely to the skipper; keen to learn more about the birds she had come to see. She had no idea baby puffins were called pufflings. *What a cute name*, she thought. And how hazardous for the guillemots. She had no idea so many of them drowned. What a precarious life. As the boat was skilfully navigated between the rocks Caroline stared up in wonder at the ledges, or stacks, as they were known, that were crammed with these black and white seabirds.

Finally the boat came in to dock and the passengers started to disembark. A man coming down the stairs from the top deck had a camera on a tripod. There were some serious photographers and wildlife enthusiasts among them. The skipper gently grasped her arm and helped her and the other passengers off the boat before herding the stragglers together. He asked them to remain in a group until the warden arrived. However, his call wasn't heeded by a group of three who had walked off up the coast path towards the visitor centre. Their confident strides and expensive professional looking equipment made Caroline think this wasn't their first visit to the island.

'Be careful as you walk. It's slippery here on the rocks. Take your time.' The skipper lowered his voice as he addressed Lofty. 'That's odd. There's usually someone to greet them.'

'Aye. It would have to be Tom. The others were on the mainland last night. There was quite a party. One of them was celebrating finishing her PhD. I'll tell you something – that Sylvie's a fair bonny lass.' Lofty's face fell. 'They were supposed to be on this crossing going back. I was looking forward to seeing her again but three of them got blootered last night. Couldn't face the boat. Apparently Justin's taking them back later.'

The skipper was clearly unimpressed. 'More money than sense. What have I told you about drinking the night before we take the boat out?'

'Aww come on, Skip. We take the boat out seven days a week.'

'Mebbe we do but you dinnae work seven days a week, do you?'

'Aww, are you telling me I cannae ever go oot? I'm young. I need to let my hair down once in a while. I didnae have that much to drink. Anyway, I'm no' like you old sea dogs. I can get over a hangover in a blink of the eye.'

Lofty winked at the skipper who just rolled his eyes dramatically. 'Get after that wee group and bring them back, will you and see what's keeping Tom. I wonder if he's still on Fluke Street.'

'Aye, but I'm burstin' fura pee.' Lofty rolled his eyes at the skipper. 'Expect it was all that beer.'

The skipper screwed his face up in a grimace. 'You may be able to recover from a hangover quick enough but ye clearly cannae hold yer piss.'

Caroline stood patiently with the rest of the disembarked passengers as she watched Lofty make his way up the path. Her attention was quickly diverted from the younger man when one of the passengers, who was getting impatient, approached the skipper to ask when they could start the walk.

'How long are we going to be held here? When can we start walking? We're not going to spend as much time on the island as we were told, so will we be in line for a discount?'

Caroline, who had been listening to this exchange tried not to smile. *There is always one*, she thought.

The skipper put his hands up to placate them. 'We're usually greeted by either the warden or one of his volunteers. I understand that there was a bit of a shindig on the mainland last night so you're in for a treat, as the warden himself, Tom Ramsey'll greet you. He's very knowledgeable and you're lucky to have him talk to you.'

The skipper then looked at the passenger who had asked if they were in for a discount. 'And no, you'll no' be in line for a discount.'

Caroline felt ridiculously pleased that the skipper had put the man in his place. The skipper looked at his watch then, through narrowed eyes, up the path but there was no sign of the warden, although Caroline saw the three individuals who had gone ahead begrudgingly make their way back to the group.

'To save some time and while we wait for Tom to appear I'm going to tell you a bit about the island and the work of the warden and volunteers...' He rubbed his hands. Caroline wasn't sure whether it was with cold or with enthusiasm. She stamped her feet. Her toes were feeling numb. She wondered if the warden of the island was already out looking for the missing fisherman and that's why he wasn't down at the harbour.

5

Fletcher stretched her arms behind her head and arched her back. She glanced around the office. Helen Lennox was having an earnest conversation on the phone. She hoped it was work-related. Gayle Watson was bent forward, looking at something on her computer.

Fletcher felt she should go up and say something more about the DS's bereavement but she had already given the older woman her condolences. However, it just didn't feel enough. *Why oh why, in the face of death, do we feel so useless?*

She thought back to her late-on miscarriage. There had been certain friends and family members whom she felt had avoided her. Too awkward a conversation to have, she supposed. She frowned. At the time it had done nothing but increase her sense of loneliness. And she didn't want that for Watson. Carruthers had been good during her miscarriage. He'd tried to reach out to her, but she had shut him out. She glanced over at his empty chair. His jacket was on the back of it, so she knew he was still in the station. She supposed he too had gone for coffee. She hurriedly got up. There was something she wanted to ask him out of Helen Lennox's hearing. Before she left the office, she went over to Watson's desk. She placed a hand awkwardly on the woman's shoulder.

'Gayle, I'm just going to get a coffee. Do you want anything?'

Watson looked up from her computer. The strain was showing on her face but she still managed a smile. Fletcher noticed the smile didn't touch her eyes but there was gratitude in them. 'No, I'm good. Thanks for asking though.'

Fletcher caught up with Carruthers at the coffee machine. She was also worried about him. He'd been a lot quieter these last couple of months, not like his old self at all. She worried that it had something to do with his coming across his ex-wife again. Perhaps it had unsettled him. She knew he still had feelings for Mairi because every time she asked about her he changed the subject. If that wasn't a giveaway sign she didn't know what was. She also knew that, despite the fact Carruthers had saved his ex-wife's life in their last major case, he hadn't acted on the feelings he still had for her even though Mairi had now split up from her boyfriend. Although she hadn't known him when he and his wife had first separated she knew how much he had loved her. She wondered if he had decided to let sleeping dogs lie. Perhaps he was trying to move on with his life. Without his ex-wife.

She looked up into his face once more while trying to read the emotion in his blue eyes. 'Are you okay, Jim?'

His expression was unfathomable and a thought crept into her head that he had cultivated this on purpose by way of protection. She wasn't the only one who didn't like to feel exposed, especially at work in front of colleagues.

Perhaps it wasn't anything to do with his wife. It was just as likely to have something to do with his mum or his brother, neither of whom had been keeping particularly good health. His brother was still recovering from a heart attack and his mum had recently gone through surgery for lung cancer. Thankfully his brother had now returned to his own home back in Glasgow. Fletcher knew that he had definitely outstayed his welcome in Carruthers' Fife cottage.

'I'm fine, Andie. Just going through a spate of insomnia. It happens.'

'Are your mum and brother okay?' *I really want to ask about your ex-wife but the last time I did you bit my head off.*

He smiled down at her. 'They're both doing much better, thanks.'

She decided to push a bit. 'You must be relieved that they caught your mum's lung cancer early.'

He nodded. 'She's making a good recovery.'

'And your brother?'

'Much better after that second op.'

Having decided she wasn't going to get much more out of him by way of personal information she hovered awkwardly. 'I just wanted to ask – are you going to be part of the drugs bust?'

Carruthers face visibly relaxed. 'I was speaking with the NCA this morning and it's on hold.'

Fletcher's face fell. 'I thought it was definite. I was going to ask if I could come along.'

'I'm waiting to hear back from them but they've got intelligence to suggest there's a vessel currently crossing somewhere into the North Sea. Gus thinks it's bound for Fife laden with drugs.'

'Shit.'

'The tip-off's come from the French Customs Agency. They've got a Border Force cutter alongside a frigate and a spotter plane all ready to intercept. Only problem is that they've switched off the AIS so we don't actually know their current location.'

'They're taking a risk by switching that off. I know they want to stay undetected but if anything were to go wrong...'

'Unsurprisingly they're willing to take the risk to protect their haul of drugs.'

'I guess they've weighed up the risks and rewards. From what you've said it sounds like the NCA are undertaking a massive operation. Let's face it, if this vessel does get intercepted they'll have a lot more to worry about than just violating maritime law.'

Carruthers sipped his coffee. 'Yeah, you're right. They will. Long prison sentences. Do you remember a case a while back? Five fishermen from the Isle of Wight arrested for allegedly smuggling a huge haul of cocaine from a container ship in the English Channel?'

'It was one of the biggest drugs hauls in UK history, if my memory serves.' Fletcher leant against the drinks machine as she spoke. 'Didn't they get well over 100 years in prison between them?'

'Yep, although I seem to remember evidence coming to light casting doubt on their guilt.'

A frown furrowed Fletcher's forehead. 'I'm surprised the boat is bound for Fife. They usually go into Aberdeen.'

'I said the same thing to Gus, but Fife is what the intel is telling them. You still want to come along if I can swing it? The problem is that this is no longer a simple drugs raid. I may not be able to get you involved.'

Fletcher smiled. Her DI almost sounded like a wee boy he was so excited. *I most definitely do want to be involved*, she thought. *I hate missing out on the action. And there's no way I want to talk about the latest development in front of Helen Lennox. Let Lennox think it was still going to be a simple drugs raid in Glenrothes.*

Fletcher's thoughts then turned to Watson. As much as she wanted to be the one who was in on the collar perhaps it should be Gayle Watson. Her face became serious. 'I was just wondering if you were going to ask Gayle instead. If we can make some arrests it might help her process what happened to her niece.'

There was a time Fletcher wouldn't have given a second thought to Gayle Watson. She'd hated that the older woman had been brought in as her replacement when she'd been off after her miscarriage and had hated it even more when she'd come back to work only to find that the superintendent had miraculously found some extra money from their so called non-existent budget to make Watson part of the team. Hugely resentful and pushed out is how she'd felt. However, over time Fletcher had warmed to the flamboyantly dressed officer. It hadn't been an easy ride but now she couldn't imagine Edenside Police Station without her.

Carruthers looked fondly at Fletcher. 'Well, it's possible the interception might be as early as tomorrow. I would suspect we won't get much notice. And if it does end up being tomorrow Gayle's going to be at the funeral.'

'Oh shit. I didn't realise the funeral's tomorrow.' Fletcher looked at the options on the drinks machine. 'Christ, any idea how the family's coping?'

'No, not really. You know Gayle. She's a bit of a closed book. Have you spoken to her much?'

Fletcher shook her head. 'No, I've tried but I don't know what to say, to be honest.' *I've known Gayle for over two years now and I still don't know the name of her partner*. She noticed that Gayle Watson always kept her language gender neutral when speaking about her other half. It was probably something the Fifer had learned to do by way of protection. Being a lesbian in today's police force would still have its challenges. At the end of the day the woman was very much a closed book.

Carruthers sipped his black coffee slowly. 'I know what you mean. What do you say when it's been such a sudden death? And it's the manner in which the young girl died, isn't it? She did say they were all feeling numb. Do you know how Gayle's sister is coping?'

'No, I don't. Badly, I would assume. At least that's how I would be coping if it were my daughter.'

'You actually going to get a coffee or just stand here talking to me?' Carruthers looked amused as he said this.

Fletcher jumped into action, pressing the button for white coffee.

Carruthers blew on his own coffee before he took another sip. 'I get the feeling Gayle's organising the funeral.'

It didn't surprise Fletcher. 'She's a very capable cop,' she found herself saying. 'I can imagine her being good at the practicalities and being useful to the family might help her get through.'

She started as Harris approached them. 'Call's just come in,' said the older cop, shuffling his feet as he walked. 'Unexplained death in Glenrothes. Possibly drugs related. McTavish wants you two to go. Don't think you'll be needing that.' He took the coffee cup out of Fletcher's hand and, grinning, took a swig.

Fletcher sighed. *Shit. I should have grabbed a sandwich from the canteen when I had the chance.*

6

The front door, which was awash with graffiti, was ajar. The house was filthy. Fletcher could smell the dirt and decay even before she stepped inside. She was now grateful she hadn't eaten any lunch as the pungent smell was making her feel nauseous.

Carruthers had a problem even properly opening the front door and when he finally gave it an almighty push they found out why. Behind the door was a mound of unopened mail. Months of the stuff by the looks of it. The carpet was dirty and stained. Everything spoke of a life or lives on the edge lived in unbridled chaos.

Carruthers spoke to the nearest uniformed PC. 'How many people live here?'

'We're not sure,' answered the blonde female officer who wrinkled up her nose when she spoke. 'We think it's being used as a squat. Everyone's scarpered. There's just the one poor bugger in the living room. Dead.'

Carruthers and Fletcher followed her through to the dark living room. Now they were properly inside the smell of urine and vinegar was even more overpowering. *Most likely heroin,* thought Fletcher. She knew that when manufacturers transformed opium into heroin they boiled it with the chemical acetic anhydride. A by-product of this chemical reaction was acetic acid – the chemical that gives vinegar its distinctive smell.

Fletcher opened her mouth in an attempt not to breathe through her nose. 'The light's out.' She shone a powerful torch, the beam picking up the seated pale body on the discoloured couch. The strap was still on the user's thin arm; needle in the skin. The deceased was male; looked to be in his late thirties, although Fletcher knew he was likely much younger. His white T-shirt was more than a little grubby and was full of holes; his once blue jeans were black with filth. His face was hollow and gaunt indicating years of addiction.

'Shit,' Fletcher said with feeling.

There was a high-pitched cry from another room. Fletcher's stomach somersaulted. It was the unmistakable cry of a baby.

'Jesus,' said Fletcher. She turned to the PC. 'You didn't tell us there was a baby here.'

The PC looked flustered. 'I'm so sorry,' she stammered. 'I d-d-didn't know. I thought the rest of the house was empty. The light's dreadful and the batteries in my torch have given out. I've been using the light from my mobile phone.'

The PC's face had drained of colour. Her eyes were fixated on the body of the drug user. Fletcher suspected that this was her first time seeing a dead body. Another urgent wail pierced the silence.

The officers sprang into action, covering the space quickly to follow the baby's cries to a dingy bedroom. Carruthers tried the light but that too was out. As Fletcher's eyes adjusted to the gloom at first she couldn't see anything but she followed the cries round to the other side of the bed. There on the floor was a sight that made her pull up short. The baby was lying in the arms of a young woman who was still bent over it. Her straggly blonde hair covered the top of the baby's head. Fletcher's eyes lighted over the syringes and heroin cooking pots. Everywhere on the floor around them was evidence of drug paraphernalia. The eyes of the woman were expressionless. In that instant Fletcher knew she was dead.

The uniformed officer gave a sob and covered her mouth with her hand. She stood transfixed; eyes wide.

Carruthers spoke first. 'Get the baby to hospital immediately.'

The PC seemed unable to move so Fletcher stepped forward and prised the urine-soaked baby out of the arms of the dead woman. She plonked it into the arms of the uniformed PC before turning back to look at the body on the floor.

'Two more deaths. Christ. Must be a bad batch,' said Fletcher. 'I wonder what this lot's been cut with.'

Fletcher knew that dealers had become even more creative with their cutting agents, creating sometimes sinister and deadly mixes to stretch their supply. There had been cases of heroin being cut with quinine and Fletcher had been witness to the terrible effects it could produce – blindness. She gazed sadly at the body seated on the floor. She had seen some sights in her time but for as long as she lived she would never get the sight out of her mind of the dead woman clutching her baby.

She shone her torch directly at the uncapped needles. Fletcher wrinkled her face. Some still had blood in them. Carefully she picked up the drugs paraphernalia with her gloved hand ready to bag it and hand it over to the labs. 'We'll have to get it tested. Thank God the baby's still alive but with this little lot it could have all sorts. Hepatitis; HIV; you name it.'

She searched the rest of the house, noting the laminate flooring in the kitchen and bathroom pulled up like scattered jigsaw pieces. They walked back into the kitchen. The sink was full of unwashed dishes. Flies buzzed around and the smell was overpowering.

'About as bad as I've seen,' said Fletcher, grimly.

There'd been a spate of drug-related deaths in Fife over the last few months but none of the officers present had ever come across a scene as heart wrenching as this before. Fletcher became aware of another noise. A new noise. She turned round. The PC, still rooted to the spot and cradling the now quiet baby, was crying.

Fletcher came out of the ladies where she had been scrubbing her hands. She took a sniff of the sleeve of her dark blue blouse. Carruthers fell into step with her. 'Thank God I'm wearing a dark colour,' she said. 'I feel really dirty.'

'Are you okay?'

The dark-haired detective had her face turned away from him as she mumbled her answer. 'Christ, I still stink of baby piss.'

Carruthers wondered if that was really what was bothering her, or if, like him, she felt she stank of the neglect and death from the property they had just visited. The despair seemed to cling to his clothes and hair. He couldn't wait to get home and have a shower. He felt utterly depressed and looking over at Fletcher knew without asking her that so did she.

As they walked back to his desk they were met by Helen Lennox. She looked at Carruthers and ignored Fletcher, apart from sniffing unpleasantly, something that was not lost on the DI. He wondered what was going on between the two women. Lennox turned to Carruthers. 'You've had a missed call on your mobile.'

'Oh?'

'I just happened to be walking by your desk, Jim. Caller ID said Mairi. That's your ex-wife, isn't it?'

Carruthers felt his stomach tighten. He would have to make sure that he took his mobile with him or put it in his desk drawer if he was ever away from his desk, even if it was just for a coffee. He didn't like the fact Lennox had got close enough to see the caller ID. *Just happened to be walking past the desk, my arse. Snooping more like.*

Although he hadn't seen his ex-wife recently, he wondered why she had split from her boyfriend. He hadn't called her as he wanted to give her some space. He was curious why she had rung him.

Lennox's face lit up. 'I wonder what she wants? Maybe she wants to get back with you?'

Carruthers could feel a flush of annoyance creep up his neck. He inhaled.

'That's what Willie Brown is saying, anyway.'

God, she really didn't know when to stop. 'Oh, is he?'

'Well, yes. Hasn't she dumped the boyfriend? It's all round the station.'

Carruthers saw Fletcher throw Lennox a dismayed look. Meanwhile he threw a sharp look at Fletcher. He'd told her in confidence about Mairi splitting from her boyfriend. He was going to have to speak to her about her indiscretion.

Two spots of colour appeared on Fletcher's cheeks as she snapped, 'I don't think it's any of our business what the call was about, do you?'

Carruthers stole a glance at Fletcher. She had the good grace to turn crimson. The station was shocking both for gossip and nosy colleagues and, where the latter was concerned, DS Andrea Fletcher was by far the worst. However, she also happened to be his friend.

Lennox wasn't letting them get back to work just yet. 'Is it true that there were *two* deaths at the property and you found a baby still alive in its mother's arms?'

Words got round the station quick enough, he thought. Fletcher took a slow, deep breath. Carruthers saw that she was irritated by the younger woman's thoughtless question. He wasn't immune to the fact that Lennox was almost making it sound like gossip. He decided she would have reacted very differently had she actually been there herself.

Fletcher scowled at their newest recruit. 'Helen, don't you have some paperwork to do, or something?'

'Okay, okay, I'm going.'

As he watched Lennox walk away, head slightly bowed, Carruthers turned to Fletcher. 'Andie, don't be too hard on her. I think she's just trying hard to fit in.'

'I think she's a nosy cow.'

Carruthers snorted. 'Don't take this the wrong way but three words: pot, kettle, black. I've never met anyone as nosy as you.' His face suddenly grew serious and he dropped his voice. 'And by the way, if I tell you something in confidence, I don't expect it to be broadcast all round the station.'

Fletcher's earlier blush deepened.

7

'The warden's still not shown up. How long are we going to wait?' Lofty looked at his watch as he spoke to the skipper of the *May Princess* before jerking his head towards the murmuring passengers. 'They're getting restless.'

Scott Gardner also glanced at his watch, mindful of the stirrings of discontent. If nothing else they were all starting to get cold.

'Do you still need a pee?'

'Aye, it's getting worse,' Lofty whined. 'I'm aboot to piss myself.'

Gardner rolled his eyes. 'Haud yer weesht.' He could see a couple of his English passengers looking at him curiously. He wondered if they knew he had just told Lofty to be quiet. He lowered his voice so only Lofty could hear him. 'If yer desperate use the toilets at the visitor centre and while you're up that way nip up to Fluke Street and see what's keeping the warden.'

Lofty walked off, taking long purposeful strides on the path towards the visitor centre where he knew there were the only toilets on the island.

A few minutes later he approached the wooden hut but as he

did so he saw a huge cloud of birds all swooping and dive-bombing something on the ground about a hundred feet away from the hut towards the cliff edge. Likely a dead rabbit. He'd seen plenty of them on the island. He idly wondered how they had got over from the mainland. A gull was busy pecking at something. His stomach churned as he remembered a story about a small dog whose owner had claimed that it had been picked up and carried away by a huge rogue seagull. *Didn't they find the leg of the poor wee dug? Or was it just a rabbit's leg?* Curiosity got the better of Lofty and he forgot all about his full bladder. He veered away from the visitor hut towards the mass of shrieking birds eager to see what unfortunate animal had met such a cruel end.

As he approached the front of the building he saw the body of a man lying on its side in the grass. He stopped short nearly losing his balance, his eyes wide with fright. He took a sharp intake of breath before he ran at the seabirds that were swooping and settling on the body. Coming closer he recognised the body as that of the warden of the island. Tom Ramsey was wearing his familiar grey and black Gore-Tex jacket. The man's binoculars were still slung round his neck but it was the blood that had Lofty's eyes widen. The man's jacket had all but turned red.

Feeling nauseous Lofty turned away and vomited. After a few moments he steadied himself and approached the still figure. He half knelt, running the back of his hand over his mouth before turning once more to the terrible sight. The warden's body was covered in gashes and blood soaked all his clothes. He called the man's name but the warden didn't move. It was when he saw the dead man's face that he let out a shriek. The birds had pecked one of his eyes out. Shakily he stood up and ran skittering back to the safety of the boat.

'Right, so where was I?' The skipper was standing, legs askance, and arms folded, clearly enjoying stepping into the role of warden.

'You were telling us what the volunteers do on the island,' encouraged an elderly grey-haired woman wrapped in a green cagoule. 'By the way, I don't mean to be rude but at what point can we actually start our tour? You've kept us here for a good wee while now. I'm starting to get really cold.'

There were mutterings of agreement and nods. The group were now huddled together, hoods up, trying to keep warm.

Above the cries of the birds Caroline thought she heard a scream. She cocked her head to one side but there was no further noise and she wondered if she had merely imagined it. However, when she looked at the faces of her fellow passengers and crew she knew that they had also heard something. Several had looked up and a couple had turned round.

The skipper was faltering. Finally he continued with his talk but he didn't sound quite so confident. As he spoke he kept an eye on the path. 'Every year there's far more volunteers apply for the posts than are places and they do everything from seabird monitoring to helping with the guiding and enquiries from the general public.'

'How long has the island been a nature reserve?' Caroline noticed that the voice belonged to the earnest-looking young woman who had been talking to Lofty on the boat. She decided the passenger was most likely an ornithology student.

The skipper tried to smile at her but he appeared distracted. 'I believe there has been a research programme on the Isle of May since 1956 which is when the island became a nature reserve.'

He certainly knows his stuff, thought Caroline, impressed, even if his mind isn't completely on the job.

'The island has accommodation for up to sixteen–'

A shout stopped the skipper mid-track from finishing his sentence. This time all the passengers looked up and a few moments later they saw Lofty running full pelt towards them kicking up the small stones on the path as he went.

Caroline stared in horror. *Oh my God what's happened? He looks totally spooked. Perhaps he was the person I heard screaming.* Lofty's mouth was open but no words came out. He reminded Caroline of a goldfish. The young man's face was ashen and there was a sheen of sweat on his brow. She couldn't tell if that was from exertion or fear. An awful thought entered her mind. Had he stumbled on the body of the missing fisherman? She offered up a silent prayer that that wasn't the case. But what else could have spooked him on this uninhabited island?

Lofty rushed his words which all came out in a tumble. To Caroline's horror she saw that the young man was shaking. The skipper grabbed Lofty's arm and steered him away from the group so that they could have a private conversation. She strained to hear what they were saying over the noise of the seabirds. She noticed that everyone else had stopped talking.

'Dead... Birds... Blood... Eye.' That was all she heard but it was enough to know something terrible had happened.

A grim-faced skipper made his way back to the group leaving a shaking Lofty standing rigid to the spot. 'Okay, listen up. I'm going to have to leave you for a few minutes. You are to stay *exactly* where you are. I don't want *anyone* to move from here. Understood?'

There were nods from the group but nobody made a complaint about there being a further delay. Fear mingled with anxiety so palpable it hung in the air. The skipper looked around him. His eyes settled on Caroline. 'What's your name?'

She stuttered out the words 'Caroline Young.'

'Right. While I'm gone, Caroline Young is in charge.' And with that he turned heel and followed Lofty up the path. Caroline, who had never considered herself leadership material was less concerned about the prospect of being put in charge of one hundred complete strangers and more worried about the fact that, as he turned away, Lofty, apart from shaking, now appeared to be crying uncontrollably.

Carruthers finally extricated himself from the conversation with Fletcher and hurried back to the office. He picked up his mobile under the watchful eye of Helen Lennox who, much to his embarrassment, gave him a thumbs up sign, and headed out to the car to listen to the message and phone his ex-wife back. There was no way he wanted his conversation overheard and reported to the entire station.

After three rings Mairi answered her mobile. Suddenly he was nervous. How ridiculous. Why should he be feeling nervous talking to his ex-wife?

'Mairi, it's me, Jim. You rang?'

'Oh, Jim, thank you for calling me back. Are you busy this week? Can we meet?'

Carruthers almost had to smile. She'd never been one for small talk. He thought quickly, pushing the tragic visit to the squat out of his mind. There was currently nothing pressing except writing up the report. The forecasts and budgets could wait. The RNLI were out looking for Paterson and hopefully the warden of the Isle of May had just slept in and would be found slumbering in his bed.

He found himself agreeing immediately, if for no other

reason than out of pure curiosity. 'Yes of course. Is everything okay?'

'Everything's fine. Don't worry, but I would like to see you.'

'Today?'

'If you can fit me in?'

'Today is better for me.' He thought of what Gus from the NCA had said. There was no way the planned interception of the vessel would be organised for as early as that same day but if he arranged to see his ex-wife tomorrow, what was the betting that's when the interception would take place? In this job he knew that when you had a window you had to go for it. Things didn't stay quiet in CID for long. He glanced at his watch. 'Okay, how about a coffee? I could get away for forty minutes or so.' It was handy they were now working in the same town.

'Yes that would be great, Jim. How about we meet in the Pilgrims Arms in an hour?'

Carruthers could picture the Pilgrim's Arms. It was a local's pub. Mairi had probably chosen it as she knew none of her students would be seen dead there. She'd recently returned to academia after taking a break from teaching philosophy and she was back teaching in Castletown. An image came into his head of the last time he had been in a pub with his ex-wife – of her slim leg and ankle bracelet. In fact, hadn't it been the same pub? He swallowed hard. What did she want? Well, he would find out soon enough. As Carruthers cut the call he contemplated whether he should change for his coffee date into the clean and pressed white shirt he always kept in his locker for emergencies.

'Is he dead? It's Tom Ramsey, isn't it?' Lofty wiped his wet nose on his sleeve. His eyes were moist. 'There were so many birds.

He was surrounded by them.' He let out some more choking sobs and a line of snot ran from the end of his nose.

A grim-faced skipper stepped closer to the prostrate figure. It was lying in short grass that looked like the surface of a billiards table, thanks to the island's rabbits. He stooped to feel for a pulse in the man's neck even though he knew it was useless.

A cloud of birds dive-bombed them. They were excited as they knew they were in for a feeding frenzy. Lofty chased them off.

'There's so much blood,' sobbed Lofty, his teeth chattering with shock. 'What's happened? Could he have tripped and fallen?' His eyes widened as he took in the ripped Gore-Tex jacket of the warden. 'What type of birds would have done that to him?'

The skipper straightened up slowly. He too had turned white. Even in his army days long before he had gone into the fishing industry he had never seen anything like this. 'I don't think those marks have been made by birds, Lofty.'

Gardner knew that some seabirds were aggressive and would think nothing of attacking vulnerable prey but as someone who had seen active service he knew knife wounds when he saw them. He counted at least eight of them on the man's torso but kept quiet. He swallowed hard and grasped Lofty by the shoulders. 'Go back to the boat; grab my jacket, will you? We need to protect him from the birds.'

'Shouldn't we move him? We can take him indoors.' Lofty picked up a foot encased in a bloodied boot and started to pull him across the ground.

'Don't touch him,' the skipper snapped.

Lofty let the foot drop.

'We need to leave him exactly as we found him for the police.' The skipper straightened up so he was almost eye level with Lofty. 'When you get to the boat radio for help then go and find Justin.' He thought of the red-headed crew member who was a few years older than Lofty. 'Make sure all the passengers are back on board. Follow the instructions that the police give you. They may want you to leave the island. But if they do want you to leave you must come and tell me first. And mind, remember to bring the jacket with you.'

Lofty was open-mouthed. 'We can't leave you behind what will you do?' The sentences came out as one long string of words.

The skipper had made his mind up. 'Someone needs to stay with him.'

Lofty gasped. 'Aren't you afraid? What if whoever's done this comes back and attacks you?'

The skipper looked over at the body of what had once been the warden. He then looked around him. All he could see was the bleak beauty of the now uninhabited island. 'I think whoever attacked Tom Ramsey is likely long gone.' At least he hoped they were long gone. He said it with a lot more conviction than he felt. But the thought of staying on the island with only a dead man and a bunch of frenzied birds wasn't a prospect he relished.

Lofty appeared unable to move.

'Lofty, get going,' the skipper snapped. Lofty didn't need to be told twice and he skittered away, arms flailing, stumbling briefly over some small rocks.

Gardner wasn't a religious man but he looked with both pity and revulsion at the dead warden. He made the sign of the cross on his chest before looking upwards into the sky. All he could see overhead was a mass of birds.

8

Carruthers switched off his computer and picked up his jacket. He had a couple of jobs to do before he met Mairi but there was plenty of time. Just as he was leaving his desk his phone rang. He doubled back to pick it up. With a bit of luck, it might be good news about the fisherman. By now the whole of Anstruther would most likely know Robert Paterson was missing. It was some comfort to think that many would be rallying round the man's wife in her hour of need.

It was the voice of DCI Sandra McTavish on the line. 'Jim, drop what you're doing.' Carruthers noticed the urgency in her tone. She snapped out the words in staccato fashion. It sounded like machine-gun fire. 'Get over to the Isle of May, pronto. Take Fletcher with you. And we'll need the SOCOs.'

Carruthers' heart sank. 'Have they found the missing fisherman? I take it you don't think it was an accident?'

McTavish's voice was curt. 'There's been a body discovered on the island. It's believed to be that of the warden, Tom Ramsey. He's been identified by Scott Gardner, skipper of the *May Princess*.'

'Christ.'

Carruthers paused in case his boss had anything else to add. He didn't have long to wait.

'It's being treated as a suspicious death, Jim.'

'You're joking?'

'I wish I was. Looks like he's been stabbed.'

Carruthers was dumbstruck. What could have happened to the warden? Who would have killed him? He felt sorry for the chatty skipper of the *May Princess*. He often had a wee blether with him when he was strolling down by the harbour and the *May Princess* was in dock. He imagined he wouldn't be quite so chatty now.

'I have no idea what's going on,' continued McTavish, 'but we have one missing fisherman whose boat has been found in close proximity to one dead warden. We need to get on top of this situation and fast. Mark my words, the press will be on to this in double quick time. Get Paterson's boat brought in ASAP and I want a full forensic sweep of both boat and island. And I don't want this information to get into the domain of the public yet – not until we know what we are dealing with – so if you see any press brief them to this effect and be firm about it. If we are talking about a murder, then we don't want them impeding the investigation.'

So much for worrying about being bored to death having to deal with forecasts and budgets. While standing he put a call through to the booking office of the *May Princess* to see if he could commandeer the RIB. He was lucky. The rigid inflatable boat called the *Osprey*, was available.

It was one of two methods of ferrying passengers over to the island and being an inflatable it was much faster than the ferry. It only took ten people but he, Fletcher, Dr Mackie and the SOCOs would be given priority and anyone else would just have to take alternative transport. Carruthers put on his jacket and filled Fletcher in with the latest news.

As they left the building they bumped into Helen Lennox. She looked at them through narrowed eyes. 'What's the excitement? Where are the two of you going in such a hurry? Has there been another drug death?'

Carruthers was still struggling into his jacket as he walked. 'We're needing to get over to the Isle of May. A man's been found dead.'

'Can I come?'

Neither Fletcher nor Carruthers stopped walking or even slowed down. Instead he shouted over his shoulder, 'Someone has to stay here, Helen. I want you to get on to the Dive and Marine Unit. It will be worth them doing a dive around the island. If Robert Paterson's gone over there his body could have snagged on underwater rocks.'

Lennox followed them to the station's reception. 'Ooh, so the body found isn't that of the fisherman then?'

'They think it's the warden.' Carruthers tossed the words over his shoulder.

Lennox shot past them and opened the front door. 'The warden of the island? No way. But that's not fair if I can't come along. I never get the exciting jobs.'

Carruthers left Helen Lennox looking indignantly at their backs. Honestly, sometimes it was more like working in a sixth form college than in a police station. He was actually starting to wonder how the hell she had been promoted to CID.

They had walked halfway across the car park to Fletcher's little green Beetle before Carruthers remembered he was supposed to be meeting Mairi later. 'Oh shit.'

'What's wrong?'

He expelled a quick, frustrated breath. 'If I tell you I don't want it all over the station this time.'

'Look, Jim, I'm really sorry about that. I promise I'll keep it to myself.'

'No, I mean it, Andie.'

'Scout's honour.'

'Okay, I was supposed to be meeting Mairi for a coffee in Castletown. She's asked to see me.'

Fletcher let out a squeal of excitement. 'Ooh, I wonder why?'

'No idea.' Carruthers stared out of the window. He was too busy wondering what butchery had happened on the Isle of May to spend much time thinking about his ex-wife. Fletcher started the car, drove out of the police car park and navigated her way confidently through the streets of the ancient Scottish town. She was a good driver, and Carruthers knew that she had enjoyed her advanced police driving course, but she did tend to drive fast.

They left the university town behind them with its silhouette of cathedral and castle ruins and in no time at all got out into the open flat countryside.

'Give her a quick ring now. I'm sure if you explain the situation she'll understand.'

Would she understand though?

His mind flitted from his ex-wife back to the shock news of a body having been found on the Isle of May then back to his ex-wife again. *Wasn't this, in part, why she left me in the first place because I always put the job ahead of her? So typical we've been relatively quiet at work for the last couple of months and the first time I get a chance to meet up with Mairi this happens.*

He sighed and reached into the back of Fletcher's car to grab his jacket. His mobile phone was in the pocket. He grasped it and made the call. Mairi's mobile went to answer machine. He kept the message short. He sighed as he put his phone back.

Fletcher glanced over at him. 'If it's important you'll get to meet up with her. I'm a firm believer in the expression "What's meant for you won't go past you".'

He could only hope she was right. But then again Fletcher didn't know his ex-wife.

'Did Sandra say any more, Jim, about what we might expect to find over on the island?'

Carruthers looked across at his younger colleague seeing the determination in her face. He knew she enjoyed working on big cases with him. He shook his head. 'No. Only what I told you. A body of a man has been found on the island. Scott Gardner's identified it as that of the warden. It's being treated as suspicious.'

Fletcher glanced over at him as she drove. 'I *knew* there was something wrong when I couldn't get hold of him. I could *feel* it in my water. I take it there's been no news about the missing fisherman?'

Carruthers shook his head.

They arrived in Anstruther and Fletcher parked up in the main car park at the harbour. It was such a familiar scene to Carruthers as it was just two minutes from his house. Looking across the car park they could see Dr Mackie gingerly get out of his old battered Land Rover. He was taking an age doing so and Carruthers knew the older man was having problems with his joints. Fletcher opened the boot of her car to get out two sets of protective suits.

Mackie nodded a greeting to them. 'You never know where this job will take us, do you, laddie?' said Mackie. The Highland lilt of the pathologist's voice was still in evidence even after all these years of living and working in Fife.

The old boy isn't kidding, thought Carruthers.

Mackie shut his driver door. 'This is one of the more interesting places to find a body, that's for sure. Haven't been to the Isle of May for a while. Who's the victim?'

Carruthers produced his notebook from his trouser pocket.

'We believe it's thirty-eight-year-old Tom Ramsey, employed as warden on the island.'

Mackie nodded sadly. 'I know him.'

Carruthers snapped his notebook shut. He wasn't surprised Mackie knew Tom Ramsey. Mackie lived locally, was a keen walker and birdwatcher like himself. A pang of guilt coursed through Carruthers. How many times had he promised his ex-wife they would visit places like the Isle of May and they never had? He had always been too busy. Even after they had split he had promised himself a trip to the island – 'the May' as locals called it – and still he hadn't made it. Normally when he had time off he went further afield, hillwalking in the West Highlands.

He glanced over at Mackie who was busy getting out his nitrile gloves and protective cover-all kit from the boot of his Land Rover. Aside from being one of Scotland's top pathologists and active walker he was also a keen bletherer and Carruthers could imagine that if he had half a chance he would have bent the ear off the warden.

He thought of Mackie's role on the island. With any death there was a procedure to be followed. Before next-of-kin could be notified a certified doctor first had to pronounce that all signs of life had been extinguished. But it sounded as if that wasn't in question.

They walked silently together towards the boat that would take them to the May. They were greeted by the skipper, a ruddy-faced man in his sixties with a shock of white hair who gave each of them protective waterproof gear.

'Is this necessary?' Liu, the Chinese police photographer asked.

'We provide it for all passengers. You're liable to get wet from the sea spray but it's up to you.'

Carruthers watched Liu struggle into his bright yellow

waterproofs and step gingerly onto the *Osprey*. 'I don't like water or boats. Why couldn't he have died on the mainland?' he grumbled. 'And I have my photography equipment to think about.'

As she zipped up her waterproof Fletcher looked at the police photographer sharply. 'I don't think he expected to die at all. But if he had to die perhaps it's a fitting place for him. Surrounded by the birds he loved. If it is the warden, that is.'

'They would have pecked him half to death,' muttered Liu. The wiry man shook himself. 'Can't stand seabirds. Awful things. So aggressive.'

'Sounds like he was dead already, which is why we're heading over there.' Fletcher ignored the look Carruthers threw her.

Liu settled himself in his seat and placed the camera equipment, which was in protective waterproof casing, by his feet and looked around him. 'What type of boat is this?'

'It's a ten metre rigid inflatable boat.' The voice came from behind them.

'How long will it take to get to the island?'

'Twenty-five minutes. You'll be travelling at around twenty-five knots.'

'Is that fast?' asked Liu.

The skipper laughed. 'Faster than the *May Princess*.'

Liu looked anything but reassured. 'Are you sure this thing is safe?'

The skipper laughed again. 'It's fine as long as you're not pregnant and you don't have a back condition. I know you're not pregnant. Reckon your back is up to it?'

Liu nodded but he looked less than convinced. Carruthers wondered if the pathologist's back was up to it. He was clearly experiencing a few niggles if his cumbersome attempt to get out of his vehicle was anything to go by.

9

Scott Gardner stood and watched from his vantage point high up on the cliffs as the *May Princess* set sail. As far as he knew he was now all alone on the island with the corpse. He watched his boat being buffeted by the choppy waves as it navigated its way back through the jaggy rocks.

Lofty had returned with Gardner's jacket, which had been carefully placed over the victim. They had tried not to alarm the passengers when Justin calmly asked them to get back on board but they had inevitably caught wind of the reason for the hasty departure, according to Lofty. Not all of them were happy about having to leave the island. Gardner imagined that the mood would be naturally subdued, a mixture of disappointment at not having their planned day out and shock that a man's body had been found.

The skipper glanced at his watch, wondering how long it would be before the police arrived. Fearfully, he looked back to where the body of the warden lay. The legs and blood-spattered outdoor boots stuck forlornly out from under the waterproof as the wind rippled over the jacket.

Lofty Sykes had been a mess but he couldn't blame the poor

lad. The boy had stumbled back to the group; his face ashen. Gardner would need to check up on him later when he got back to the mainland. He was unsure how the youngster would feel about returning to the May in the future and he would likely need time off work after making the grisly discovery.

Who would be heading up the police investigation? He hoped it would be Inspector Jim Carruthers – but then remembered that the Glaswegian was no longer a DCI. There was now a woman heading up the team. By all accounts she was good at her job. She would have to be to find out who had killed Tom Ramsey. He couldn't think of any obvious reason why someone would want to kill the warden of a nature reserve. In any case Gardner hoped Carruthers would be part of the investigative team. He liked him and trusted that he would do a good job.

He wished he'd got a coffee on board the boat before it had set sail. If truth be told, though, he could do with something stronger. It wasn't every day you came across the bloodied body of someone you knew. He rubbed his bare arms and stamped his feet. Despite being of bigger build he was starting to feel chilly and wished he had chosen to wear trousers rather than shorts.

Gardner was always happiest when he was out at sea with the big rolling waves. The expanse of the ocean, even with all its inherent dangers, gave him a deep sense of peace. But being here on the island was altogether a different matter. He was already starting to feel claustrophobic. Now the boat had left there was no way of getting off the island. He watched it sail further out to sea until it completely disappeared. He looked fearfully at the shrouded body. A shiver passed through him. He hoped whoever had committed this terrible act of violence was long gone.

Had it been a bit rash insisting that he stayed with the body? There hadn't been time to do a sweep of the island. What if the murderer *was* still here, lurking in or around one of the Victorian buildings or hiding out in the ruins of the ancient priory?

What could have got Tom Ramsey killed? And, more importantly, what had happened to the murderer? He tried to calm his mind, which was going into overdrive. Would this be a one-off killing or were there more intended victims? It all came back to motive. He glanced around him, viewing it as the police might view it. With well over a hundred people visiting, it would be a forensics nightmare. He could just imagine how many pairs of muddy boots had walked around the visitor centre, the short walk from where the body had been found. Gardner took a deep breath and sat down stoically to wait for the police. He checked his mobile for a signal and was relieved when the bars appeared. Unless he went to the warden's accommodation this was now his only means of communication with the outside world. His large hand closed protectively round his phone.

After about five minutes a thought niggled him. His eyes widened. He had forgotten all about Robert Paterson's boat. What if the fisherman had been washed ashore half dead but still clinging to life? He stood up, unsure, wondering what to do. He looked across at the shrouded body of Tom Ramsey. Should he leave the victim to go look for any sign of Robert Paterson? He hesitated but only for a moment. The man was dead. There could be a second man who was still alive but needing help. But only if he left now. The decision had been made. He pocketed the mobile and hurried up the path.

Fletcher watched Liu's face carefully. He was starting to turn green. It was obvious that not everyone shared her and Carruthers' love of wildlife and the great outdoors. However, Liu did have a point. Seabirds, particularly in coastal towns, were becoming highly aggressive. She had noticed, since she was last in Anstruther, that the bins outside the fish and chip shops had been replaced with enormous new high-tech seagull-proof bins.

Fletcher watched Liu as he sat ramrod straight in the boat. He looked unnatural in his posture. His knuckles were white as he gripped the sides of the RIB. A thought occurred to her. She shouted over to him, 'Are you worried about seasickness?'

Liu nodded.

'Apparently you're not seasick on this boat. Something about it being at a lower centre of gravity than that of the *May Princess*,' shouted Carruthers.

'Tell that to my stomach,' the police photographer replied, looking unconvinced.

Fletcher tried not to smile. They hadn't even left the harbour yet. What was Liu going to be like on the open water?

The skipper started the engine up. Fletcher heard Liu muttering to himself. She didn't know if he was religious but she was convinced he was saying a prayer. They navigated out of Anstruther harbour then picked up speed.

'Hang on to your hats,' cried Fletcher, gleefully as adrenaline coursed through her body. She noticed Liu kept his head down. Conversation was all but impossible as they bumped and zipped along. If they hadn't been going to the island on police business it would have been a fun day out. She marvelled at the skill of the skipper as he skimmed through the waves. This was great fun.

Fletcher spent most of the time on the boat trying to push back her unruly hair that was constantly blowing in her face. Very quickly it became wet from the sea spray and she could taste the salt on her lips. *At least I'll get the smell of death out of my clothes after visiting the squat. Just as well we were given these water-proofs to wear otherwise I'd be absolutely soaking*, she thought. She wondered idly how Carruthers' ex-wife would receive the news that her meeting with Jim had been cancelled.

She spotted another vessel coming into view. As it drew closer she saw it was the passenger vessel, the *May Princess*, with its cargo of sightseers. From the bowed heads and unsmiling faces she saw how dejected they were. She hoped they understood why they had been ordered back to the mainland. They would have a story to tell tonight but it wouldn't be a happy one. The boats sounded their horns at each other as they passed and for some strange reason this gave Fletcher a small sense of comfort.

After only about twenty-five minutes they landed at the sheltered harbour at Kirkhaven. Fletcher spotted the skipper of the *May Princess* standing by the visitor centre. He cut a lonely figure. As soon as he saw them begin to dock he hurried towards them.

Carruthers helped Fletcher step off the inflatable before disembarking ahead of Dr Mackie whom he also helped off. The police photographer, Liu, who clearly hadn't exaggerated when he said he didn't possess a pair of sea legs, stepped off gingerly then promptly threw up. *So much for passengers not being seasick on the RIB.* All four of them peeled off the waterproofs provided for them by the skipper, apart from Liu. The Chinese man wiped his hand over his mouth and remained bent double. Fletcher took her rain hat off and tried to smooth her wayward hair down with one hand. The waterproofs that had been supplied to her were soaking, as was the hat.

'Bloody hell. Never been on one of those things before. Not for the faint-hearted. It was exhilarating though.' As she spoke Fletcher had an eye on the grey-looking police photographer. In comparison she felt her face positively glowing. It felt like it did when she got too close to a campfire.

Carruthers commented, 'Looking at poor Liu, I don't think it's something he's going to be doing again in a hurry.'

'Apart from on the way back you mean?' Fletcher threw Carruthers a mischievous grin. It was a light-hearted moment in what was clearly going to be a serious visit.

~

A large ruddy-faced man wearing a blue T-shirt and a pair of baggy blue shorts came bounding over to them. Carruthers saw the relief etched on the skipper's weather-beaten face as he jerked his head in the direction of the island. As he struggled out of his waterproofs and into his coverall kit and paper shoes he kept an eye on the police photographer.

'Good to see you again, not in these circumstances though,' Scott Gardner said, thrusting his large hand out to Carruthers and then to Fletcher. The man's grip was strong and confident.

'No, indeed,' agreed Carruthers. 'It's a bad day. Any news of Robert Paterson? I take it his body's not been washed up on the shoreline?'

Gardner shook his head. 'I've done a quick sweep. Not the easiest when you're carrying the extra weight.' He patted his well-covered stomach ruefully. 'I've found nothing. That's not to say he's not here, though. He might have been swept into one of the many caves or rocky inlets. In that case it could be almost impossible to find him.'

'I guess it was always a long shot,' sighed Carruthers. 'We've got the Dive and Marine Unit arriving soon. They can check the caves out.'

The skipper directed his next comment to Carruthers. 'The body's back there, not far from the visitor centre. I'll warn you it's not pleasant. From what I can see there's several stab wounds and it's definitely not been done by birds.' By way of explanation he said, 'I used to be in the army.'

Carruthers hadn't known that fact. But having ex-army as first on the scene was useful.

They waited until the last SOCO had got their protective kit on and as a group walked carefully along a stony track. Carruthers and Gardner in front, Fletcher slightly behind and Mackie and Liu bringing up the rear. Liu, grunting as he walked, had the heavy camera equipment still in its protective plastic slung over his shoulder.

Carruthers turned to the skipper of the *May Princess* once more. 'What can you tell me about what happened?'

Gardner's eyes were downcast. 'Not much, Jim. As you know we were less than half a mile off the island and the first thing that happened was that we came across Robert Paterson's boat. We shouted out to him but there was nothing. He wasn't on board.'

'His wife called him in missing first thing this morning,' Fletcher said.

'So I believe.' Gardner glanced at them and stopped walking. 'But what was he doing taking his fishing boat out at night?'

Carruthers stopped dead in his tracks and faced the skipper of the *May Princess*. 'My thoughts exactly, although I believe he left at first light. Would that make any difference?' He thought of Paterson's creels stacked against the harbour wall.

Gardner rubbed his hand over the bristles on his chin. 'Might do. I know some of the boys from Anstruther have started fishing for prawn. He might be one of them.'

'Would you take out your boat at first light for prawn?'

'Possibly. Your best bet is to ask Frank Dewar.'

Carruthers knew of Dewar. The man was another local fisherman and friend of Paterson.

'Scott, if he had been fishing for white fish then I could

understand it, but the white fishing industry ended here years ago.' That much Carruthers did know. 'I was under the impression that if you set out from Anstruther now it would be mainly lobster you'd fish for.'

Gardner scratched his head. 'That's true. It is still mostly lobster being fished from Anstruther but, like I said, recently I heard some of the fishermen are also starting to fish for prawn. Ach, bugger. I hope he's still alive, but I can't imagine how it might be possible. The winds are starting to pick up. If the body's at sea God knows where it has drifted.'

As if to emphasise the point Carruthers felt himself being battered by a strong head wind. 'You're right. The current could have carried him much further out.' He thought of Helen Lennox's words that the body might be out in the North Sea by now. 'If so,' he continued, 'it might be months before we find a body.' *If they find one at all*, thought Carruthers.

'Anyway,' Gardner continued, 'when we found Robert's boat and realised it was empty we called the coastguard in Aberdeen and carried on to the island.'

Carruthers nodded. He knew that everything was directed from Aberdeen.

The skipper walked round a dead seagull. Carruthers wondered how it had met its end. 'When we arrived, I thought it strange as there was nobody to greet us. Usually we get one of the volunteers, if not Tom, but then young Lofty told me about the celebration over in Anstruther.'

Carruthers nodded. 'That's right. The volunteers were over on the mainland. One of them was celebrating getting her PhD. Ramsey must have given them permission to all leave the island together.'

'Lofty was fair upset about that. He fancies one of them.' Gardner panted as he climbed the now steep path. 'He was hoping to see her this morning but apparently they were all pretty hungover. They didn't make the crossing.' The skipper grabbed Carruthers' arm. 'By the way, watch where you're stepping. The ground is teeming with puffin burrows. You dinnae want to crush a chick.'

Carruthers adjusted his footing so he was safely back on the stony path and now walking slightly behind Gardner.

'I didn't know puffins lived in burrows, did you?' hissed Fletcher. 'I thought they had nests.' She flattened her wet hair against her head.

'Tut tut,' said Carruthers, turning round. 'I thought you were the nature lover.'

Fletcher pulled a face.

Gardner threw his comment over his shoulder. 'To get back to what happened, I sent Lofty ahead to locate the warden. A short while later he was back with the news that he'd found a body. The boy was really shaken up.'

'You're definitely sure it's Tom?'

''Fraid so. No doubt at all. I see him when the boat docks three or four times a week.'

As he walked Carruthers kept an eye on the sky. It was a dark mass of swooping, swarming birds. A tern got so close he felt the swoosh of the wings and ducked. He wished he had brought a hat.

'The Arctic terns nest on the ground close to where the boat is tied up,' said Gardner. 'They'll be the ones dive-bombing you and trying to peck your head. He hasn't been moved, the warden I mean, but I've covered him with my jacket. The birds were showing too much interest in him.'

'Have you touched him at all?'

'Just checked for a pulse, Jim, to see if he was dead, but when I saw the state of his face, well, I knew it was game over.'

Carruthers felt his gut heave.

'To be fair, I'm no' really sure why I checked for a pulse.'

10

The body of the man lay on his side, one arm bent beneath him. His jeans were blood-soaked as was his grey and black Gore-Tex jacket.

Fletcher tried hard not to recoil at the disturbing sight but, being the professional that she was, within seconds her police instincts kicked in and she surveyed the scene with an expert critical eye.

The second thing she noted was that he had a pair of binoculars around his neck. *Killed in the line of duty* was the expression that sprang to mind. A bloody notebook lay open close to the body. Carefully she picked it up and flicked through it. Under today's date a list of birds had been written carefully with a ballpoint pen and the times they had been seen. The last entry had been a fulmar at 7am.

She handed the notebook to Carruthers. 'I think he was killed just after 7am.'

She started doing an immediate assessment. As she knew only too well, you couldn't assume a victim had been killed where they are found. They would need Dr Mackie to confirm that. However, with the amount of blood that had pooled around the body and soaked into the ground her guess would be that he had been killed not far from the visitor centre.

Fletcher took a closer look at the man's jacket. *Expensive*, she thought. *I'm surprised he's not wearing hillwalking trousers, though. Much more quick drying than jeans.* He would need the best outdoor kit in this line of work. She felt a spit of rain. She gazed at the jacket again and at the amount of blood that had seeped through. Either the murderer had stabbed him many times over or he had got lucky and had pierced an artery. A strong metallic smell hung in the air that mixed with the saltiness of the sea.

Dr Mackie knelt by the body and set to work almost immediately with a visual examination while Fletcher and Carruthers kept their distance. The pathologist worked silently and efficiently.

Fletcher stared at the tears in the fabric of the jacket. The attacker was either someone who was strong or someone who had been overcome with rage. Or both.

The position of the body interested Fletcher. It looked as if the victim had used his last breath to try to get up. The birds had pecked at his face and the closest eye to them had only the bloodied socket remaining. If this was indeed the warden of the island Fletcher felt a strange sadness that the birds he had spent his life protecting had treated him so badly in death.

But this is nature, she thought. *Nature in all its glory. Beautiful. But brutal.*

Once again she looked upwards to see a puffin flying past, its beak full of small fish. It was that old truism that in the midst of death life still carries on.

She directed her gaze back to the body, counting the number of wounds. It was difficult though, what with the amount of congealed and dried blood. Unexpectedly she felt sick and turned away to swallow down the bile that was threatening to rise. She took a deep breath of sea air and returned her gaze to the corpse when she felt a bit better. It would be hard to perform the job she was paid to do if she felt sick every time she looked at a dead body. And usually she was okay. What had got her so rattled about this death? Perhaps it was because it was so at odds with the natural surroundings and sense of isolation. What a solitary death. To die alone on a small island surrounded by raucous seabirds was certainly not how she would want to depart this world.

Then she remembered the young dead woman still cradling her baby back at the squat.

She thought about Ramsey's family and whether he had a partner and how they would come to terms with his terrible end.

She resumed her scan of the victim's torso, noting the multiple deep lacerations. As she watched Mackie straighten up and walk round the corpse she kept an eye on the circling and swooping birds. The sky was full of them, an encroaching blackness as they dipped and dived. The noise was fearsome and she had to shout over them to be heard. Like Carruthers she loved birds but she had always found the more aggressive seabirds rather menacing.

Liu seemed to be shaking so much he could hardly set up the camera equipment. If any of the birds got too close he would duck and let out little shrieks. She wondered if he actually had a phobia of seabirds. If so, it was most unfortunate that the victim was surrounded by thousands of them.

Mackie expelled a deep breath. He turned briefly to Carruthers. His voice, when he finally spoke was slow and measured. 'On first examining him, this looks like stab wounds. It's unlikely he's inflicted them on himself. Some of them look pretty deep and I would suspect a number of them could have killed him.'

Carruthers took a swift look round. 'There's also no knife unless he's lying on it or it's embedded inside.'

Liu managed to set up his camera and took a series of photographs of both the body and the surrounding area. His shakes subsided. Fletcher was glad. If he did indeed have a phobia of birds it was no laughing matter.

Mackie called out to the photographer. 'Have you finished photographing him in this position, Liu? Can I turn him round?'

'No' yet. Nearly. Aww fuck.' A seagull had swooped and deposited its excrement on the Chinese man's shoulder. It would have looked comical if the situation they were in hadn't been so serious. Liu dug into his bag and, muttering, wiped the bird poo off with a white handkerchief.

'Supposed to be a sign of good luck.' Fletcher gave Liu what she hoped was a supportive look. Liu kept quiet but didn't look too impressed.

Liu returned to photographing the body and indicated to Mackie when he had finished. With a great deal of gentleness, Mackie, with Carruthers' help, turned the body round so the man was now on his front.

'There are stab wounds all over the body,' said Mackie.

Fletcher pondered this. She wondered if the warden had been murdered by someone he knew. Statistics said in all probability he had. It was a violent attack.

'He's even been stabbed in the back.'

Stabbed in the back smacked of cowardice. In an effort to lighten the mood just for a brief moment Fletcher said, 'It would be too easy if the murder weapon was inserted in his back and covered with fingerprints, wouldn't it?'

Mackie's response was harsh. 'We're not playing out an Agatha Christie novel. What I will say, though, is that this has been a frenzied attack, but then you don't need me to tell you that.' The pathologist bent down on one knee and examined the dead man's hands. 'There's only a couple of defensive wounds to the palms.'

Poor sod, thought Fletcher. She looked round her. There was a hell of a lot of blood. Fletcher wondered which puncture wound had finally killed him. Most likely a stab wound had punctured an organ but they would know more when John Mackie conducted the post-mortem. The more important question was, who would want to kill the warden of the Isle of May?

'And you definitely think he was killed here?' Fletcher addressed her remark to Mackie, although she had a strong feeling she already knew the answer.

Mackie looked up. 'It's likely from the amount of blood that he *was* killed here.'

'Can you give an estimate for time of death?' Carruthers leant over the body as he asked the question.

'Within the last twelve hours.'

'Can you be any more precise than that? It looks likely according to his notebook that he was alive and well at...' Carruthers took the book from Fletcher. '7am.'

'I'm not giving you any more until I get him back to the lab, Jim, but if you've got his notebook you most probably have your answer.'

The detectives both wanted to know if Ramsey's death was within the same window of time as Paterson's disappearance. Her money was on it being early morning. It would be useful to know what time the volunteers left the island.

She knew Gardner had already done a cursory sweep of the coastline in his attempt to locate Robert Paterson. Thinking of Paterson also got her thinking of the man's boat. 'We need the island searched, Jim, and to get one of the fishermen to take Robert Paterson's boat back to the shore . We also need a full forensics sweep done on it.'

'That's right,' agreed Carruthers.

'This is really strange. Paterson goes missing close to where the warden's body is discovered. Is it a coincidence? What's going on, Jim?'

'I only wish I knew. One thing's for sure though. Press are going to have a field day.'

Carruthers gazed down at the body of the island's warden. 'I don't know what to think at the moment,' he said, 'but we have one dead warden and one missing fisherman.' He looked up at Fletcher. 'We need to find Paterson.'

At that moment there was a shout and Fletcher looked up to see the rest of the SOCOs had just arrived. They snaked their way up to the visitor centre in their white suits. Fletcher watched Carruthers leave their group to direct some of the SOCOs to fan out across the wee island.

'Get the team to start looking for a murder weapon,' he shouted. 'I want every inch of the island combed, including all the buildings, the lighthouses, keepers' houses and the priory. However, you need to remember this is a nature reserve. Be careful where you tread as there's scores of puffin burrows.'

The SOCOs nodded and began to fan out to start their painstaking fingertip search.

Fletcher couldn't imagine how they could do a thorough job without crushing some of the burrows.

Finally Mackie stood up. As he straightened he put his hands in the flat of his back. 'Christ, it gets harder and harder to do this job. Why can't they all die indoors?'

He batted away a diving tern that had got too close. 'We're going to have to move the body as soon as possible and get it back to the lab. This scene is like something out of *The Birds*. And in all seriousness I think Liu is about to have a meltdown. It's one of the more challenging places I've been called to, if I'm honest, although I did have to go down a mineshaft once. God knows how I got back up again. I wasn't young then either.'

Fletcher ducked as another tern swooped. 'Jesus. That was close. I felt that on the back of my head. Will they attack us?'

'I think they're particularly aggressive when their chicks are newly hatched,' said Scott. 'It's just the parents being protective.'

Carruthers got to his feet, dusting himself down. 'Have you seen a sign of anyone else on the island?' He addressed his remarks to the skipper.

'No, but I'll be honest with you, Jim, there were moments I was crapping myself once the *May Princess* had left. It suddenly hit me that I was alone with a murder victim. I then started to worry that mebbe the murderer was still on the island and that I'd be next.'

11

Carruthers tapped Fletcher on her shoulder. 'C'mon. Let's go and take a look round. Leave the SOCOs to do what they do best.'

Fletcher gazed around her. 'Where do we start?'

'We'll start with the warden's accommodation. It's closest to the visitor centre.'

They walked the five minutes up the rough path to Fluke Street. The accommodation was housed in practical white-washed bungalows. The warden's accommodation was the second building on the left after that of the volunteers.

Carruthers turned the metal handle of the gate, which made a rusty squeaking noise, walked up the path and tried the blue painted wooden door. 'It's unlocked.'

'Probably thought he was alone on the island. No reason to lock it.'

Somehow the fact that Tom Ramsey had left his accommodation unlocked on his last trip outside, if indeed he had been killed outside, made his death even worse, thought Carruthers. *Totally unsuspecting.*

'We're looking for general impressions at this stage. We don't want to compromise the scene for the SOCOs. No doubt they'll want to fingerprint later.'

They walked into the property and for a moment stood still in the hall. So far there was no sign of any disturbance. Or blood. Very quickly they found themselves in the warden's cosy living area. Two comfortable brown leather armchairs faced a wood-burning stove. A soft brown rug was placed over the blue-carpeted floor.

'This is nicer than my own living room,' remarked Fletcher. 'He's made it a real home-from-home. I can't believe he's got a wood-burning stove here. Reckon the wood for it would have to come over by boat.'

Carruthers picked up a crime novel from a small wooden table. 'I guess when you're spending several months of a year on a small island it's important to have a few creature comforts.'

'There's no TV though,' said Fletcher. 'I don't know if that's a blessing or a curse. What would he do of an evening, especially on those nights he's on his own?'

'Read a book?' Carruthers pointed to the shelves of crime fiction books. 'He's obviously an avid reader.' He took out a few, flicked through them and replaced them in the shelves. Most of them were written by Scandinavian writers like Jo Nesbo and Camilla Lackberg. 'He's obviously into his Nordic Noir. It's bleak stuff.' He shook his head. *How ironic that a man who was into crime fiction characterised by brutal crimes and often shocking violence would end up going the same way.* 'There's nothing in this room. Let's try the next.'

They walked into the warden's study. There were several bookcases full of files and paperwork and a large wooden desk on which sat a computer and keyboard. But the walls were what interested Carruthers the most. On an enormous corkboard were pinned maps, sheets and photographs. Next to a large-scale map of the island were various daily site reports.

Carruthers went up to the board, took down a sheet and studied it before passing it over to Fletcher. It was a list of dates and bird names. On it were details of when the first egg had been produced and the first chick of each species hatched. The inspector noticed with interest that the egg of the first puffin had been discovered on 14th April and the first chick recorded was on the 22nd May. Next to it was a guidance sheet for usage of the Cisco telephone system and next to that a sheet about water tank levels. The neat handwriting denoted a man who was both careful and methodical. Carruthers' eyes drifted across the board until he came to a set of photographs.

'There are photographs of each year's volunteers,' he said. 'That's handy. I guess they change every season.'

'They change but the warden stays the same. I wonder how long Ramsey has been doing this job.' Carruthers took down that year's photograph of the warden and his volunteers and passed it to Fletcher.

'Easy to find out.'

'Hang on to that,' said Carruthers.

'Don't worry. I was intending to.'

Another photograph caught Carruthers' eye. He pulled it down and stuck the pin back in the board. This time it was Tom Ramsey on his own. His head was thrown back and he was laughing. The dark-haired man looked animated and happy. The inspector recognised the gate. It had been taken outside his accommodation. Carruthers looked closely at the photograph. The warden had his telltale binoculars around his neck. And he was smiling. 'I think he had a real passion for this job. Take this one as well.' He handed it to his DS.

Fletcher's eyes lighted on the warden's desk. A mobile phone was sitting next to the computer. She reached out but he stopped her.

'Leave it for the SOCOs,' instructed Carruthers. 'They'll

want to take both the mobile and computer and dust for finger-prints but more importantly we need to leave as much undis-turbed as we can.'

The nod told Carruthers she understood. A map, partly wedged under the warden's computer was pounced on by Fletcher. 'This will be useful though, Jim. It's a map of the island. Reckon it would be okay to remove that?'

Carruthers gave his permission. 'I'd rather we left everything untouched but given we don't know our way round I think it would be helpful. Yeah. Go on. Grab it. Let's leave this room. There's nothing here.'

Fletcher pulled the map from under the computer. They walked out and into the warden's fitted kitchen casting their eyes around the small space. 'There's no sign of a struggle in any of the rooms,' said Carruthers. 'And he certainly wasn't killed in here.'

A row of brightly coloured mugs hung from hooks over the tabletops. Carruthers cast his eyes around but if he had been hoping to come across two used mugs showing Ramsey had entertained a visitor before he was killed he was disappointed. There was nothing obvious in the room that could be passed on to forensics.

'Mackie felt he was killed where he was found,' said Carruthers. 'Perhaps there was no reason for the killer to come in here. After all, he found what he wanted outside.'

'Looks that way and it would be borne out by the amount of blood at the scene.' Fletcher glanced round the kitchen. Last night's dinner plates had been washed and left on the draining board. Everything was neat and tidy. A drained tea mug stood on the old wooden breakfast table. There was no sign of a struggle or a fight.

'No sign of any breakfast things,' observed Fletcher.

'Perhaps he doesn't eat breakfast. Maybe a cup of tea was enough.'

Fletcher opened the fridge door. There was milk; a lump of cheese; some cold meats and two bottles of champagne. She pointed out the bottles to Carruthers. 'Seems a bit extravagant.'

Carruthers peered into the fridge. 'Perhaps he's got a weakness for the finer things in life.'

'Apart from the basics and the champagne there's not much in here.' She closed the fridge door.

'Well, perhaps he was running low on stock. You can't just pop out and buy a loaf of bread. And let's face it; no Tesco delivery here.'

Fletcher touched Carruthers' arm. 'C'mon. Let's go. Next room.'

Their search of the bathroom produced nothing out of the ordinary. Carruthers noted a toothbrush and tube of toothpaste on the white sink. He opened a small cupboard attached to the wall but there was nothing of interest. Just the usual paraphernalia that you would find in a man's bathroom – paracetamol, plasters, cold remedies, soap and a razor. All in all the room was spotless but utilitarian.

Next they walked into Ramsey's bedroom. This was the only room in which there was anything remotely personal. Fletcher walked round the side of the bed to pick up the first of two framed photographs on the bedside table. It was of an older couple. She passed it to Carruthers who stared at the picture. The resemblance to Ramsey was uncanny. The warden had the same square-set jaw and dark hair as his father but he had his mother's almond-shaped eyes.

'His parents, do you suppose?'

'Looks like it.' He looked around him. 'No photograph of a girlfriend though.'

'Maybe he was single.'

Fletcher picked up the second photograph and smiled. It was of a golden retriever. 'The family pet.'

'So you've got an animal-loving island warden who is most likely single and close to his parents. And yet he ends up getting murdered. Why? There must be a clue here somewhere.'

'Not if it's a nutjob.'

'We all know that's not very likely.'

'Not very likely but it happens.'

Carruthers replaced the photograph on the bedside table. 'A nutjob who just happens to be on the island on his or her own. How would they even get here? I think he's been targeted. This killing is deliberate. It's not like Ramsey was in the wrong place at the wrong time. He's on a frigging small *island*. C'mon. Keep looking. There must be *something*.'

They opened drawers and cupboards. Finally after discovering nothing but Ramsey's penchant for Marks and Spencer boxer shorts Carruthers shut the drawers. 'Let's go. There's nothing here. At least nothing for us. The SOCOs might get more.' As they opened the front door they saw a long line of the space-suited officers wending their way down the path towards the buildings.

Carruthers shut the door on the now dead man's life. He felt a moment of great sadness that the next people to set foot in the building would be the scene of crime officers and not the warden. Fleetingly he wondered who would drink the champagne.

He nodded to the first officer as the man passed him.

'You didn't touch or move anything?' The scene of crime officer asked the Glaswegian policeman.

'Nothing.' Out of hearing of the officer Carruthers hissed, 'Let's see that map,' as he sidestepped one of the SOCOs.

'Your nose growing longer, Pinocchio?' Fletcher handed over the map to Carruthers as she spoke, a wry smile playing on her lips. He opened it and, heads touching, they both studied it. 'I want to cover the whole island,' said Carruthers, 'but let's go to Pilgrim's Haven first.'

'There seems to be several ways of getting there. Which way do you want to go?'

'Via the priory. And then we'll take a look at the bird observatory. I want to get a good feel for the whole island.'

12

They doubled back to the visitor centre then took a path to the right, which led them to a steep climb up to the ruins of the priory.

'I had no idea there was such a maze of paths on this island,' said Fletcher a little while later. She knelt down to look at a mound of earth. 'Almost looks like a rabbit warren but those must be the puffin burrows they were talking about.' She stood up and continued to walk. 'Oh look, I think that's an eider duck.' A large contented duck was nesting just a few feet away from them on the ground. 'God, they're huge. And really tame.'

'Keep your mind on the job, Andie,' Carruthers remonstrated.

They carried on walking until they came to the ruins of the priory. Fletcher gazed at the tumbledown stone and then out to sea. She expanded her lungs as she took in a deep breath of fresh sea air. 'I can imagine a community of monks on the island. It feels like a very spiritual place. But if the ruins are anything to go by, what's the betting they came to a grisly end?'

Carruthers who was hunched over among the stones

shouted at her. 'Don't forget we're looking for a knife or some sort of bladed implement. This isn't a geography field trip.'

'I know. I know.' She made her way to Carruthers and started ferreting around the vegetation with her gloved hands. 'I *can* multi-task, you know.'

'As amazing as the wildlife and ruins are, Andie, can you just *focus?*'

He sounds irritable, thought Fletcher. *Maybe he's pissed off because he's had to cancel seeing his ex-wife.* She got down on her haunches but after a few minutes called out, 'I don't see anything here.'

'I can't see anything either. Okay, let's keep walking.' He took the guide out of her hand and pointed at a landmark. 'Let's take this path to Pilgrim's Haven. The bay is the location for the puffins' webcams.'

'I know about them,' said Fletcher. 'They look out to the cliff and the beach. It's worth viewing the footage. You never know what might be seen. It's live streamed to the Scottish Seabird Centre in North Berwick but you can also see it live on the internet.'

Carruthers started walking and Fletcher caught up as they made their way to Pilgrim's Haven.

'It's not going to show us Kirkhaven though,' remarked Carruthers, 'and that's where the body's been found.'

'God, these cliffs are impressive,' she said as she looked down one. Several medium-sized black and white birds with blunt black beaks caught her eye. 'Crikey, look at all those birds. What are they? Razorbills?' There was no answer from Carruthers who was crouched down examining something on the ground.

As Fletcher surveyed the cliffs and inlets something caught her eye, lying at an angle in a precarious position. She marched towards it.

'Jim, come and have a look at this.' Fletcher stood next to one of the webcams. 'Look, it's been smashed.'

Carruthers joined her. 'Good spot.'

'Why would it be smashed? Did the murderer do it? If so, why? It might be live streaming but it's nowhere near the murder site.'

Carruthers rubbed his bristles. 'We can find out from the volunteers whether it was in working order yesterday.'

Fletcher scribbled in her black notebook. 'C'mon. Let's walk on.'

As he led the way he shouted over his shoulder. 'How many volunteers are staying on the island at the moment?'

'Five I think. Three women and two men.'

'And that's it? There's nobody else?'

'I don't think so. Apparently the island can also house small groups of visitors but there's nobody else staying just now.'

'It must be a strange existence.'

'The night sky would be amazing.' Fletcher knew Carruthers enjoyed looking at the stars. 'And let's face it. It gives a whole new meaning to the term "going out for a quiet pint". A quiet pint really would be a quiet pint.' She puffed as she kept walking. Her calves were feeling the strain. 'Everything that you needed would have to be brought on the island by boat. I can't imagine it, can you?'

There was an ear-splitting shriek above them. Carruthers looked overhead to see two large seabirds. 'I'm not sure it would be that quiet with the noise from those birds. Do you think you ever get used to it? I think all that squealing and squawking would do my head in. I wonder if they ever shut up or if they're like this all night long?'

'I spent a weekend in Peterhead once,' said Fletcher, thinking about Britain's most north-easterly seaport. 'They were pretty loud all night. At least that's how I remember it.' Catching

Carruthers' look of surprise, she added, 'I know it's not the first destination you'd think of for a weekend by the coast.'

'What took you up there?'

'I was visiting a friend.' She thought of dark-haired Nicky. Another friend she'd lost contact with since she'd joined the police. Most of her old friends were hitched with young kids now. She didn't know about Nicky though. She pulled a face. 'God, it was seriously noisy in Peterhead.'

'You talking about the fishermen coming out from the pub drunk?'

'No. I was talking about the bloody seagulls and the foghorn. The seagulls started screaming at 3am and never stopped. And the foghorn went on all night. I couldn't get a wink of sleep.' Fletcher didn't actually remember meeting any fishermen but she definitely remembered the hotel she had stayed in. *Was it with Mark? It had been a mistake booking the cheapest.* When they checked in mid-afternoon she remembered the bar full of drunken men. Perhaps they had been fishermen. They had taken the narrow staircase to the rooms above and found that none of the lights in the corridor were working. The small window at the back of their room had a large crack running through it. And to cap it all the lock on their door was broken. They reluctantly stayed the night but after a fitful sleep had left before breakfast, worried about the possibility of food poisoning if the cleanliness of the room was anything to go by. She shuddered.

'Have you ever been back? To Peterhead?' Carruthers asked.

'No. Our friend moved back to Glasgow. And there was no reason to return. I can't remember much about Peterhead at all except for the hotel, the seagulls and the foghorn.'

'I've never been there,' Carruthers admitted, 'but it must be like a lot of fishing communities in Scotland. Pretty much every-thing would be based around the fishing.'

Fletcher stopped walking for a moment and gazed out to sea. 'I would go seriously stir-crazy if I had to live on this island. Imagine what it's like in bad weather? You would have those strong north-easterly winds bringing heavy seas and rain. The visitor boats must be cancelled quite regularly. Imagine if the weather is so bad you can't even get outside to do your volunteering. You wouldn't be able to get off the island in bad weather either, even if you wanted to. It must take a special type of person to enjoy this lonely existence.'

'I don't know. I think I'd quite like to spend some time here. Just you and nature. Really getting back to basics.'

Fletcher could see that this would appeal to the man who loved his wild camping, Scottish hills and solitude. 'It wouldn't just be you and nature if the volunteers were here. There must be arguments and fallouts from time to time when you're confined to such a small space. The warden's more likely to have been killed by someone he knows.'

'We need to find out more about his death. Hopefully the post-mortem will tell us. We'll start by interviewing the volunteers, although I don't see how one of them could have killed him if they were all on the mainland. One thing's for sure though. They won't be getting back to the island any time soon. Not until the SOCOs have finished their search.'

'I think it's amazing there was a settlement here at one time,' said Fletcher, studying the guidebook. 'I don't know the details but wasn't it one of the earliest Christian communities?'

'Maybe that's why there's place names on the island like Bishop's Cove and Pilgrim's Haven,' Carruthers ventured.

She laughed. 'There's also somewhere called Shag Rock and Willie's Hole, which sound positively rude. Look at this. Slipped Disc and Foreigner's Point. I wonder how they got those names?' Fletcher felt a tug at her jacket and a gust of wind propelled her along the path. 'Oh God, the wind's picking up again. Hope we don't get stuck here. I wonder how Liu's coping.'

'He'll be glad to get back to the mainland.'

Forty minutes later they had had enough. 'I think we should call it a day and try to get back to Anstruther. Let's leave the rest to the SOCOs. That's what they're here for.'

Fletcher readily agreed. A light rain had started to fall and the weather was closing in.

13

'Findings?' Sandra McTavish looked around the room before her gaze settled on Carruthers. The full team were in the newly set-up incident room with McTavish standing near the board at the front.

'No murder weapon's been found so far,' said Carruthers. 'The SOCOs are still conducting their search. It might be a small island but it's full of cliffs, caves, inlets and havens, not to mention grassy knolls.'

'I think we need to be realistic and accept that we may never find the weapon,' said McTavish. 'It could easily have been thrown into the sea or onto a ledge.'

As she said this Carruthers thought about the dizzying height of the cliffs and the numerous ledges that precariously housed the seabirds.

'Mackie has confirmed that Tom Ramsey was killed where he was found,' said Fletcher. 'This is also borne out by the fact we found no evidence of a fight or any sort of disturbance back at the warden's accommodation. We've given his laptop and mobile to forensics. A notebook and binoculars were also recovered at the scene. It looks like Ramsey was out logging birds when he was attacked.'

Where was the pen he was using, though? thought Carruthers. *He would have used a ballpoint pen to take the notes and it hadn't been found with the binoculars or notebook.*

He spoke aloud, half to himself. 'No pen was found.'

'Sorry, Jim,' said McTavish, her brows knitting together. 'What are you talking about?'

'When we found Ramsey. He still had his binoculars slung around his neck and we picked up a notebook lying by his body. But there was no pen. Where did the pen go?'

'Must still be close to where he was found.'

Carruthers was surprised Fletcher hadn't picked up on the missing pen. Usually her attention to detail was excellent.

'We have Ramsey's parents heading to Scotland for the formal ID. They're only in Northumberland so it won't take them long to get up but both Scott Gardner and Lofty Sykes have identified the body as being that of the warden.'

'What we need to do now is talk to people close to Ramsey,' said McTavish, looking solemn. She stared intently at the photograph of the body. 'Who would want to kill the warden of a nature reserve?' She stared at the faces around her. 'Build up a picture of his last movements. Find out who the last person was to see him alive–'

'Surely that would be the volunteers before they left for the mainland?' said Lennox.

'What time did they leave the island?' There was a steel edge to McTavish's voice. 'I want them interviewed. As soon as possible. Did Ramsey have any fall-outs with anyone?' She stared at the photograph of the bloodied body of the warden. 'This was a frenzied attack and we need to find the perpetrator. And make sure you interview them separately so they can't corroborate each other's stories,' she added.

Fletcher and Lennox nodded, both busy scribbling in their notebooks.

Lennox looked up. 'I've run Ramsey's name through the database and he has no criminal record.'

'Good work, Helen.' McTavish stood for a moment with her back to the room full of CID while she studied the photograph of Ramsey with his latest group of volunteers. She turned round to face them. 'What we now need to find out is what his relationship was like with each one of the volunteers. Did he get on with all of them? I can imagine when a small number of people are living in such proximity to each other like that there will be niggles and misunderstandings. Did a misunderstanding blossom into a feud before it got nipped in the bud? Did anyone have an axe to grind? Were any of them having affairs with each other?'

Helen Lennox patted her spiky hair. 'Doesn't the warden spend several weeks on their own on the island out of season without the volunteers? God, you'd be so lonely. I'd end up going nuts.'

McTavish ignored Lennox's remark and started to pace up and down. 'I want to know more about Tom Ramsey's background. Where was he before he got the job as Isle of May warden? Was he warden elsewhere? Look at his personal relationships with those close to him. Does he have a girlfriend? Or a boyfriend? Had that relationship gone sour?'

There was some whispering among those assembled.

'I don't think there's a current partner,' said Fletcher. 'At least there were no signs in his accommodation.'

'What about an ex? And let's not forget we've also got a missing person's enquiry ongoing. There's still been no sighting of Robert Paterson – alive or dead.'

Helen Lennox's hand shot up in the air. 'Are we treating the two as connected?'

'It's hard to say at this stage whether they're connected or not,' said McTavish, 'but let's be frank – ordinarily I'd say no. We have no evidence to suggest they are. However, it does look suspicious that Robert Paterson's boat is discovered less than half a mile from the island where Tom Ramsey's body's been found. And what was Robert Paterson's boat doing so close to the Isle of May in the first place? The island is a nature reserve. Aren't there restrictions for fishing vessels?'

There was another murmuring.

'We're assuming there *are* fishing restrictions but it'll be worth double checking.' She looked over at Carruthers. 'Jim, you live in Anstruther. Find out, will you?'

Carruthers nodded.

'And if there are restrictions, we also need to find out what those restrictions are. But remember the tide could have taken Paterson's boat to within the restricted limit. There's nothing to say he was illegally fishing there.'

'There's one other thing I need to chase up too,' said Carruthers.

'Which is?' McTavish sounded impatient.

'Why did he take his fishing boat out overnight?'

'Cos he's a fisherman,' said Helen Lennox.

Carruthers was calm in his response. 'Anstruther fishermen mainly fish for lobster, Helen. They don't take their boats out overnight. You'd fish for lobster during the day.'

That silenced Lennox, who turned away looking embarrassed.

'However, what Scott Gardner did say is that some of the local fishermen in Anstruther have started to fish for prawn. If Paterson was one of them then it's entirely possible he'd take his boat out at first light.'

'First light?' McTavish looked thoughtful. 'About 4am at the moment, then?'

'Middle of the night to the rest of us,' put in Harris.

'I got told to talk to Frank Dewar,' said Carruthers. 'I know him. Friend of Paterson's and another fisherman.'

McTavish's voice was firm. 'Make it a priority.'

Carruthers also made a mental note to speak with Paterson's wife as soon as possible and find out where her husband regularly took his fishing boat. He also thought it might be instructive to have another word with Scott Gardner. After all, he was a gregarious person who lived locally and being an ex-fisherman perhaps he would know if any of the locals were in the habit of disregarding the regulations about fishing too close to the May. He kicked himself for not asking earlier.

Fletcher sucked the end of her pen. 'I've been doing some research on Fife fishermen,' she said.

'Are you going to share the findings with the rest of us?' said McTavish.

'Fishermen in the East Neuk of Fife are represented by the Fife Fishermen's Mutual Association.'

'Meaning?' McTavish asked. 'I don't come from a long line of Fife fishermen, Andie.'

'It's a co-operative, which means–'

'I know what a co-operative is.'

Sandra's getting tetchy, thought Carruthers. *And I don't blame her.*

'Well, it just means that the East Neuk fishermen sell their daily catch as a group rather than as individuals. They must be doing something right: apparently it generates around £3.5 million per year.'

'Do we know how many prawn and creel boats work out of Anstruther?' McTavish looked at both Carruthers and Fletcher when she asked this question.

Fletcher read from her notes. 'I think there's about forty.

Anstruther has got a long fishing tradition. Apparently it's been a port since the thirteenth century.'

'As interesting as that may be let's stick to the case. First of all, we need to know why Paterson was fishing at night.'

Carruthers jumped in. 'Leave that to me. Like I said, I can find that out.'

Fletcher continued reading from her notebook. 'Okay, well this is quite interesting too. Apparently it's been at least fifteen years since overfishing resulted in the last white fish being commercially landed in the East Neuk. It's now all about prawns and langoustine, crabs scallops and lobsters. I also found out that the prawn boats operating out of Pittenweem mainly fish within fifteen miles of the harbour but they also sometimes spend periods off the north-east coast of England or the west coast of Scotland.'

'I suppose it's a bit like fishermen travelling to follow the herring shoals,' said Carruthers. He could imagine the boats from the East Neuk making their way further north or south in pursuit of the now lucrative langoustine.

McTavish scratched her head. 'None of that helps us in understanding why Paterson took his boat out at night, though, unless as Jim said he was fishing for prawn and starting at first light.' She sighed. 'It would, however, be useful to know if a good living can still be made from being an East Neuk fisherman. We don't yet know why Paterson has disappeared or why Ramsey has been killed but we do know one thing. Most murders are committed due to jealousy or greed.'

'Do you think the murder could be tied up with drugs?' Harris asked.

'We found no evidence of drug-taking in Ramsey's accommodation,' said Fletcher.

Carruthers thought about what Gus from the NCA had told

him. 'Is it just coincidence we have a drugs shipment expected to be coming in to Fife in the next couple of days by boat?'

McTavish looked thoughtful.

'We already know that the drug aspect is definitely worth pursuing,' urged Carruthers.

McTavish made a quick decision. 'Yeah, you're right. If a shipment is expected into Fife it would be smaller boats which would pick up the drugs most likely in the middle of the night.'

'And that's *exactly* when Paterson went missing. During the night. Gus from the NCA said the same about it being smaller boats which would pick up the drugs haul.'

'At the moment we have absolutely no evidence that either the warden's murder or Paterson's disappearance is connected to the drugs trade but I think it's worth considering.' McTavish stood with her arm against the incident board. 'We have no motive at all at the moment so we need to keep an open mind. The one thing we do know though is that his murder was brutal and bloody.'

'And possibly premeditated.' All eyes were on Carruthers. 'The other thing is one of the webcams was smashed. They live stream to the Scottish Seabird Centre in North Berwick and apparently also on the internet.'

Fletcher cleared her throat. 'I've made a phone call to North Berwick and I can confirm that the webcams were all working the day before the murder.'

McTavish tilted her head to the side. 'You think it was deliberately smashed then?'

'Bit of a coincidence otherwise,' said Carruthers. 'However, having said that the webcams were nowhere near where the body was found.'

'That doesn't make sense then,' cried Lennox.

'If the webcam was smashed by the murderer then it's looking likely Ramsey was killed by someone who had intimate knowledge of the island,' said Fletcher. 'I mean, how many people are going to know where those webcams are even located?'

McTavish looked thoughtful. 'It also tells us something else. If the webcams were smashed by the perpetrator I agree the murder was more likely to have been premeditated.'

There was a low murmuring among those present in the incident room.

McTavish gazed round the room. 'Right, time to assign jobs.' Her eyes alighted on Fletcher. 'Andie, I want you and Gayle to interview the volunteers. Jim, I want you to talk to anyone who is close to Paterson. Start with his wife and his best friend. We need to know why he was fishing at night. Also find out about any fishing restrictions. It might just be coincidence that the boat has been found so close to the island but we need more information. Also find out what his state of mind has been like recently and–'

'You think it could be suicide?'

'Not ruling anything out at this point, Jim.'

The door to the incident room opened and Brown put his head round. He looked straight at McTavish. 'Ma'am, you'll want to read this just in from the lab. The preliminary forensic report on Robert Paterson's boat.'

'Well, hand it over then. No good standing at the door with it.' She put her glasses on and as she read it she exclaimed loudly. She licked her lips and drew in a deep breath. A hush descended around the room. She looked up at the sea of faces. 'Blood spatter has been found on Robert Paterson's boat.'

'He must have had an accident,' cried Helen Lennox. 'Perhaps he tripped over some of his fishing gear, lost his footing and toppled overboard. He wouldn't be the first.'

A second voice called out. 'Or just mebbe he's been killed by the same nutter that's killed the warden.'

McTavish put her hand up for silence as she skim-read the report a second time. 'Apparently forensics believe there's been a lot of blood.' She frowned.

Various cries and comments came from around the incident room.

'Too much for an accident?'

'If he'd bashed his head... We all know head wounds bleed a lot.'

Brown was still hovering at the door awaiting his next instruction. He didn't have long to wait.

McTavish turned to him. 'Get on to the lab. We need to see if the blood on the boat is Robert Paterson's. We'll need his DNA.'

'Yes, ma'am.' Brown retreated out the room and shut the door.

McTavish took her glasses off and pinched the bridge of her nose. 'Okay, so what does this tell us?'

'Not much until we know whose blood it is,' exclaimed Helen Lennox.

McTavish's shoulders dropped as she spoke, a bit quieter this time. 'I don't think it will be in much doubt that the blood will belong to our missing fisherman. I think, given that the boat was found out at sea and there has been a lot of blood on it, it's unlikely Paterson is still alive.'

'Do you suspect foul play?'

'To be truthful I've no idea, but it's definitely suspicious.'

McTavish looked over at Carruthers. 'Jim, any news about Tom Ramsey's post-mortem?'

Carruthers stopped checking his mobile and looked up. 'The Procurator Fiscal is fast-tracking it. It will be done later today. But when I last spoke with Mackie some of those cuts were deep. And his preliminary examination showed that several could have killed him.'

'Good. Okay. I feel we are finally starting to progress things.'

She shuffled her notes. 'Okay, what was I going to say before that interruption?' She looked around her and her eyes fell on Helen Lennox. 'Helen,' the woman started to attention, 'I want you to build up a picture of our warden. What was he like? Was he currently in a relationship? Where was his last post?'

'On it, but can I tag along with Andie when she interviews the volunteers?'

McTavish appeared to be thinking this over.

'I'm happy for Helen to go instead of me,' said Watson. 'After all, I've got the press release to draft up.'

That's nice of Gayle Watson, thought Carruthers.

'Yes, all right, that makes sense but let Andie take the lead.'

McTavish turned to Watson. 'Can you get the press release done by close of today?'

'Aye, no bother.'

The briefing broke up and the officers drifted out of the incident room. McTavish turned to Carruthers. 'I need to fill Bingham in with the latest findings but I'll be in my office if you need me.'

14

Carruthers tapped on his DCI's door half an hour later and put his head round. 'Sandra, have you got a minute?'

She wore her harassment like a shroud. 'Sorry, Jim, I'm a bit busy at the moment. Can it wait?'

'I just wanted to say I'd like to go to the post-mortem.'

McTavish took her glasses off and held them in her hand. She pinched the bridge of her nose. 'I know you like to be present at PMs, Jim, but we can't spare you at the moment. Mackie will ring us just as soon as he has any results.'

'I'd still like to be there.'

McTavish glared at Carruthers. 'I'm the DCI and I make the decisions.'

Carruthers was shocked at her outburst. It wasn't like her to pull rank. He thought they'd settled into a good working relationship. However, her outburst did remind him of the early days when she had first joined their team and how difficult the relationship between them had been then. In retrospect, it hadn't helped that even after he'd been demoted he'd still got to keep his office. Until Sandra McTavish had turned up, that is. He'd then been pushed out to join the other members of CID.

'Sandra, is everything okay?'

She shook her head and wiped the back of her hand over her face. 'I'm sorry. That was uncalled for.' She looked up at him and he could see the exhaustion in her face and the pain in her eyes. 'It's unprofessional of me to take my bad mood out on you.' She stood up. 'This case is taxing to say the least and I have a few problems on the home front, that's all.'

Carruthers hovered awkwardly. 'Happy to listen if you want to talk.' Even to his ears his answer hadn't sounded that convincing. It wasn't that he was unsympathetic. It was just that he was out of his depth talking to his new boss about her emotions.

She shot him a grateful look. 'Sorry. I really shouldn't be bringing my personal problems to work. Or to you.'

Carruthers could see her hesitate. He wondered whether McTavish's long hours and busy family life meant she had lost touch with any friends.

'It's my husband.'

Shit. She does want to talk.

She'd obviously decided Carruthers deserved an explanation. The DI wondered what the woman's husband had done now. He had known that they had been having marriage difficulties. Occasionally she had confided in him. He thought back to one excruciating visit to a restaurant with her in their last murder case when she had talked candidly to him about her marriage problems. It had surprised him that she had chosen him as her confidante and he still hadn't figured out if that was a good or bad thing.

'The marriage is over, Jim, in all but name. My bastard of a husband says he's going to be fighting for custody of the kids.'

Carruthers' eyes widened in shock. He had no idea things had got so bad between McTavish and her husband. And having been through a divorce himself he didn't wish it on anyone. He looked at her with serious concern. She looked like she might burst into tears at any moment. He almost wanted to go and find Fletcher. She'd know how to deal with this situation much better than him.

However, he also knew he had to say something and pushed the words out. 'Sandra, I'm so sorry. I don't know what to say.'

'Look, if you want to go to the PM, then go. I'm not going to stop you. But I want you to make it a priority to interview the man's wife. So do that first. Okay?'

McTavish had obviously decided that she didn't want to talk about her marital problems any further so a relieved Carruthers followed her lead. Truth was he couldn't wait to get the conversation back on to a work footing. 'Do we tell her about the blood spatter on the boat?'

McTavish appeared to be thinking this over. 'Not yet, not until we get confirmation of whose blood it is.'

'Well, surely it's going to be Paterson's? Doesn't she have a right to know?'

'What purpose will it serve at this stage? It's unlikely it's something she'll be able to keep to herself and I don't want that information out in the public domain at the moment. If Paterson has come to a sticky end, I don't want the murderer to know we're on to him. Oh, one other thing, Jim, make sure Lennox gets to go with Fletcher when she interviews Ramsey's parents. After all, I did instruct her to find out what she could about his life so it makes sense that she's present.'

McTavish didn't wait for an answer but put her head back down, so that a sheet of black hair obscured her face. She riffled through her papers. Carruthers knew he had been dismissed and that McTavish was back to thinking whatever dark thoughts she had under the guise of work.

Carruthers drove the short distance back to the picturesque village of Anstruther. He tracked down Paterson's address. The fisherman and his wife lived in an old fisherman's cottage aptly named 'Fisherman's House'. It was set back from the harbour in a little row of cottages. It had the traditional red pantiled roof so typical of the old buildings in this part of Fife – a nod to Scotland's trading links with the Netherlands.

He was aware, as he parked up, that his mind wasn't solely on the interview he was about to conduct with Paterson's wife. He was still thinking of his DCI; moved by the ravaged look of pain on her face as he had left her office. Not for the first time he was glad he was single. His thoughts then turned to his ex-wife and the possible reasons for her wanting to see him. There was only one thing he knew for certain: with everything going on at the station that meeting was going to have to be put on hold.

He stooped to right a potted geranium plant that was lying on its side on the path to the door. It reminded him that the wind had picked up since morning. He placed it carefully with the others; admiring the attractive line of brightly coloured flowers before he rang the bell.

The door opened and the anxious and drawn face of Robert Paterson's wife greeted him. She wrapped her worn green cardigan protectively around her frame as she looked up at him. *Eyes are the gateway to the soul*, thought Carruthers. And Mrs Paterson's eyes held so many different emotions: fear, anxiety, resignation and hope.

I am just so sorry I have no good news for you.

Was it just going to be a waiting game until it was official that she was a widow? So far there had been no positive news from the coastguard and the man had now been missing for well over five hours. Carruthers wondered how long it would be before they called the search off.

He pushed his morose thoughts away as he flipped open his warrant card. 'Mrs Paterson?'

She looked at him with a pleading look in her eyes. 'Is there any news of my husband?'

'I'm sorry. No. Not yet. Would I be able to come in please? I would like to ask you a few questions about Robert.'

'Yes, of course. I was just taking a break from the housework to have a cup of coffee.'

Carruthers admired the way the woman was trying to keep busy. *It can't be easy but having a routine must help*, he thought.

Mrs Paterson stepped aside and let Carruthers enter the hall. As she led him towards the living room she turned round and said, 'I heard about what happened to the warden on the Isle of May. It's a terrible business.'

Carruthers knew that news had a way of travelling fast around a small community. He was surprised that the press weren't already sniffing round. *Give them time. They'll be here soon.*

He was ushered into the small attractive living room. The carpet looked as if it had just been freshly vacuumed and he could smell the sweet earthy aroma of beeswax. *She's been busy.*

'The police told me that my husband's boat was found adrift just off the island. Do you think the two events are connected?' She picked up her cup of coffee and took a sip.

That's what we all want to know, thought Carruthers. *It's the million-dollar question.* But it helped that she was the one to ask that question. It gave him an easy lead in. He started his line of questioning carefully. 'Do you know whether your husband is in the habit of sailing his fishing boat so close to the Isle of May?'

Mrs Paterson bit her lip.

Carruthers studied her carefully. *She's worried that people are going to think that her husband's disappearance and the fact his boat was found so close to the murder scene had something to do with*

Ramsey's murder. 'I need you to be honest with me, Mrs Paterson. Where did your husband usually fish?'

'Call me Mary. He mostly fishes for lobster so he wouldn't take the boat out far, especially in the summer.'

'Mostly?'

'Like some of the other fishermen he'd also started fishing for prawn.'

That answers the second of my questions.

Mrs Paterson offered an explanation in answer to Carruthers' quizzical look. 'In the winter the lobster go further out as the water gets colder and the fishermen follow them.'

That makes sense. I should have listened more carefully when the fishermen were chatting in the pub. Carruthers chose his words carefully. 'Would it be unusual to find his boat fishing off the May? I take it there are fishing restrictions around the island, given it's a nature reserve?'

Mrs Paterson shook her head. 'There are no fishing restrictions. Never have been.'

They had all assumed that there would be. Carruthers was surprised. He would have to double-check that but at least he was getting through his questions.

The woman's hands were shaking as she put her coffee cup down. He didn't blame her. It must be hard being the wife of a fisherman at the best of times and these weren't the best of times. She covered her face with her hands. 'I just don't understand it. Where is he? The weather was fine and he's a careful man. It doesn't make sense unless–'

'Unless–?'

She swallowed hard and Carruthers saw the pained expression in her eyes. 'Unless he had an accident and fell overboard.'

That's one possibility. Carruthers thought of the blood on the boat. Had the fisherman had an accident, after all? However, he still couldn't shake off the thought that something more sinister had happened to Robert Paterson. *But I only think that because of the amount of blood discovered and because his boat was found so close to the site of Tom Ramsey's murder.* 'Can I ask if you've had any news reporters sniffing round?'

Mrs Paterson frowned and shook her head. 'No. Nobody.'

'Good. If you do, please say nothing to them. And we'd really appreciate it if you would notify us.'

'What can I tell them?'

Carruthers chose his words with care. 'Obviously at this stage we're still hoping your husband will turn up alive and well.' Even as he said this Carruthers knew that with every passing hour time and hope were running out for the fisherman. He changed tack. 'I'm led to understand that if you're fishing for lobster you would take the boat out during the day. You've mentioned your husband had also started to fish for prawn. Do you know why he took his boat out overnight?'

'Robbie doesn't sleep well. Ever since our son died.'

'I'm so sorry to hear that. How did you lose him again?'

'He got hooked on drugs. There was nothing we could do to save him. In the end he committed suicide.' She looked down at her hands. 'A big part of Robbie's life ended the day our boy died. He was an only child and my husband loved the bones of him. Like I said, he doesn't sleep well. He used to get up and just sit in the living room staring at the wall, sometimes for hours. Taking the boat out at first light fishing for prawn gave him something to do.'

She's talking past tense, thought Carruthers. *She thinks her husband is already dead.* Carruthers had every sympathy with insomniacs. After all, his sleep wasn't always good. However, he did wonder just when Paterson got any sleep. Did he have naps during the day if he was out fishing at first light? Another thought entered his head. *Had tiredness led to the man's accident?*

'I told him just sitting in the dark here in the middle of the night wasn't healthy. But then some of the Ainster fishermen started to fish for prawn and they often go out at first light. So that's what Robbie did.'

Exactly what Scott Gardner said. Carruthers noted Mrs Paterson's use of the local term for Anstruther.

'That's what he would have been doing at 4am, inspector. It might be the middle of the night for you but it's still first light.'

That makes sense. Carruthers imagined Paterson in the early hours of the morning firing up the engine, switching on the navigation lights and letting the ropes go from the quay as he slipped into darkness. *What a lonely existence.*

'How is your husband's health? The reason I'm asking is, if the worst has happened and your husband has fallen overboard, could there be any underlying medical reasons for it? Or do you think tiredness could have played a part?'

'He was a smoker but he didn't drink alcohol when he was out at sea. He took warfarin but generally he was in reasonable health.'

Carruthers knew that warfarin was a blood thinner. 'Do you mind me asking why he was taking warfarin?'

'He has a blood clotting disorder.'

The police officer digested that piece of information. He also knew that the main side effect of warfarin was bleeding more easily than normal. Could this account for the volume of blood on the boat? He made a note in his black notebook.

15

'You think that's important? That he was on a blood thinner?'

'I don't know, Mrs Paterson. Did your husband have any other medical problems?'

Mary Paterson shook her head.

'I need to ask, how well did your husband know Tom Ramsey?'

'For God's sake, you don't think he had anything to do with the warden's death? My husband is missing, inspector. Shouldn't you be out helping the coastguard find him?'

Carruthers hadn't been offered a seat so he stood near the window. Out of the corner of his eye he saw a blurry image outside the Patersons' home. He turned to see an elderly woman walking slowly down the front path. When she saw that Mrs Paterson already had a visitor she hesitated then turned round and walked away.

No doubt coming to offer Mary some support. She'll need it.

'I understand you're upset, Mary, and it must be a particularly hard time for you but I do need to ask these questions.'

Mary Paterson seemed to calm down. 'Of course you do. I'm sorry. He knew him in passing. That's all.'

'No need to apologise. Okay, that's fine,' said Carruthers, still maintaining eye contact with Mary Paterson. *What is my gut instinct telling me? That she is genuinely baffled by her husband's disappearance and that she is telling the truth.* 'Can I ask what your husband was wearing the last time you saw him?'

Mrs Paterson let out a short sigh. 'I've already been asked what he was wearing. He'll be wearing what he always wears on the boat.'

She's starting to get frustrated and I don't blame her. Like everyone else she just wants to know what's happened to him. And no doubt she thinks I should be out with the search.

'His orange oilskins and yellow wellington boots.'

'Is he in the habit of wearing a PFD?' Carruthers was referring to the personal flotation devices that fishermen were being urged to wear.

She shook her head. 'No. He's old-school. We talked about it and certainly the FMA urges their members to wear them but he felt it hampered his movement on board the boat.'

'The FMA?'

'Robbie belongs to the Fishermen's Mutual Association.'

The co-operative Fletcher had mentioned in the meeting. 'Oh I see. So Robbie was a member.'

'They all are.'

'I'm guessing he wouldn't wear a tracking device?'

Mrs Paterson shook her head.

Pity. Carruthers knew only too well that there had been a recent spate of accidents in the Scottish fishing industry and that a good number of those who had drowned hadn't been wearing a PFD.

'Can I borrow your husband's toothbrush? I'll probably just need it for a few days.'

This question seemed to throw the fisherman's wife. 'What on earth do you need his toothbrush for?'

He had been instructed not to mention the blood on Paterson's boat so what could he say to her? 'It's just routine.'

Mrs Paterson looked vaguely confused but nodded. She left the room. Carruthers took the opportunity to look around. His gaze settled on several framed photographs on the mantelpiece. But he didn't have a chance to get a proper look as, within a few moments, Mary was back holding her husband's toothbrush. Carruthers brought out an evidence bag and popped it in, sealed the bag and put it in his jacket pocket.

'What was your husband's state of mind like before he took the boat out?'

The woman opposite him clattered the coffee cup back onto its saucer, clearly angered by his question. 'You're not trying to ask me if I think he took his own life, are you?' She walked across to the window and stared out at the sea. 'I lost my own father in a fishing accident. His body was never recovered. It's still out there somewhere.' She turned back to face the policeman. 'Robert knew what that did to me. He'd never put me through something like that. And then five years ago, as I said, we lost our only son to suicide.'

'I'm so sorry, Mrs Paterson... Mary.'

Carruthers had to remind himself that he hadn't been in Fife that long. Sometimes, like now, he felt at a disadvantage at not being a local. The woman was biting her lip and when she looked back at Carruthers he could see there were tears in her eyes. He hated being the one responsible for dredging up painful memories but he had a job to do.

He noticed the woman's hands shake again. He didn't need to be told that Mrs Paterson was right on the edge. He had to tread carefully. Clearly her life had been full of tragedy. She turned to face the window again. Carruthers took the opportunity to look more closely at the photographs on the mantelpiece while the older woman continued to stare silently out to sea.

There wasn't a mote of dust on them and Carruthers suspected that she dusted them every day. He recognised a younger Robert Paterson in one of the photographs with his arm round a young man. The young man was the spitting image of him. Both had the same powerful build and broad shoulders. *It must be their son.* Carefully he picked up an old black-and-white photograph of a weather-beaten man standing next to a boat. He had his arms crossed over his thick sweater and he was smoking a pipe. *This must be Mrs Paterson's father. No, wait. The photograph is older than that.* The man in the photograph must be the grandfather or perhaps great grandfather. He looked up to see Mary Paterson still gazing despairingly out of the window. *I wonder how long they kept a vigil for her father?*

He replaced the photograph quickly. His eyes lit on another photograph and carefully he picked that up. From the hair and the clothes it looked as if it was from the mid-eighties. It showed a group of people at a party. Carruthers spotted Robert Paterson at the back of the group. He took a closer look at the individuals in the picture. A youthful and smiling Mary Paterson looked up at him. *She would have been mid-thirties in that photograph. She was bonny in her youth.* There was a man with his arm round her. He thought he recognised him as Frank Dewar.

'Who's this?'

Mary Paterson turned round. She walked over to Carruthers, took the framed photograph out of his hand, looked at it with something resembling a wistful smile then replaced it on the mantelpiece. 'It's Frank. Frank Dewar.'

Carruthers' ears pricked up. So it *was* him. The missing fisherman's best friend, according to Scott Gardner, and a man he needed to talk to.

'Looks like it's been a long friendship.'

'That's right. It has. The four of us have known each other a long time, well over forty years. Irene doesn't keep the best of health now. Frank's practically become her carer. He's very good to her. Do you know, he's even installed a stairlift and wet room for her.'

Carruthers took a closer look at the photograph. The way Mary leant into Frank Dewar piqued his interest. There was an intimacy about them that he had failed to see at first. He wondered if, at any point, Frank Dewar and Mary Paterson had been more than just friends. He filed this nugget away in his mind to bring out another time. Now was definitely not the time to talk about lost loves. 'I'm not for a moment saying that your husband has taken his own life or even that he has been contemplating suicide. I just need to build up a picture of his movements the last few days and what his state of mind was like. You mentioned your husband had sleep problems. Would you say he's been suffering from depression?' Carruthers knew what he thought but he wanted to hear it from Mrs Paterson.

'Like I said, he's never really got over our son's death. Neither of us has. Do you have children, inspector?'

'No.' He felt a moment of sadness. He knew Mairi had wanted kids. If he'd been more attentive to her needs and not so obsessed about his police career perhaps they would still be married. Perhaps they would even have children by now.

At last she turned round to face Carruthers. 'It's funny. I grew up in this house. My mother was born here. I've been through this before, staring out of this very window hoping the sea would give us back our loved one. And here I am doing it again.' She managed a sad smile. 'You know there's a whole flotilla of small boats out looking for him. All his friends. The folk he drank with. The folk he fished with. The folk he played darts with. He'll be found,' she said confidently. And then a whisper not meant for Carruthers' ears, 'He has to be.'

Suddenly Carruthers was at a loss. This seemed such a private moment for Robert Paterson's wife. She cocked her head slightly to the side and her eyes had a faraway look in them. *It's almost as if she's hearing her mother's voice telling her as a child that everything will be all right, that daddy will be home soon. But daddy didn't come home and it now looks as if her husband won't be coming back either.*

'I'll let myself out, Mrs Paterson.'

She didn't move from the window or give him any acknowledgement that she had even heard him. She was in her own world. Carruthers walked quietly to the door. He stepped outside and shut the front door firmly behind him.

16

Andrea Fletcher shepherded Tom Ramsey's parents into the viewing area of the mortuary. Helen Lennox followed close behind.

Fletcher took in their tear-streaked cheeks and pinched white faces. She judged that the photograph of them in the warden's accommodation must have been a fairly recent one. Despite the awful news and the physical effect their son's death had obviously had on them they both still looked younger than their years. Mrs Ramsey's blonde hair was loose round her shoulders, framing an attractive face. *They must have had Tom soon after getting married,* she thought. Both were casually dressed in blue jeans and fleeces. *They look outdoorsy. I wonder if that's where Tom got it from.*

As the curtain parted Fletcher noticed Mr Ramsey grasp his wife's hand and give it a squeeze. This was one of the hardest parts of policing and Fletcher felt a lump in her throat at the gesture. She found herself holding her breath.

Fletcher nodded at Mackie who took his cue and carefully uncovered the victim's head and shoulders with the sheet. As the couple gazed at the mutilated face of their son Mrs Ramsey let out a shrill scream and shouted her boy's name as she placed her palms on the glass partition. She slowly sank to her knees, her damp hands leaving traces of sweat on the glass. Mr Ramsey knelt down to comfort his wife.

Mr Ramsey spoke in a quiet voice, full of restrained emotion. 'That's Tom. That's the body of our son.'

'I'm so sorry,' whispered Fletcher. 'I promise we'll do everything to apprehend the person who did this and bring them to justice.' Fletcher couldn't think of anything else to say. Together they helped Mrs Ramsey back to her feet. Fletcher put her arm round the older lady's shoulder while Lennox stood uselessly by looking completely out of her depth.

With her arm still round Mrs Ramsey's shoulder Fletcher guided her out of the viewing area. 'Let's go to the visitor's room. It's more relaxing there. My colleague can bring you both a cup of tea.' Fletcher thought she heard Lennox click her tongue in annoyance but she ignored it, filing it away to the back of her mind to bring up once they were on their own.

'A cup of tea won't bring Tom back, will it?' Mrs Ramsey cried. 'I just don't understand. Why would anyone want to kill our son?' The look of bewilderment on her face told its own story. She had no idea who had killed her son.

Why indeed? What the hell is the motive for murder? And such a frenzied murder at that?

At some point the police would have to tell the Ramseys more of the details of their son's violent death before they were splashed all over the tabloids but in the meantime they were still trying to process the shock of seeing their son for the last time on a cold clinical slab.

Fletcher knew that it was never going to be the best time to ask probing questions during a mortuary visit but in a murder enquiry time was of the essence, the first forty-eight hours being the most crucial. *And let's face it, their son has been brutally murdered. There's never going to be a good time.* And the more time that went by the less likelihood there was of catching the perpetrator.

Tom Ramsey's parents sat together on the couch in the room set aside for grieving family members. Fletcher had left them alone for a few minutes under the guise of helping Lennox with the tea but in reality she knew they would need some private time together, even if it were just a few moments.

She returned to find Mr Ramsey rubbing his wife's back rhythmically with his hand. It was a touching gesture of comfort. Fletcher started off slowly. 'I'm really sorry to ask these questions now, Mr and Mrs Ramsey, but do you know of anyone who would wish your son harm?'

The grieving couple shook their heads and Mr Ramsey dropped his hand from his wife's back to hold her hands in his instead. They remained silent for a few moments until Mrs Ramsey said, 'No. Nobody. We never had any trouble with him. He was always a good boy.'

Fletcher had heard this numerous times since joining the police force, often from the parents of hardened and brutal criminals who just would not believe their children had turned bad. However, Ramsey had no criminal record.

'I can't think of anyone who would want to kill him,' said Mr Ramsey. 'He always had lots of friends when he was at university. And he absolutely lived for his work. He loved being warden on the Isle of May. It was his dream job. He must have been killed by a complete stranger. I mean, you hear about this sort of stuff happening, don't you? Do you think he was just in the wrong place at the wrong time?'

'You do hear about it, but it's still very rare. In most cases the victim knows the–' she was going to say murderer but at the last minute changed it to, 'the person who committed the crime.'

Fletcher thought of Mr Ramsey's words that Tom had been

in the wrong place at the wrong time. It was something the investigative team had already discussed. At the time of his death the warden had been completely alone on the nature reserve, apart from the murderer, that is. How could he, therefore, be in the wrong place at the wrong time? Surely somebody had deliberately gone out of their way to visit the island to extinguish the life of this popular man. *How could it possibly be a random murder?* She knew that Ramsey's parents were clutching at straws. It was likely they didn't believe their son had been killed by a knife-wielding stranger any more than she did.

'You said Tom had a wide circle of friends when he was young. Was there anyone he was particularly close to while he was warden on the Isle of May?'

Mr Ramsey spoke for both he and his wife. 'Most of his time was spent with the volunteers on the island but occasionally he would go to the mainland. He'd sometimes have a drink with the fishermen.'

Helen Lennox finally found her voice. 'Do you know if Tom had a girlfriend?'

It was Mrs Ramsey who answered. 'Not currently, no. He split up from his last girlfriend before taking his present job. He always joked that his work was a demanding mistress.'

'What was the split like?'

Both parents glanced at each other. A look passed between them. 'You know what these things are like. Splitting up's never easy.'

Fletcher made a mental note to chase this up. *It was a bad split, then.* She brought her notebook out. 'Can you give me the name and details of his ex?'

Once again Ramsey's parents glanced at each other. A shadow passed over them. 'We'd rather you didn't contact her. She's somewhat... unhinged,' Mr Ramsey said finally.

'When you say "unhinged"...?' urged Lennox, exchanging a look with Fletcher.

'She accused Tom of all manner of things.'

'None of which he had done,' put in Mrs Ramsey.

'Can you give me an idea of what sort of things?'

Mrs Ramsey looked at her husband. 'We'd rather not say. It was a bad time in his life. And now he's dead. Doesn't seem much point in going over it all.'

Mr and Mrs Ramsey obviously aren't fingering their son's ex for his murder, thought Fletcher. 'Please let us be the judge of that. We will most likely need to interview her, I'm afraid, given the circumstances.'

Mrs Ramsey nodded but she didn't look too happy. Mr Ramsey remained silent but gave his wife's hand a squeeze. Finally he said, 'If you think it's necessary we'll give you the contact details.'

'Where does this ex-girlfriend live?'

'Ellie moved back to Bristol.'

Perhaps a trip to Bristol was on the cards then. The police budget could stretch to that. Fletcher wondered if McTavish would let her go personally.

'Ellie?'

'Ellie Robertson.'

The way Mr Ramsey said the name interested Fletcher. She had the feeling he had met the woman and not liked her. *At least she isn't living in Iceland or Estonia*, thought Fletcher, remembering a couple of their previous cases.

'Where was he working before he got his job as warden on the Isle of May?' Lennox asked.

Mrs Ramsey had fallen silent and was letting her husband do the talking. 'Not far from where we live, actually. The Farne Islands, off the Northumberland coast.'

'How long was he there for?' Fletcher asked.

'Just a year.'

'That's not a very long time. Any reason he left after a year?'

'He just fancied a change.'

Fletcher wasn't convinced. It was a strange answer to give.

'He's a bit of a restless spirit. Finds it hard to settle.'

'Has he had any liaisons with any of the volunteers, as far as you know?' Helen Lennox stood poised with her notebook.

Fletcher swore under her breath at Lennox's directness. She also knew that even if he had got together with one of the volunteers, Ramsey's parents would probably be the last people to know.

Mr and Mrs Ramsey exchanged looks. Neither appeared happy. 'Tom was married to his work. I don't think he'd want the distraction and I really don't think after his experience with–'

Fletcher cut in, knowing that Lennox's bluntness was putting them on edge. 'He was obviously passionate about his work. Do you know how he got on with the volunteers? Were any of them particularly difficult to work with?'

It was Mr Ramsey who answered. 'Tom was always appreciative of the work the volunteers did. They were an invaluable resource.'

Fletcher was beginning to think that Tom Ramsey sounded too good to be true and then she remembered the ex-girlfriend. *Everyone has skeletons in their closet. Could Ellie be one of his?* 'He must have had some frustrations?'

'The weather, mostly. Everything he did was weather dependent.' As he spoke Mr Ramsey looked at his wife who nodded. 'It could be wild. And of course most of his work was outside. I think they all got frustrated when it was so bad they were confined to barracks. Yes, I'd say the weather was the biggest frustration.'

Fletcher was starting to build up a picture of the warden. He sounded like a conscientious man whose love of birds and wildlife were now his main, if not only, passion in life. Fletcher was coming to the conclusion that being warden on a small island like the Isle of May was rather more than just a job. It would be a vocation. And the weather would be the dominating force that shaped the lives of all those on the island. But she also couldn't help but feel that living on a remote island would be a great place to be if you were also running away from something. Or someone. Had it been true in Tom Ramsey's case?

17

Dr Mackie mumbled to himself as Carruthers pushed open the door to the mortuary room. Mackie's assistant, Jodie Pettigrew, was nowhere to be seen. The policeman was grateful for that at least. That brief relationship hadn't ended well. A stupid error on his part in one of their early dates signalled the end of yet another romance. Perhaps he should just stay single.

Mackie looked up from the trolley on which the male victim lay. 'It's fortunate we've been able to fast-track the post-mortem for you. Now his parents have had the viewing and left the building let's get cracking, eh, Jim. I know you'll be keen for answers and if I'm honest, I can think of better places to be of an evening.'

Carruthers wasn't sure if 'fortunate' was the right word. True, nothing more pressing had come in but then it would have taken a lot to trump the savage murder of a man, killed during the despatch of his work duties.

The body of Tom Ramsey was naked except for the white sheet. Two bare feet stuck out from the end of the table, a label with Ramsey's name tied to the end of one of them. Mackie carefully took the sheet away. Carruthers had noticed in the time he had been at the station that the pathologist was a very careful, methodical man, for which he was grateful.

This was the first time Carruthers had seen the victim naked. When Ramsey was lying dead on the island he had looked the part of the island warden dressed in his Gore-Tex with binoculars hanging round his neck. *Now he just looks like a man. A dead one, stripped of all identity.* The skin had a bluish tinge; the lips lifeless. Aside from the multiple places Carruthers believed the knife had been thrust there were several smaller marks where the birds had pecked. Carruthers tried not to look at the face.

As if to echo Carruthers' thoughts Mackie said, 'There are thirteen knife wounds. This attack was frenzied. That's the only word I can find to describe it, Jim. Ten to the torso, one to the neck and two to the back of the head. I'll show you those later once we get him turned over.'

The body had been cleaned and the stab wounds showed up clearly.

'And then this is interesting. We also have this.' Mackie circled the dead man like a bird circling his prey.

Carruthers could see the pathologist's attention was fixed on Ramsey's left ankle, which the pathologist picked up in his gloved hand. 'Bruising and puffiness to the ankle and spreading into the foot.'

'What could have caused that?' Carruthers leant over the torso.

'It looks as if he twisted his ankle just before his death.'

'Trying to get away from his assailant, perhaps?'

'It's possible.'

'Maybe he fell down a rabbit hole.' He thought back to his visit. 'There were enough of them on the island.'

Mackie was still examining the ankle, prodding it gently through nitrile gloves. 'You wouldn't think there'd be rabbits on the Isle of May, would you, but they were introduced in the early 1400s as a source of food for the early settlers.'

Carruthers had long ceased to be amazed by Mackie's knowledge of Scottish history. The man was a veritable encyclopaedia of information but when you knew him for any length of time it was just something you accepted about him. If he didn't throw a nugget of history Carruthers' way, albeit at the most inappropriate time, the police officer figured something would be very wrong.

Mackie circled the victim until he was back near the upper body again. He looked straight at the stab wounds. 'Unless we find something surprising it's more than likely one of the stab wounds killed him.'

'Can you tell what sort of knife was used?'

'You're looking for a fixed blade knife with an approximately three-inch serrated edge.'

The pathologist picked up the man's hands one by one and examined the palms. Carruthers saw a couple of slashes. 'Only a few defensive wounds to the hands, as I said at the locus. And the only other thing of note to tell you before we open him up is that he has a previous nasal fracture.'

Carruthers looked confused.

'Broken nose to you, laddie. Not sure if it will be relevant to your investigation but worth telling you all the same.'

The pathologist picked up his scalpel. 'Right, let's open him up.' With practised ease the pathologist opened up the chest after performing a large, deep Y-shaped incision from sternum to pubic bone.

'Of course they have no natural predators on the Isle of May, apart from the gulls. The rabbits, I mean.'

Carruthers stared down at the cadaver on the slab finding it now hard to reconcile that this had been a living, breathing man only a few hours before.

'Talking of predators,' Mackie looked down sadly at his charge, almost forgetting the inspector was in the room with him, 'who's preyed on you, eh?' He took a deep breath in through his nose before he continued to speak. 'Who extinguished your life?'

The two men were disturbed by a ringing phone. Carruthers slipped his hand into his lab coat.

He heard Mackie draw in a sharp breath. 'No mobiles allowed in here, laddie. You know the rules.'

'Sorry,' mumbled Carruthers. Caller ID told him it was his DCI. 'It's the boss, I need to take it.'

'Outside.'

Carruthers nipped out and took the call. He had a brief conversation with McTavish, then slipped back into the room.

Mackie looked up as he spoke. 'He was stabbed through the thorax, the blade piercing the intercostal muscles, then the left ventricle of his heart. This is most likely what killed him, barring our toxicology results.'

Carruthers leant over the corpse. 'A three-inch blade could do that?'

'It's possible on deep exhalation when the ribcage deflates. At that point the ribcage would be closer to the heart. If he took a blow to the stomach, for example, which caused winding then followed through with the knife that might do it.' Mackie peered at the body, gently tracing a gloved hand over the stomach. 'If you look very closely this looks like a bruise.'

Carruthers looked at the man's stomach and he thought he could detect a faint bruise. 'Can you tell by looking at the wounds whether the perp could have been a man or a woman? Or right or left-handed?'

'He was wearing Gore-Tex with a T-shirt underneath when he was killed. Gore-Tex is a lightweight waterproof material also known by its trademark name of Teflon. Some folk think it hard to pierce the material but it's surprisingly easy. You could be looking at either man or woman committing this act. I also believe that you are looking for a right hander.'

Carruthers needed to be clear in his mind about the train of events. 'So Tom Ramsey is out on the island with his binoculars and notebook logging birds believing himself to be the only person there at that point when he's set upon by a knife-wielding assailant. And at some point just prior to death he twists his ankle, most likely in an attempt to get away from his vicious attacker.'

Mackie walked round the body. 'Seems that way, Jim.'

Almost to himself Carruthers muttered, 'Where *the hell* did that person come from? There was nobody else on the island.'

'That's your job, laddie. Not mine. Can't answer that one I'm afraid.'

Carruthers pursed his top lip. How had the murderer got on the island? He must have arrived by boat. But how? Whose? He couldn't have come over as a day-tripper on the *May Princess* as all passengers were carefully logged and there was only one sailing a day. And hadn't Scott Gardner said that each passenger was accounted for at all times? Carruthers knew that if one of the passengers hadn't turned up at the pickup point on the island to get the boat back to Anstruther the crew would have known about it.

He found himself speaking his thoughts aloud. 'The perp must either have had his own boat or he must have hired one.' He made a mental note to check whether there were any outlets or fishermen who had hired their boats out to anyone recently.

Mackie looked up, scalpel in hand. He was frowning. 'When

we were on the May I didn't see Tom's boat, *The Invicta*. It's usually moored at Kirkhaven harbour.'

'Then perhaps our perpetrator made his getaway using the warden's boat. Thanks, John. That's really helpful.' *Why didn't I think about whether the warden of an island would have had his own boat?*

18

Andrea Fletcher and Helen Lennox stood in the Bank Hotel, ready to conduct their interviews. The Neo-Greek B-listed building in Anstruther, which had been built for the headquarters of the National Bank of Scotland in the mid-1800s, made for a lavish, imposing venue. However, they had chosen it as it was now friendly and family-run, plus it had a large sunlit glass-fronted breakfast room.

The police officers took the five volunteers through to the airy breakfast room and indicated for them to take seats. The two female officers remained standing.

'When can we go back to the island to collect our things?' Fletcher watched the young blonde woman in front of her, whom she judged to be in her mid-twenties, wring her hands. 'I want to go home.'

'And you are?'

'Patricia Cummins.'

I bet you do want to collect your belongings and go home. And it's a fair enough response, thought Fletcher. The young woman probably hadn't long since left university. *If I were that age, I'd also want to go home. I certainly wouldn't want to keep working on an island where my boss had just been butchered.*

'I need to get back to the island. There's work to be done.' This from an auburn-haired young woman.

'Sorry? You are?'

'Nicola Reid.'

Her accent was Glaswegian.

She's being very pragmatic, almost cold, thought Fletcher. Not the response you'd expect from someone who worked alongside a murder victim. But then again Nicola hadn't been the one who had come across the body and, as Fletcher knew only too well, the shock of a sudden death did strange things to people.

She remembered the statement she'd taken from the shaking Lofty Sykes. Life had to go on and the boat would be running again before too long but she judged from his reaction that he'd be off work for a while yet. He'd clearly been traumatised.

'I'm afraid the whole island is currently being treated as a crime scene,' said Helen Lennox. 'Nobody can set foot on the Isle of May at the moment. But we'll let you know when you can return.'

Patricia Cummins bit the skin around her fingers. Fletcher noticed that they were bleeding. 'Do you – I mean, do the police think this attacker will strike again?'

It was a reasonable question. The subtext being, do you think we are in danger? thought Fletcher. *Well, who can blame them?* It was a particularly horrifying crime. And as yet there was no motive. Not an obvious one anyway. Fletcher had rarely dealt with anything quite so gruesome, although their last big case of the 'Student Slasher', as the press had dubbed him, had, in a lot of ways, been much worse. Fletcher cast her mind back to the young female students who had been the Slasher's victims. That had been her first case where a murderer had taken trophies from the bodies. She shuddered from the memory.

Although the police were trying hard to keep the details of this latest murder from the newspapers, in a place like the East Neuk of Fife, the gossip would be rampant.

Fletcher chose her words with care. 'We have no reason to believe anyone else is at risk, however, as you are also aware, the perpetrator is still at large, which is why it's vital we get your statements as soon as possible.'

'God, they must be seriously unhinged. Who would attack Tom?' The young man who spoke had a large red birthmark on his face.

Helen Lennox was poised with her notebook and pen. 'And you are?'

'Ben Homan.'

'That's what we are trying to find out,' said Fletcher. 'As I said, we're needing to interview you separately.'

'Are we all under suspicion?'

Fletcher tried to smile reassuringly. 'This is just routine. While I'm getting your statements, my colleague, DC Helen Lennox, will keep you company until it's your turn to be interviewed. Just out of interest, who else used the island apart from the warden and volunteers?'

Ben Homan answered. 'Members of bird watching organisations–'

'We've had the occasional scuba diver and yachtsman,' put in Nicola Reid.

Homan nodded in agreement. 'Yeah, that's right. There was a scuba diver just last week.'

Fletcher chewed the end of her pen as she listened. That needed to be chased up. If private individuals were allowed to visit the island that widened the circle of potential murderers.

'And the marine equivalent of the SAS conducts secret operations off the island but that's supposed to be hush hush.'

Interesting, thought Fletcher.

Fletcher took the first volunteer, the dark-haired Ben Homan to one of the bigger bedrooms in the hotel. It was a relaxing space and had a round polished table and two comfortable chairs. *This beats sitting on the edge of a hard bed*, she thought. Holding the interview in a more comfortable space was much less of an ordeal than dragging the volunteers to the police station to take their statements. And, as she knew only too well, people generally were far more accommodating when relaxed.

Fletcher leant forward out of the seat as she spoke, pen poised. 'Ben, when did you last see Tom Ramsey?'

Ben Homan shifted his weight as he got comfortable. He was a pleasant-looking man with an open face. 'Well, we all last saw him just before we left the island to go over to Anstruther.'

'Which was what time?'

'Five-ish. We got picked up at about five so we got to the mainland the back of six.'

Fletcher scribbled the time in her notebook. 'And you were picked up by?'

'Angus McCrae. A friend of Lofty Sykes. Lofty helps crew the *May Princess*.'

And they would need to talk to Angus McCrae. Fletcher made a note in her black book as she watched her charge carefully. Most murders are committed by someone close to the victim and for the five months they were on the island there would be nobody closer to the victim than the five volunteers. 'What was his mood like?'

Ben tilted his head to one side. He shrugged, showing his surprise at the question. 'Fine. He appeared normal. Just like any other day. Most of the time he was a pretty happy-go-lucky guy. Easy to get on with.'

Most of the time. That needed to be explored but there was a more pressing question to be asked. 'Why did Tom stay on the island? Had he not been invited to join the celebration?'

'Oh, he was due to come with us but in the end he felt he had too much work to do.'

'So it was a last-minute decision to stay behind?'

'Yes. We felt it was a shame. He would have really enjoyed it. And the pub had a live gig on by King Creosote. It's Tom's favourite band. They were brilliant.'

Fletcher knew the band. The singer, Kenny, came from the East Neuk of Fife. She'd run into the gregarious man a couple of times. And King Creosote was, she knew, one of Carruthers' favourite singers. 'And I understand you were celebrating one of the volunteers getting their PhD?'

'That's right. Pat has just got her PhD. Zoology. We're all really chuffed for her. Tom told us he even had a couple of bottles of champagne for us. We were going to have another celebration back on the island a bit later in the week.'

So that's why there are two bottles of champagne in Tom Ramsey's fridge. He sounded like a thoughtful man. *And Pat must be older than she looks*, thought Fletcher. *I put her in her mid-twenties but if she's just finished her PhD it's likely she's a few years older.*

A faraway look came into Ben's eyes. 'I can't believe he's dead. I wonder who's going to take over his job?'

Fletcher shifted in her seat. She was struggling to get comfortable. 'The appointments are made by Scottish Natural Heritage, aren't they?'

'That's right and Tom was just perfect for the post. He really knew his stuff. He'd been a warden before, you see. He was also good with people, both the volunteers and the general public. Like I said, he was just an easy-going guy. We're all stumped as to who would want to kill him.'

'Do you know where he worked before he came here?'

Ben Homan nodded. 'The Farne Islands.'

That chimed with what Tom's parents had told her.

'You mentioned earlier that Tom was easy going "most of the time". What did you mean by that?'

'He had this weird ex-girlfriend.'

Fletcher flicked back through the pages of her notebook. 'An Ellie Robertson?'

'Yes, I think he left his previous post because of her. She sounded absolutely demented.'

'What did he say about her?'

'That if he didn't use the washing machine to do their laundry on the right day of the week she'd throw his clothes out of the window into the street, for one.'

Controlling behaviour. In a healthy relationship the two partners allowed each other to manage chores in their own ways. She thought back to her ex. He couldn't even be bothered to stick around after she had had her miscarriage.

'I think she also accused him of having an affair at one point.'

Fletcher could hardly bring herself to ask the next question given how controlling Ramsey's ex had sounded. 'If she thought he'd had an affair, how did she exact her revenge? Did he ever say?'

'By cutting all his clothes to pieces. I think he said that was the last straw. That's when he decided to get out.'

But would she let him go? Ellie Robertson was fast becoming their number one suspect. She certainly had motive. *A woman scorned and all that.* But the question was, did she also have opportunity? And if she had who had taken her over to the island?

19

Fletcher poured herself a glass of water. She was starting to feel warm. The room was airless. She stood up and lifted the large sash window before she sat back down and sipped her water. 'Did he ever tell you how Ellie Robertson felt when the relationship finally ended?'

'He never really said.'

'Was he happy here?'

'Well, for starters it got him away from her.'

So he had been running away. I was right.

'And he loved his work. So it was a win-win.'

Fletcher was continuing to build up a picture of the warden. He sounded like an outgoing and dedicated lover of nature who was passionate about his post as warden on the Isle of May. However, it also sounded like there had been a cloud hanging over his head in the shape of his ex. She had exhibited some controlling behaviour, if Ben Homan was to be believed, but was she a killer? And would she travel all the way from Bristol to do it? It seemed unlikely. But someone had killed the warden and Fletcher instinctively felt that that someone was still out there, lurking in the shadows.

On the other hand, Fletcher didn't believe the perpetrator of the crime was an outsider to the area so that would rule out Ellie Robertson. She firmly believed – based on no more than a hunch – that he or she was local, maybe even living on the island, which would then make him or her one of the volunteers. *Who else had known about Tom Ramsey's last-minute change of plans other than them?*

The more she thought about it the more it began to bother her that Tom Ramsey hadn't been expected to be on the island. Ellie Robertson wouldn't have known that, would she?

Fletcher then interviewed an earnest-faced blonde with baby blue eyes whose name was Sylvie White.

'How did you get on with Tom Ramsey?'

'Fine.' Sylvie settled herself in her chair. Like all the volunteers she was already dressed for a day of work. Hillwalking trousers, outdoor boots and a fleece top. 'I didn't really get to know him. There's probably very little I can tell you, to be fair.'

'Please let us be the judge of that,' said Fletcher. She noticed the girl sat bolt upright, shoulders tense, hands clenched. She didn't blame her. It was most probably the first police interview she had ever given. No doubt she'd be terrified.

After an awkward pause Sylvie White spoke again. 'I'm not really one for socialising and I was there to do a job, not make friends.'

Fletcher's eyes narrowed as she scrutinised the girl closely. *Probably happier with the birds than with people. She's certainly not comfortable with being interviewed.* It was possible that the girl suffered from social anxiety. Not for the first time she thought what a hard place the May would be if you felt the need to get away and couldn't find any solitude. A small island sounded like the perfect place in theory, but in reality? There weren't even many buildings you could choose to spend some time in on your own. *And being in Scotland we're not blessed with the fine weather that the south of England is blessed with so any time outdoors other than for work purposes would most probably be limited.* Fletcher couldn't imagine anything worse than being stuck on the Isle of May with a small group of other people for weeks, if not months, on end. Like Carruthers, she had grown to love her own space.

'What about the birds? We're right in the middle of some important monitoring.' The earnest look on the face of the young woman confirmed to Fletcher that she was more concerned with the wildlife than the warden but then again everyone dealt with bereavement differently. She was most probably finding the news hard to take in.

'We'll let you get back to your work as soon as it's possible. In the meantime, I do have a few more questions. As a volunteer, what are your duties?'

'Oh it's very varied. Everything from species monitoring and ringing the birds to visitor management. When we first set foot on the island we're getting ready for the arrival of the terns. To be fair there's also always quite a bit of general maintenance to do, especially when we first arrive. Path repairs are the worst. There's nobody here during the winter, you see. There's also a vegetable garden to look after.'

'How much interaction do you have with the visitors to the island?'

Sylvie White pulled a face. 'I'm not so keen on the meeting and greeting of visitors; I'm not chatty that way. I like to just be with the birds and nature. But Tom was great at it. Oh, and I don't really like the toilet cleaning either.' She wrinkled her nose. 'We have to do that as well.' Her face dropped. 'I still can't believe he's dead.' She put her head down and burst into tears. Fletcher passed her a tissue from a box that was sitting on the table.

She is finding it hard to process the fact Ramsey had been killed.

Not surprising. 'I can imagine cleaning the toilets wouldn't be anybody's favourite job,' said Fletcher in a bid to get the girl on side. 'And how long would the volunteers be on the island?'

Sylvie sniffed. 'Roughly from April to August. As you probably know the island is closed to visitors from the end of September, although the warden stays on for a few months. In the winter it becomes a seal colony.'

'What birds are you currently recording?' Even as Fletcher asked this question she had no idea how this would further the investigation but, with so little to go on, she felt it was still worth asking. And if she could get this quiet, tense girl to open up and feel relaxed, it could only help.

Although tear stains streaked her cheeks the girl's face lit up. 'This is the best time of year to be on the island. There are literally thousands of birds.' As much as Fletcher loved her wildlife she had never seen anyone so animated talking about seabirds. 'We're particularly interested in the puffins. But we're also recording the cormorants and the guillemots. The Isle of May is a really special place as it's a staging post for birds in the spring and autumn. We've even had a sighting of a blue throat in the last few days. That's a very rare migrant.'

As much as Fletcher enjoyed hearing about wildlife she couldn't help but feel they were getting off subject. However, she noticed that the girl's shoulders had relaxed and she was now much more engaged. 'What sort of people become volunteers?'

'Well, I want a job in conservation so it's great experience for me. I haven't really got any proper work experience. And I was so excited when I found out that the Isle of May has Scotland's oldest bird observatory. Both Pat and Nicola's backgrounds are in Zoology. And then there's Ian. He's a fair bit older than the rest of us. Apparently he wants a career change.' She leant into Fletcher and dropped her voice. 'He's been in banking.' She raised her eyebrows when she said the word banking as if it was a dirty word.

The volunteer looked worried. 'We really do need to get back to the island.'

Fletcher felt like saying that the birds were going to have to fend for themselves as they were dealing with a murder investigation but she remained quiet. 'Were you aware of any tensions between anyone?'

'There have been a few minor arguments.'

'About what?'

'Usually who's doing the washing-up or cleaning the accommodation.'

No different to any other household, then. 'So no major flare ups?'

'Not that I know of but I'm usually the first to retire to my room. I like to read. If anything happened after I left for the evening I probably wouldn't know about it.'

Yes, but surely you'd be aware of tensions and an atmosphere the next morning over breakfast, thought Fletcher. It seemed to her that Sylvie White didn't want to get involved. She wondered why. But then again perhaps with her nose in a book she really wouldn't notice. She was curious how a girl, who, in all likelihood did suffer from social anxiety, had got on in the pub the evening before. Had she found it an ordeal?

Fletcher smiled at the volunteer sitting opposite her. 'You sound a bit like me. Happier with your own company. What made you go out last night and join in the celebrations?'

'Oh, yes, you're right. It was a bit of an ordeal but Pat is really nice, and, well, it would have looked really off if I had been the only one not to have gone.'

Except that you wouldn't have been. You would have been on the island with Tom Ramsey. Fletcher wondered if Sylvie White would have met the same fate as Ramsey or would the warden still be alive if someone else had been on the island? 'Ben Homan said there was a good band playing? King Creosote?'

The girl laughed. 'I don't know why he said that. He missed it. He came back in after they'd finished. As soon as we got to Anstruther he told us he had to meet someone and disappeared. Thought that was a bit rude, to tell you the truth.'

Fletcher's ears pricked up. 'Do you know who he was meeting, out of interest?'

'He didn't say.'

Fletcher mulled this over. Homan had said nothing about leaving the rest of the group to meet up with someone else.

'Okay, thank you for your time, Sylvie. Can you send in–' she glanced at her notebook, 'Ian Gaunt?'

While she was waiting for the next interviewee Fletcher nipped to the en suite bathroom.

She no sooner had shut the bathroom door a few minutes later and returned to her seat when there was a tap at the door of the bedroom. The door opened and in walked a tall, thin man. Fletcher couldn't help but notice how aptly named he was.

'Ian Gaunt?'

He nodded. She extended her hand and shook his. She was curious as to why his hand was so moist. It smacked of nervousness. Fletcher was interested in Ian Gaunt. He was much older than the rest of the volunteers. Fletcher guessed that he was older than even the murdered warden. And she remembered that he had been a banker. Interesting career change to go from banking to birds.

'Have a seat, Ian. Thank you for your time. I just need to ask you a few questions. It's standard procedure in cases like these. Can you tell me when you last saw Tom Ramsey?'

'Just before we left for Anstruther. To tell you the truth, I thought he was coming with us.'

'But he changed his mind last minute.'

'Yes, that was really unfortunate.'

'Unfortunate?'

'Well, I'm assuming if he'd come with us he'd still be alive, wouldn't he?'

'Indeed.' Fletcher noticed that Ian Gaunt's bloodshot eyes darted about the room. She struggled to make eye contact with him.

'You're a fair bit older than everyone else. I hear that you used to work in a bank?'

'That's right. I stuck it out for ten years but I was never happy in that environment. It's too rigid and hierarchical.'

Fletcher didn't know anyone who worked for a bank but she could imagine that might be the case. She wondered if it could be anything like the police force.

'So you left the bank and retrained?'

'Yes.'

As he spoke Fletcher scribbled notes in her black notebook, which was fast filling up.

Fletcher was still thinking about her interview with Ian Gaunt when Nicola Reid knocked on the door. She asked the young woman to take a seat. Fletcher explained that she needed to start building up a picture of Tom Ramsey and the volunteers who had worked with him on the island.

'You're asking me to rat on the people I work with?' Nicola Reid looked up at Fletcher with big, round blue eyes. Fletcher noticed that she had put her auburn hair up in a ponytail.

Fletcher put her pen and notebook down on the table next to them. She was starting to feel tired. The room still felt stuffy despite the fact she had opened the window. 'I don't think I would call it "ratting" on them. And I'm sure I don't need to remind you, Nicola, that this is a murder investigation and a particularly violent one at that.' She wasn't about to tell the student that Tom Ramsey had been stabbed thirteen times. Doubtless she'd hear all sorts of horror stories as soon as the press arrived. She considered showing the girl the photographs of the dead Ramsey but hoped to get the information she needed without upsetting the young woman. She reminded herself that everyone reacted differently when faced with a sudden and shocking death, especially murder, and the slightly disinterested air might just be a front.

That was the other thing. They needed to speak with anyone who had a boat. Doubtless the press would try to find any way imaginable to get over to the island to take photos of the scene of the crime. The police needed to warn the locals not to talk to journalists or allow them to hinder the investigation.

Thinking about boats brought something to mind. She turned to the volunteer once more. 'I understand Tom Ramsey had his own boat?' No boat had been discovered on the island when they had found the warden's body.

The girl nodded.

'But his boat wasn't used to take you to the mainland for the party?'

'No. We all got picked up by Angus McCrae.'

'Do you know where Tom Ramsey's boat is?'

The girl looked surprised. '*The Invicta*? It should be over on the island. It was there when we left.'

And now it isn't. Fletcher felt a wave of excitement coursing through her veins. This could be important. Where was Tom Ramsey's boat? There could only be one answer to this question. The murderer had used Ramsey's boat to escape from the island. The girl all but forgotten Fletcher then thought of the next obvious question. How had he or she got to the island in the first place? Then it hit her. A third party might have dropped the murderer off. The murderer could have had an accomplice. Finally she felt they were getting somewhere.

'Can you describe Ramsey's boat?'

'I'm not an expert in boats but it was small, painted yellow and white.'

The interview continued. Her stomach rumbled sounding like thunder. She glanced at her watch. It was eight in the evening and she hadn't eaten anything all day. She had survived on nothing more than tea and coffee and, up until now, hadn't even noticed. She had one more interview to go. She stood up and had a good stretch before she started her interview with Patricia Cummins.

20

Carruthers spied Frank Dewar, the owner of the oldest creel boat in Anstruther, coiling some ropes on the quayside. When the fisherman saw Carruthers approaching he sat down on a lobster pot and lit a cigarette with a calloused hand. *Doubtless he knows he's in line for some questions*, thought Carruthers.

The fisherman, who had a strong-looking physique despite being in his early sixties, looked up at Carruthers, a mixture of confusion and sadness on his weather-beaten face. He was also sporting a cut over his right eye.

He waited for Carruthers to draw close before he spoke. 'I've spent my life on the boats, Jim. I'm sixty-two years old and I started when I was sixteen.'

Carruthers waited for Dewar to continue.

'I've lost friends at sea. She's a cruel mistress. I've seen men drown right in front of my own eyes and not been able to do a thing about it. I've even known men to go missing never to be found, but this is something different.'

Carruthers couldn't agree more. He pulled up a lobster pot and sat down next to the old fisherman, although he was so tired all he really wanted was to go home, grab a bite to eat, shower and go to bed. It had been a long day.

Carruthers pointed to the man's face. 'That's a bad cut over your eye. How did you get it?'

Dewar managed a rueful half smile as he touched the cut. 'Hit my head on the glass shelf in the bathroom. I told Irene we should have put it higher.'

Frank Dewar offered Carruthers his cigarette. Despite being an ex-smoker Carruthers accepted it, took a long drag before giving it back to the fisherman. He tasted the bitterness of the nicotine as it hit the back of his throat.

'What's going on, Frank?'

'You tell me.' Dewar took a drag before he spoke. 'You're the cop.' He offered the fag again, but Carruthers shook his head. 'Do you think they're connected?'

Carruthers raised his eyebrows.

'Robbie Paterson's disappearance and Tom Ramsey's murder, I mean?'

'At this stage I really don't know.' He looked at Dewar. 'You know Robbie better than anybody.'

'Aye. I've known him for fifty years. We were at school together.'

'I understand Robbie sometimes takes his boat out at night?'

Dewar nodded. 'Some of the boys have started to fish for prawn. A couple go out at first light.'

'Including Robbie?'

'Aye.'

So why hadn't his boat returned. Why had it been found floating eerily in the sea? 'What sort of fisherman is he?'

'Do you mean is he a careful fisherman?'

Carruthers nodded.

'We all treat the sea with the respect she deserves.'

Carruthers noticed the use of the female pronoun. A lot of

the older fishermen were superstitious. He knew of one man who refused to have Swan matches on his boat as swans were considered unlucky! He wondered how superstitious Robbie Paterson was. 'I understand from his wife he isn't in the habit of wearing a PFD?'

'We talked about it but he felt it was too constraining. Got in the way of the work.'

That's borne out by what his wife said, thought Carruthers. 'Would he have had radar?'

Frank Dewar laughed. 'You're a bit behind the times, Jim. The Decca Navigation system shut down nearly twenty odd years ago. It's been replaced by GPS.'

Carruthers felt himself reddening. He was a city boy from Glasgow. What did he know of how fishermen navigated? Although if he had thought about it properly it made sense. After all, he used GPS to navigate when he walked in the hills, though his antiquated GPS device could be temperamental. He remembered when he had got himself lost on the Cairngorm plateau in a whiteout. He shuddered. 'Paterson's boat was found less than half a mile off the Isle of May. Did he usually fish there?'

'He mainly fishes quite close to Anstruther harbour.'

'That's not answering my question, Frank. Was he ever known to fish close to the Isle of May?'

'Aye, sometimes. It can be good fishing round the island.'

'But you wouldn't take your boat that far out at first light if you were fishing for prawn?' Carruthers stole a look at the old fisherman. *He's becoming tight lipped. I'm not a drinking pal anymore. I'm now a cop.* 'I understand there's no fishing restrictions around the Isle of May?'

Dewar nodded. 'Aye, that's right although some nature-lovers think there should be.'

Carruthers was feeling frustrated. He wasn't getting

anywhere. 'I'm not accusing Robbie of a crime, Frank. I'm just trying to establish the facts.' *Although to be fair I'm starting to think he may have committed a crime, and if you know about it, you, my friend, are colluding.*

But the fact that Robert Paterson's boat had been found less than half a mile from the site of the frenzied murder of the warden of the Isle of May was something Carruthers didn't particularly like, and glancing at Frank's pinched face and narrowed eyes, nor did Dewar.

'How far would lobster boats generally go out?'

'Most of the boats that leave from Anstruther harbour are small, Jim, which means that engine size and weather dictate how far from shore and how often we can fish, but as I said, Robbie also went out fishing for prawn. If he had taken his boat out at first light then it was prawn he was after.'

'He usually fishes alone? Has it always been like that? I understand the creel boats can usually take two people.'

Dewar nodded. 'He used to go out with another fisherman. This is going back some years, mind. Word had it they had a falling out. That's when Robbie decided he would rather go it alone. He always says to me that there's nothing like being alone on the open sea.'

Carruthers could understand that. The open sea to Robbie Paterson was obviously what the Scottish mountains were to him. A chance to be alone in silence in nature with his own thoughts. He wondered about the man Paterson used to fish with. Was this a potential lead?

'Where can I find the man Robbie used to fish with? I'd like to ask him some questions.'

Dewar laughed mirthlessly. Carruthers couldn't see what was so funny.

'You want to know where to find him? Anstruther Cemetery. He died in 2015. Cancer.'

Another dead-end, then. No pun intended.

They sat in silence for a few moments before the fisherman spoke again. 'You know Robbie's wife, Mary, lost her dad at sea, don't you?'

'I didn't until I spoke to her recently. She told me. What happened?'

'He was skipper on the boat, the *Endeavour*. It went down in a storm in '72. Lost with all hands.' He shook his head. 'And then five years ago they lost their son to suicide. The poor woman must be going out of her mind.'

Carruthers was surprised to learn that Frank Dewar hadn't visited Mary Paterson since her husband had gone missing. He wondered if this could be meaningful.

'The fact is, Robbie's missing, Jim, and the police should be pouring all their efforts into finding him if he's still alive. He's no' a well man.'

'How do you mean?'

'I don't know the details. I just know he doesn't keep the best of health.'

Carruthers frowned. According to Mary Paterson her husband was keeping reasonable health, aside from being on blood thinning medication.

'You mean the fact he's on blood thinners?'

'I think he has heart problems.'

So which was it? Did he or did he not have a health problem? One look at his medical records would tell them. That is, if Paterson had been to his doctor. Whether he had or not, Carruthers was starting to get the impression that Robbie Paterson was a man who kept secrets.

'You often find that in fishermen, Jim – poor health, that is. It's a tough life out at sea.'

Carruthers nodded. He could well imagine that fishermen, working under dangerous conditions at sea and in poor weather, often had health issues a lot earlier than the national average. 'So what are you saying, Frank? Did Robbie have a problem with his health that he hadn't told his wife about?'

'I dinnae know about that, Jim. All I know is he'd been to the doctor about something. I got the feeling it was something to do with his heart. Whether he'd told Mary, now that's another matter.'

So there would be medical records then. This put a new slant on the investigation. If Paterson had an underlying health condition perhaps that would account for his going overboard in good weather. He needed to speak with the man's wife again. And with Paterson's medical practice.

'You need to find him. I dinnae understand why you're wasting your time talking to me.'

Carruthers glanced over at Dewar and was stung by the criticism in his words. 'We've also got an ongoing murder enquiry,' he heard himself say. Dewar's criticism was making him feel defensive. 'The coastguard are out searching. If Robbie's still alive they'll find him.'

This seemed to placate Dewar. 'I've known Robbie Paterson all my life and there's no way he's involved in Tom Ramsey's murder.' He threw the cigarette onto the ground as he stood up. Its sparks hit the tarmac as Frank Dewar walked away without a backwards glance.

Carruthers stayed sitting on his lobster pot and thought about what Dewar had said. He was already forming several theories and he didn't like any of them. Either Robbie Paterson had murdered Tom Ramsey and had drowned trying to leave the island – but in that case, where was Ramsey's boat? Or somehow Paterson had been witness to Ramsey's murder and had then been murdered himself. Or Paterson knew who had killed Ramsey and had staged it to look like he had drowned so he wouldn't be the next victim. That last idea seemed unlikely, he conceded. The only theory Carruthers wasn't giving much weight to, going on gut feeling alone, was the theory that Ramsey's murder and Paterson's disappearance were just a coincidence.

His thoughts turned to Frank Dewar who had all but disappeared from view. *That man knows more than he is saying. And I mean to find out what secrets he's keeping.*

Carruthers trudged to his cottage to fix himself some supper. He felt exhausted after such a long day. After microwaving some leftover lasagne his mother had brought over, he sat and cradled his whisky, swirling the amber liquid around his crystal glass. He thought about Robert Paterson's health. Could there be anything in his medical records that would explain his disappearance? Perhaps something that even the man's wife hadn't known about. There was only one way to find out. He'd need to visit Paterson's GP. He took the heavy glass up the stairs to bed with him. He was asleep as soon as his head hit the pillow.

21

Carruthers arrived at Anstruther Medical Practice bright and early the next morning. He thought about filling McTavish in before he left his cottage, but, in the end decided against it. *What she doesn't know won't hurt her, as the saying goes.*

Anstruther Medical Practice was in fact not in Anstruther, but rather in Cellardyke. Cellardyke was another ancient fishing port. Over time the two fishing villages had conjoined, so although the Anstruther Medical Practice had a Cellardyke address, it was just a short walk away from Carruthers' cottage in Anstruther.

He had got the name of Paterson's GP from the fisherman's wife and, as luck would have it, when the inspector arrived at the practice Dr Kenzie was between patients. Having flashed his warrant card at the startled receptionist, who looked no older than a school leaver, Carruthers was given an immediate audience with the middle-aged GP.

The inspector observed the extraordinary-looking general practitioner who appeared like something out of a 1970s sitcom with his long sideburns and striped, slightly flared trousers. Unfortunately, that was where the comedy ended. As Carruthers was about to find out the man was seriously cantankerous. He frowned at the detective as Carruthers explained what information he needed.

'I'm sorry to say I can't give you access to my patients' medical records. There are protocols to be followed, Inspector. You should know that. You don't even have written confirmation from your superintendent.'

You don't look sorry at all, you old goat. Carruthers was more than ready for this standard response. 'I understand, doctor, but as I'm sure you've heard Robert Paterson is now a missing person, most likely dead and we need to try to ascertain whether he was suffering from a medical condition that would be a likely cause of him falling overboard.'

Kenzie cut through the conversation. 'I hear his boat's been found?'

'That's right. But not him. He's not been found. His wife's going out of her mind.' He deliberated as to whether to tell him about the amount of blood found on the boat but in the end decided against it. The fewer people who knew about it at this stage the better.

'Yes, poor Mary.' He appeared to be thinking it over. 'I'm really sorry, Inspector...' he looked at Carruthers' warrant card, '...Carruthers, but I can't divulge any personal details, even in these circumstances. GDPR and all that. You do understand...' He took a closer look at Carruthers, taking in the man's slightly bloodshot eyes. 'You're not one of my patients, are you?'

'No, I'm not.' *Thank God.* He was starting to feel short tempered with the man's lack of flexibility. 'I'm registered with another practice.' *Am I registered?* He couldn't remember.

'When did you last have a check-up?' He edged closer to Carruthers and peered at him critically.

Thankfully the door burst open and the harried young receptionist appeared before Carruthers had a chance to mutter the expletive, which had just formed on his lips. 'Dr Kenzie, there's a medical emergency doon by the harbour. You're needed right away. A young boy jamp from the wall.'

In her shock and panic the receptionist had slipped into local dialect. Carruthers hadn't heard the word 'jamp' instead of 'jumped' used in any other part of Scotland. He supposed it was an East Neuk classic.

Kenzie grabbed his jacket and old-fashioned medical bag. He indicated the open door with the sweep of his arm and waited for Carruthers to leave first before shutting the door firmly behind him. He then brushed past Carruthers as he called instructions out to his receptionist in a loud officious voice. 'Jessica, let my patients know I've had to leave, will you?' He turned to Carruthers. 'Duty calls. You'll have to see yourself out.'

As soon as Dr Kenzie disappeared down the corridor Carruthers made a decision. He knew he only had a few seconds at most to act. He retraced his steps; quietly opened the door to Kenzie's room, walked in and shut it quickly again. He looked around him, spotting a metal cabinet which was alphabetised. He knew most GPs now used the electronic system but he kept his fingers crossed that Kenzie was as old fashioned as he looked. He pulled out the tray marked P-R and riffled through the files. There it was. Robert Paterson. He opened the file, leafing through it. Bringing out his phone he put it in camera mode and started taking photos of the page that detailed why Robert Paterson might have fallen off his boat.

'We need to look at the relationship between Ramsey and Paterson more closely.' Sandra McTavish paced the front of the makeshift incident room back at the station. She was eating a banana. Fletcher wondered if that had been her breakfast. 'Did they know each other and, if so, how well?'

Fletcher put her coffee cup down before she spoke. 'According to Jim, both Paterson's wife and Frank Dewar said Ramsey and Paterson knew each other only in passing and I know Jim was inclined to believe them.'

McTavish arched an eyebrow. 'They drank in the same pub. If two people regularly drink at the same small local pub often they would know each other a lot more than just in passing.'

Lennox didn't agree. 'Not necessarily, ma'am. Just cos you drink in the same pub doesn't automatically follow that you'd socialise with the same people. I can't really imagine hardened fishermen having much in common with people just out of university.'

Fletcher grudgingly agreed Lennox had a point.

McTavish turned to Helen Lennox. 'Helen, what have you found out about Ramsey?'

Lennox sat up straighter and flicked open her notebook but before she had a chance to speak Fletcher jumped in.

'We need to look at his ex-girlfriend, Sandra.' Fletcher looked over at a furious Lennox. 'Sorry, Helen. I just need to say this. Not only did the relationship end badly, but according to Ben Homan – he's one of the volunteers – Ellie Robertson had accused Ramsey of having an affair. Her behaviour became increasingly controlling. She sounds like the sort of woman who could easily become a stalker. And we all know where stalking can lead when it escalates.'

McTavish peered at them through her glasses, which were perched on the end of her nose. 'Okay, this is quite a development. The ex-girlfriend needs to be interviewed and ASAP.' She glanced at Lennox who had a frown on her face. 'Get the local CID on to it, will you, Helen? They can do the preliminary interview to see if she has an alibi.'

Fletcher was disappointed. She felt this could be a good lead. 'I'd really like to interview her myself, Sandra. I just feel someone who knows the case–'

Another female voice spoke up. 'So would I.'

Oh for God's sake, shut up, thought Fletcher. Helen Lennox was becoming a total pain in the arse.

McTavish looked at each woman in turn. 'I understand how important you believe this interview is, both of you. However, with Gayle at the funeral today that leaves us a person down. Let the local CID do it and liaise with them for now. We agree on one thing: we do need to interview the woman as soon as possible. But it can't be done by any of my team. We're far too busy up here. However, if we feel a further interview is needed then,' her gaze settled on Fletcher, 'Andie, happy for you to go.'

The DCI leafed through her notes. 'Have we heard back from IT yet? Do we know if they have gained access to Ramsey's mobile and computer?'

'Not yet, Sandra,' said Fletcher.

'That needs to be chased up. I want to see if this Ellie Robertson has sent any recent text messages to Ramsey.' McTavish switched her attention to Lennox who now had a face like thunder. 'You were going to give me Tom's background, Helen?'

'Yes, I was until I got interrupted.' Lennox took a short sharp sniff. 'He has a first degree in biology followed by a masters in environmental science. His job prior to being warden of the Isle of May was warden of the Farne Islands.'

'Do you know why he left the job?'

'No, not yet but he doesn't appear to stay in one job for very long. His last–'

Fletcher broke in. 'I actually think it might have something to do with his ex.' She avoided eye contact with Lennox, remembering that she had elicited this piece of information from one of the volunteers without Lennox being present. She felt a momentary pang of conscience that she had neglected to fill her younger and more junior colleague in on some of the important details in their debrief afterwards.

McTavish was still speaking. 'So relationships might be his Achilles heel. That's interesting. Helen, find out if there was any other reason why he left the post. Anything else?'

'One of his duties was to oversee non-residential volunteer work programmes. He also undertook survey and species habitat monitoring work.'

'I don't need his resume, Helen. I need to know what got him killed.'

Lennox reddened. She chewed her lip. She threw Fletcher a filthy look.

'The best lead we've got is this ex-girlfriend,' said McTavish. 'Now, what about the volunteers?'

'There are five volunteers: Patricia Cummins, Nicola Reid, Ben Homan, Sylvie White and Ian Gaunt.' Lennox rattled their names off.

Fletcher suspected that Lennox had talked quickly to avoid her thunder being stolen for a second time.

McTavish scratched her forehead. 'Are their backgrounds consistent with them volunteering on the island? I'm just wondering if they were using the volunteering to try to get closer to Tom Ramsey for whatever reason.'

Lennox thumbed through her black notebook. 'Patricia Cummins is a zoologist. That's the lassie who just got her PhD. She's recently returned from Tanzania where she was working with the endangered long billed forest warbler.'

There was a snort of laughter from Harris. 'I thought she was studying zoology, not ornithology,' he burst out.

Fletcher shot him an irritated look. 'Ornithology *is* a branch of zoology, you muppet.'

Lennox resumed speaking. 'Nicola Reid, from Glasgow, is also a zoologist. Apparently, the reason she undertook volunteering on the island is to expand her knowledge of seabirds. Before her post here she was working with native mammals.' She skim-read the rest of her notes before looking up. 'All of them, bar one, have the sort of backgrounds you would expect to find in those volunteering on this programme.'

'All but one?' McTavish looked up, interested.

'Ian Gaunt doesn't really fit the stereotype of volunteer if you can call it that. For one, he is a lot older than the others.'

'Isn't he older than Ramsey?'

'By five years,' said Fletcher. 'And his background is in banking.'

'We can't judge him for that. But I do want to take a closer look at him. It's an interesting career change. Has his path ever crossed with Ramsey, for example? Helen, I want you to examine Gaunt's background in further detail and run a check on all the students. See if any of them come up on our database.'

'Will do, although I would much rather–'

'There was one other thing about Gaunt.' Fletcher tucked a stray tendril of dark hair behind her ear as she spoke. She was aware she had just interrupted Lennox again but knew the younger woman was about to make yet another complaint. She, for one, didn't have the patience to listen. 'The interview with Gaunt was a bit strange.'

'In what way?'

'I can't put my finger on it. He didn't make eye contact with me. His eyes were bloodshot.'

McTavish was dismissive. 'They did have a heavy night the night before by all accounts. I'm sure someone in their late thirties wouldn't weather the amount of booze those students put away as well as someone a decade younger.'

'True. But bloodshot eyes can also be a sign of something else.'

The DCI's response was sharp. 'You think he's taking drugs?'

'I don't know.' Fletcher bit her nail. 'But there's also something he said, although it might be nothing. He said something about how unfortunate it was that Tom Ramsey changed his mind last minute about going over to the pub on the mainland.'

'And?'

'Well, that was it.'

McTavish peered at Fletcher critically. 'I don't think there's anything wrong with that, do you?'

'Well, no, sorry, just ignore me. The only other thing that bothered me about the interviews was the interview with Ben Homan.'

'What of it?'

'He said that there was a good band playing in Anstruther that night.'

'So?'

'So according to Sylvie White, Ben Homan didn't see any of the performance. He disappeared as soon as the boat landed and they didn't see him again for...' she consulted her notebook, 'four hours.'

'And he definitely made it sound as if he had seen the band?'

'Yes. He said the warden would have enjoyed it.'

'Okay, that might be worth chasing up. Helen, can I put you on to that?'

Lennox nodded. She seemed subdued.

McTavish peered over her glasses at the officers. 'How did they get over to the mainland – the volunteers?'

'They got a lift over with an Angus McCrae. Local fisherman but occasionally he gives lifts to folk who want to go over to the May. He's clean. No record and he was with two other fishermen at the time of Ramsey's murder.'

'Where's Jim at the moment, by the way? It's not like him to be late for a brief.' McTavish glanced at her watch.

'I believe he went to see Robert Paterson's GP over in Cellardyke.' As she spoke Fletcher looked at her mobile to see if Carruthers had sent her a text but there was nothing.

McTavish frowned. 'He never said.'

Shit, thought Fletcher. *I've just dropped Jim right into it.*

'Well, perhaps he'll grace us with his presence when he's good and ready.' McTavish's sarcastic tone did not escape Fletcher. She turned back to the incident board. Underneath the photograph of the warden was a map of the island.

The DCI pointed to the map. 'The tide could have carried the boat closer to the island. Tragedies at sea happen all the time. And Paterson's body could easily have drifted out into the North Sea.'

'True,' put in Helen Lennox, 'but the weather was fine, so what made Paterson go overboard?'

DCI Sandra McTavish turned back to face the officers in the incident room. 'Theories?'

'He'd been drinking?'

'Human error then? Okay. That's one possibility although, according to Jim, his friend, Frank Dewar, said he never drank when he was going to sea. Keep going. Throw things at me.'

'The boat collided with another vessel?' This from Brown who was stroking his comb-over.

'The *Maid of the Mist* was undamaged so I think we can rule that theory out,' said Fletcher.

'Another vessel could still have been involved.' Brown was insistent. 'What if the *Maid of the Mist* was on a collision course with another vessel and had to veer out the way last minute and Paterson ended up being thrown over?'

The DCI looked at Brown with interest. 'Are you saying another vessel could have *deliberately* manoeuvred itself so that the *Maid of the Mist* would be forced to change its course last minute?'

'Mebbe. It's the best suggestion so far, isn't it? And if another boat was involved it more than likely would have been deliberate. It didn't stop, did it?'

22

There was a hush that descended over the incident room as the various members of CID contemplated the latest theory. The door opened and Carruthers walked in. 'Sorry I'm late.'

'Take a seat, Jim. We're just brainstorming about what might have made Paterson fall overboard. Brown suggested another vessel might have been involved.'

As soon as he heard this the words of Paterson's friend, Dewar, came into Carruthers' mind. He needed to tell McTavish the latest development. He had meant to do it last night by phone but he had been so tired he'd forgotten. And then this morning he had gone straight to the medical practice. At least the young jumper was fine. Carruthers had hung around long enough to make sure it wasn't a police matter. He left when he found out that the boy had rowed with his girlfriend. *Bet he's feeling like a real idiot now.*

McTavish arched her eyebrow at him. 'Fletcher told me you've been to see Paterson's GP this morning? Presumably that's why you're late for this brief? Did you get anything useful?'

Carruthers caught McTavish's frown. *Bugger. She's annoyed.*

And I can't blame her. I thought I was going to change my ways and keep her more in the loop but I just can't seem to help myself, he thought gloomily.

'When I spoke to Frank Dewar he told me Paterson wasn't keeping the best of health. It's been confirmed by the practice that Paterson has a heart condition.' *No need to tell them that I've looked at the man's medical records without permission.*

'Go on,' urged McTavish.

'One of his arteries is partially blocked. It looks like he could have had a heart attack at any moment. I believe he refused medical treatment. I don't think he told his wife about the condition.'

McTavish looked thoughtful. 'So he *could* have had a heart attack whilst he was on his boat. But then that doesn't account for the amount of blood found.'

'Apparently he was on a blood thinning medication,' continued Carruthers, 'which would make any bleeding more profuse.'

'He could have had a heart attack and then hit his head on a piece of fishing equipment or on the side of the boat,' said Lennox. 'We all know how much head injuries bleed and if, as Jim says, he was on blood thinning meds...'

McTavish was thoughtful. 'So it could have been an accident then. Better for us if it is.'

There was a murmur of agreement followed by a knock on the door. A short squat man put his head round. 'The results from Robert Paterson's boat are in, ma'am.'

'Thank you, Graham.' As she spoke McTavish held her hand out for the information and Graham handed her a buff envelope. She ripped it open and pulled out the single white sheet of paper. She read it quickly then looked up and informed the room of the findings. 'Blood on the boat is a match for Robert Paterson.'

'Hardly surprising,' said Helen Lennox. 'It *is* his boat.'

McTavish took the sheet of paper away from her face and let her hand holding the paper drop to her side. 'No, perhaps not. But what *is* surprising is that forensics have found the blood of two different people, which proves someone other than Paterson was also on his boat, possibly at the time of his death.'

The room descended into animated discussion.

McTavish walked over to the board and stared at the photograph of Paterson's boat. 'We need to find out whose blood that is.' She sighed. 'This has changed everything.'

'So if there's the blood of at least two people we might be looking for someone with an obvious injury?' All eyes turned to Helen Lennox as she spoke.

Once more Frank Dewar came into Carruthers' mind. 'When I talked to Frank Dewar he had a cut to his head,' he said. 'It looked pretty nasty. He told me he had hit it on a glass shelf in his bathroom but I'm wondering if he was lying.'

McTavish's eyes flickered with interest. 'Why would he lie? You're thinking he could have had a run-in with Paterson?'

'It's possible,' Carruthers conceded.

'Well, there's one way we can find out. We need to get hold of Dewar's DNA and see if it's a match with the blood on Paterson's boat.'

'Even if it is, it doesn't mean Dewar killed him,' put in Lennox.

'True,' said McTavish, 'but if he *is* lying about where he got that cut, you have to wonder why. Start off by running a check to see whether Frank Dewar is on our database.'

Lennox nodded.

'Any news from Gus on the drugs shipment?'

'Not yet,' said Carruthers.

McTavish pulled a face. 'As soon as you hear anything I want to know.'

The rest of the day passed in a whirlwind of phone calls and meetings. By 9pm, and with no new concrete leads, a weary Carruthers headed home.

After eating a pot noodle he phoned his mum for a brief chat, and satisfied she was doing okay, he gratefully went to bed.

23

Dave Fraser listened keenly to the instructor, who he judged to be in his thirties. He was itching to get onto the water and try out his new hobby. He yawned. Early mornings weren't his favourite time of day.

'Right, you've had your safety instruction. You now know how to use the safety systems on your kite. As I said before, kitesurfing's come a long way since the early 2000s. We've also been through the theory about flying kites and the wind window.'

Dave struggled to remember everything he'd been taught but he thought he'd got enough of the drift that he wouldn't make a fanny of himself. He just wanted to get out onto the water and kitesurf.

'You've also been shown how to properly set up your kite, bar and lines.' The instructor looked round the expectant faces of the beginners. 'Can anyone tell me how to body drag?'

Dave frowned and searched his memory banks but came up with a blank.

'It's something you do every single session,' urged the instructor.

There was silence round the group. 'Whenever you try new things you'll constantly lose your board. Body dragging lets you recover your lost board so it's one of the most important things you can learn when you go kitesurfing.'

Dave had always hated any sort of instruction. That's why he'd left school early. He was starting to feel bored. He couldn't wait to get out into the sea and do his first run. His eye was drawn to a passing pretty young girl wearing a bikini. He tried hard to listen to the instructor but his mind kept drifting. A young man joined the girl and put his arm round her. Dave lost interest.

He looked out towards the sea. In a few minutes he would be out with his kite for the very first time. How hard would it be to get up on the board? He couldn't wait to try. He felt a moment of exhilaration as the adrenaline coursed through him.

'...Perfect weather conditions today.' He could hear snatches of the instruction but his mind and body were already out on the water. He was standing on the board skimming through the sea.

'...Most amazing sport on this planet.' While Dave could hear the enthusiasm in the instructor's voice his attention had been drawn to something bright orange tangled in seaweed floating in the sea. He frowned. The object disappeared for a moment only to reappear a few seconds later. Dave kept his eyes on it with an increasing sense of unease until he was certain he knew what it was. His heart pounded in his chest and he felt sick. Even from the beach he could make out how bloated and swollen it was.

'Has anyone got any questions?'

Dave got to his feet, heart in his mouth, as the realisation of what he was looking at suddenly hit him.

'Yes.' He glanced at the instructor in alarm. 'That's not... is that a body in the water?'

All the would-be kitesurfers followed the line of where his arm was pointing. Then a dark-haired girl in the group started to scream, a long piercing sound that penetrated Dave's eardrums and made his heart thud.

The team reassembled at 8am. It was a long brief. A couple of hours in, Tom Kiely put his bald head round the door. 'Ma'am?'

McTavish swung round. 'God, what is it now? Don't you people ever knock? I'm right in the middle of a brief.'

Kiely was unfazed. 'You need to know about this. We've just had a call from a member of the public. The body of a man's been found in the sea at Shell Bay. The member of the public that called it in thinks the man's been stabbed.'

The incident room erupted.

Dave found himself with a couple of the other lads and the instructor running across the sandy beach at full pelt and into the water. The instructor hit the water first, being the fittest in the group. Dave watched him dive confidently under the waves and swim using a fast crawl to where the body was bobbing up and down on its front. Dave, who was the second fittest after the instructor, wasn't far behind.

'Help me get him to land,' he yelled.

The instructor turned the body over so it was now on its back. Dave recognised the life-saving technique. As he swam closer to the floating body he momentarily hung back. The closer he got the more hideous it looked. Dave saw that it was the body of a large man with a beard. The eyes had popped out and the tongue protruded in a grotesquely swollen face. He was so shocked that he opened his mouth taking in a large quantity of seawater. He panicked, momentarily disappearing under the surface, but came up spluttering, spitting out salty seawater.

McTavish snapped into action. 'Right. We need to suspend the rest of the team brief.' She looked at Carruthers first. 'Jim, I want you and Andie to get over to Shell Bay, ASAP.'

Carruthers and Fletcher both got to their feet. Other people stood up too. 'I'm coming with you,' said Lennox as she gathered up her belongings up in record time and walked purposefully to the door.

'Not so fast. Helen,' said McTavish. 'I need you to stay here.'

Lennox looked crestfallen.

'Keep digging into the backgrounds of Tom Ramsey and the volunteers. I want you to start by finding out if any of them have a criminal record.'

'I've already looked at most of the volunteers. They're clean.'

'What about Ben Homan?'

'There's nothing in it. He sloped off to shag some girl or other in Anstruther. Story's checked out. That's why he missed the band. He joined the others later.'

'Wish he'd told us that.'

'Turns out she's married so he wanted to keep it quiet.' She bit the tip of her pen. 'I've only got one more volunteer to check.'

McTavish frowned. 'Well then, once you finish looking at them you can start looking into Tom Ramsey's background more fully. I want to know everything about him right down to where he buys his underpants from.'

'I think Jim said it was M&S.'

'I've got no time for jokes, Helen.'

'I'm not–'

'Any news on whether Frank Dewar is on our database?'

'Yes, he is. It seems he's been in a fair few scraps.'

'Good. I also want you to chase up the local CID in Bristol, will you? We need to know how the interview went.'

'Yes, ma'am.'

As the officers filed out of the incident room Carruthers approached McTavish. He spoke in a low, urgent voice. 'Do we know if the body's that of Paterson's?'

'Too early to say. All I've been told is that it's male and has a possible stab wound. Am I right in thinking Shell Bay lies about a mile from Earlsferry?'

'Yes, that's right,' said Carruthers. 'It lies in a pretty secluded area of the Fife coastline. I believe the beach is popular with swimmers as well as walkers.'

McTavish looked at her watch. 'I'm about to go into a meeting with Superintendent Bingham but I want you to keep in touch with me. SOCOs are on their way and will meet you there.'

Fletcher was filling her water bottle by the water cooler when she spied Lennox walking towards her. 'I want to talk about what happened yesterday. What was all that about?' demanded the DC.

'All what?' Fletcher's heart sank. She knew what Lennox was going to say and she had every right to be angry. Despite their difference in rank they were still supposed to be a team. She had kept an important part of the interview from Lennox. She now regretted it.

'We're *supposed* to be a team, Andie. We were *supposed* to be conducting those interviews together and yet you deliberately kept an important piece of information to yourself.' Lennox's eyes flashed with anger. 'You know what I'm talking about – namely that one of the volunteers told you during the interviews that Ramsey's ex had accused him of having an affair during their relationship. Of course you just had to keep that piece of vital information to yourself so that you could be the one to disclose it in the team brief later. I want to know why. Why would you do that? You're already a DS or are you going for DI? It's not on. It really isn't.'

Fletcher sidestepped Lennox and put the strap of her handbag on her shoulder. She glanced at her colleague's angry face. Lennox looked as if she might burst into tears. Once again the older woman regretted her actions. 'I'm sorry. I need to get going, Helen. Jim's waiting for me. We'll talk about this when I get back.'

Lennox got her parting shot in. 'We're not in competition, Andie. As women we should be helping each other get on.'

Fletcher left an indignant Helen Lennox, hands on hips, went back to her desk, picked up her keys, walked out of the station and stood by her car in the car park. Out of the corner of her eye she saw Carruthers striding towards her holding coveralls and nitrile gloves. She felt ashamed of herself. There was some truth in what Lennox had said. Did she see her as competition even though the younger woman was of a different rank? Well, no, not competition exactly, but if she analysed her feelings, she clearly didn't want her as a member of CID. The question was why?

She swept a lock of wayward hair away from her face. 'Do you mind if we go in my car? I've got everything I need in the boot.'

He looked down at her. 'I don't mind at all. Are you happy to drive?'

'Yep, sure.'

Fletcher threw her handbag on the back seat, Carruthers put his coveralls in the boot and climbed into the passenger seat. They buckled themselves in.

Fletcher put the instructions into her satnav. 'How far away is it?'

'About half an hour on the A915.'

'Stupid satnav is telling me to go via Anstruther.'

'I'd be tempted to go inland via Largoward. I think it would be quicker than the Fife Coastal route. It takes ages to go through all those wee villages.'

'I do know that, Jim. I've been living in Fife longer than you, remember?' An irritable Fletcher drove them out of Castletown. The traffic was mercifully quiet as they drove along the A915.

'You okay, Andie?'

'Helen Lennox is just getting to me, that's all.'

'Look, I know she can be a bit of a pain.'

'A bit of a pain? That's putting it mildly.'

'What's she done to upset you?'

Fletcher lapsed into silence as she thought about it. *That's just it though*, she thought. *This time it's what I've done. Not what she's done. Perhaps it's me and not her. After all, I gave Gayle a rough time when she arrived in the team. Maybe I have an issue with other women being part of the team.*

'Earth to Andie. Come in, Andie. Look, do you want to talk about it? Something's seriously bugging you.'

'Not really. After all, who wants to talk about their failings?' A miserable Fletcher saw Carruthers look at her curiously but she was keen to change the subject. She tried to keep her voice light. 'Do you know how the funeral went? I thought Gayle would be back at work today. After all we're in the middle of a murder investigation.'

'I haven't heard.'

'I hope Gayle's family's going to be okay.'

'I think it'll be a long time before they're okay. And a sudden death like that, it's not something you ever really get over.'

Fletcher suddenly felt unbelievably depressed. 'I suppose

not.' She wondered if her DI was thinking about his own child-hood, which he rarely talked about. She knew he had lost a brother at a young age in a hit and run. They lapsed into silence.

'Have you been to Shell Bay before, Jim?' As Fletcher spoke she kept an eye on her rear-view mirror as a white Mazda appeared from nowhere and tore past them on a bend narrowly missing a vehicle coming the opposite direction. Both officers gasped at the utter lunacy of the speeding driver.

'Jesus,' said Fletcher. 'That car must be going at least 90 miles an hour.'

Carruthers drew a sharp breath. 'I'll get on to traffic. The idiot will kill someone driving like that.' He pulled out his mobile and called it in.

Carruthers thought about Fletcher's question. 'I've been there once with Mairi but it was a long time ago now. As far as I remember it's a sheltered sandy beach near the Fife Coastal Path. Really beautiful.'

They heard a loud thud and as they rounded a bend Fletcher slammed on her brakes hard. Both officers jerked forward, the seat belt bruising Fletcher's chest causing her a momentary searing pain in the back of her neck. Ahead of them in the ditch was the white Mazda. It was lying on its side, all its windows smashed and the boot was open. The driver door opened and a young man tried to climb out. He was covered in blood. In the middle of the road were the mangled remains of a silver Audi. The occupants of the driver and passenger seats were unmoving.

'Oh fuck.' Fletcher pulled up by the gate to a field and both officers jumped out.

'Are you okay?'

'I'm fine,' said Fletcher, gritting through the pain in her neck.

'You call for an ambulance,' shouted Carruthers. 'I'm going to see about the occupants of the Audi.'

Fletcher gingerly leant back into the car for her mobile. A shot of pain seared through her making her feel sick. She called the accident in while gently rubbing her neck. As she finished the call she saw the driver of the Mazda crawling out of the car, limping away and trying to run into a nearby field.

'Shit. Now the perp's leaving the scene of the bloody accident.'

She saw Carruthers trying to wrench the passenger side door of the Audi open. 'Get after him, Andie.'

Fletcher cursed that she had worn a skirt to work that day but at least her shoes were flat. She tore after the youth, finally catching up with him. She wrestled him to the ground. Another agonising shooting pain went up her neck. 'Stop struggling,' she cried. 'I need to know how badly injured you are.' It didn't stop her putting a set of cuffs on him though.

From his erratic and dangerous driving to his wild unfocused eyes Fletcher guessed that he was high on drugs. Sadly the wilds of Fife were no stranger to dangerous driving. Fletcher knew only too well that there had been a spate of fatal accidents; although it seemed to her the country back roads were by far the worst. *Drugs*, she thought as her mind went back to the filthy bedsit where they had found the baby and dead junkies. *The gift that just keeps giving.*

'Have you any idea what speed you were doing back there?' As she asked the question she looked him over for any signs of serious injury. Blood was pouring down his face. 'Come on. We need to get you to hospital. Get that head wound checked out. Can you stand? And then, sunshine, you're nicked.'

The young man nodded. Fletcher hauled him to his feet and started walking him back towards the road. He half collapsed against her car. She shouted over to Carruthers. 'He's drugged up to his eyeballs. I don't think we have to worry about him going anywhere anytime soon. I also think he's been really lucky.

The head wound looks superficial.' She gestured towards the mangled Audi. 'How are they?'

'A man and woman. In their seventies. We'll need to wait for the paramedics,' called out Carruthers. 'I think the driver's okay but the passenger's going to have to be cut out. She's unconscious. It looks serious.' Carruthers talked to the conscious occupant in the car, keeping his voice low and calm.

In the distance they heard the whine of an ambulance and within moments saw the flashing blue lights of a police car. 'That's a good response time. They must have had a unit close by.' Carruthers brought out his mobile and Fletcher heard him filling McTavish in while keeping an eye on the injured motorists.

Twenty minutes later they were sitting back in Fletcher's green Beetle, having explained to the officers on the scene who they were and that they were on their way to a suspicious death. She rubbed her neck again.

Carruthers looked at her, concerned. 'Do you need to get checked over?'

'I'll survive. I might have a touch of whiplash though. I'll take some painkillers. I could always go to the hospital later if needs be.'

'As long as you're sure?'

Fletcher tried to nod but even that was painful. She pulled out a blister pack of paracetamol from the side door pocket. Carruthers offered her a bottle of water, which she gratefully accepted.

At least we're not about to go back out on the RIB boat, she thought. *All that bumping along could do my already injured neck some serious damage.* In an effort to take her mind off her neck pain she eventually said, 'I hope those folk in the Audi will be all right.'

'They're in safe hands, Andie. We can always check up on them later by giving the hospital a ring.'

Fletcher nodded. Another pain shot through her neck.

'Are you sure you don't need to get checked out? You're obviously in a lot of pain from the way you're moving.'

'I'm okay. Painkillers will kick in soon. Anyway, we don't have time to go to the hospital.' She started the car's engine. 'Oh God, I wonder if we're going to find it's the body of the missing fisherman.'

With that she accelerated down the country road leaving the flashing lights of the police car and ambulance receding into the background.

24

Carruthers and Fletcher arrived at Shell Bay and pulled up in a small car park. They both disembarked and brought out their coveralls and nitrile gloves, which they put on.

As Fletcher bent down to pull on her paper shoes Carruthers surveyed the flat stretch of beach. 'Look.' His hand shot out. 'Over there by that cluster of rocks.'

They could see a small group of young men and women in wetsuits. A solitary uniformed female police officer was taking a statement from a young man. In the distance another knot of hushed onlookers were kept back by a couple of uniform police who were busy erecting police tape. Carruthers spotted Dr Mackie kneeling on the wet sand pulling open his medical bag.

'Mackie's here. Let's go.'

The two officers jogged through the dunes and long grasses over the sand down to the rocks. Another crowd of teenagers in wetsuits were crowded round the body.

'Get right back please. Right away from the body,' shouted Fletcher. The crowd pulled back, speaking in hushed tones to each other. Three or four of them were soaking wet; hair plastered to still damp faces. One young woman was shivering. An older man passed her a towel. *Most likely the instructor.* Carruthers surmised they had been the ones who had pulled the body out of the water. He saw the kit they had with them. *Kitesurfers.*

One woman stood out in the crowd. Carruthers noticed a sharp-faced lady with blonde hair in her late thirties dressed in a dark suit standing in the group of onlookers clutching something that looked like a notebook. He frowned. Her face was familiar. She looked like a reporter. Where had he seen her before? Their eyes locked for a moment before she looked away. He glanced down at the body of the man who had been pulled from the sea. When he looked back at the crowd of onlookers a bit later on she had disappeared.

His gaze went back to the motionless figure still entwined in seaweed. His policing instincts kicked in and the reporter was forgotten. The first thing he noticed was that the body was male and clothed in bright orange oilskins and yellow boots. It had to be Robert Paterson.

The body had been in the water a while. It was bloated and had been badly battered by rocks. Carruthers hated bodies pulled from the sea when the features were so distorted that the body was unrecognisable.

Mackie stood up slowly. His knees creaked and Carruthers could hear him muttering about getting too old.

'John, what can you tell us?'

'I was going to say very little at this stage, Jim. Male, late sixties I'm guessing. He's got a lot of lacerations to his body. Some are quite deep. Likely a fisherman the way he's dressed. Looking at him I'd say he's been in the water for at least forty-eight hours.'

Well, that would fit with when Paterson went missing, thought Carruthers. The pathologist moved around the body so he was now standing and leaning over the torso's top half. 'However this is interesting–'

Carruthers leant in, excitement mounting.

The old doctor touched the side of the dead man's face and gently turned it to the side. 'See this bruising and these cuts?'

Carruthers leant further in. He could see a cut and some swelling on the lips and a further cut and bruising around the face.

Had he been in a fight?

Mackie echoed Carruthers' thoughts. 'It's possible he's been in a fight in the last few days. Some of the bruising looks older than the rest though.'

'He's had more than one altercation?'

'Because he's been in the water I can't say with any certainty but it's possible.'

Mackie straightened up and stretched. 'But I'm more interested in these other wounds.' He pointed to the wounds on the torso.

'Could they be stab wounds?' Carruthers asked.

'A couple are quite deep.' Mackie had moved round the body again and gave one a prod with his gloved hand. 'It's possible but I'd need to do the post-mortem before I could say for sure.'

'Could one of the puncture wounds have killed him?'

'Like I said I'll need to get him back to the mortuary. I don't want to conjecture at this stage, laddie.'

Fletcher straightened up from her bent-over position and hissed to Carruthers. 'We need to make a positive ID as soon as possible. From what he's wearing it's likely Robert Paterson. Do you want me to call in on Mrs Paterson? I can give her a lift to the mortuary.'

Carruthers thought about it and decided, knowing Robbie Paterson, he needed to do it himself. There was an important question he wanted to ask Mrs Paterson. 'No, I'll do it but I'll need you to give me a lift back to the station so I can pick up my car. And Andie?' She looked up. 'When you get back sort things out with Helen, will you? If you two can't get along it's not just her it will reflect badly on.'

Carruthers knocked on the Patersons' door. It was the moment every police officer dreaded. By rights it should be the job of a lower rank but Carruthers always made it his business to get personally involved. Even when he had been a DCI he had still visited the family of the missing or bereaved. He felt he owed it to the victims and their families. And when he actually knew the potential victim, well, it was a no-brainer.

A drawn Mrs Paterson opened the door to the police officer. She looked frailer and smaller than the last time Carruthers had seen her. She blinked a couple of times and shielded her eyes against the bright sun making Carruthers wonder if she had seen the light of day yet. He had noticed that her front curtains were still closed. Either she hadn't been up long or she had kept them drawn against the prying eyes of the neighbours. Although she was yet to speak she seemed groggy. Perhaps she had taken some sort of sedative.

'Mrs Paterson, I'm sorry if this isn't a convenient time to call. The news isn't good, I'm afraid. Can I come in?'

'What is it? Have you found my Robbie?'

Carruthers drew in a steadying breath. He didn't want to delay the reason for his visit a moment longer. 'The body of a man has been pulled out of the sea over at Shell Bay. We need you to make a formal ID but we think it's Robbie.'

The woman's hand flew to her mouth but Carruthers could see the look of resignation in her eyes as if she had already been preparing herself for the worst possible news.

'The description you gave us of what your husband was last wearing matches with the clothes of the deceased.'

The woman nodded slowly. 'I'll get my house keys.'

'There's one other thing.' Of course if Paterson had fought with someone on his boat the day of his death his wife wouldn't know about it but there was the possibility of the old bruising to consider. 'Had your husband been in a fight recently?'

As the significance of the policeman's words sank in Mrs Paterson dropped her eyes and nodded.

'Do you know who he had the fight with or what it was about?'

'He wouldn't say. He told me it was unimportant and to let it go.'

Why would he say that? It clearly was important. 'So you have no idea at all?'

'I didn't pursue it.'

Carruthers wasn't aware that Robert Paterson was a habitual scrapper. Remembering the cut above Dewar's eye, he was now more convinced it had been sustained in a fight with Paterson. But whether he had or not, it now left him in no doubt that the body pulled from Shell Bay was that of the missing fisherman. 'Is there someone who can come with you? Even if it turns out not to be your husband it's always good to have a bit of support.'

'I'd sooner be on my own.' Mrs Paterson's answer confirmed what Carruthers had already suspected; that since losing her only son it was likely she had, for the most part, shut herself off from the outside world.

He helped seat the fisherman's wife in his car feeling a little embarrassed that it was so dirty. He couldn't remember the last time he had given it a clean out and before she sat down he had to clear several dirty polystyrene cups and an old cloth and bottle of water off the seat. He tossed them into the back.

After a journey in which Mrs Paterson sat in silence they

pulled up at the mortuary. Carruthers parked up and helped Mrs Paterson out of the car.

'Are you ready? They've done their best but please be aware that the body has been in the sea.' It crossed his mind that for the second time in five years the woman was about to undergo an ordeal no living person should ever have to go through.

'I know what the sea can do to a body. I've lived by the sea all my life.' Of course Mrs Paterson had lost her father to the sea too. Carruthers couldn't imagine the sort of stress the families of fishermen went through. Every time fishermen set out in their boats could be the last time their families saw them. No wonder fishermen were often superstitious.

The police officer gave the nod to Dr Mackie who carefully pulled away the sheet from the older man's face. The sea hadn't been kind to Robert Paterson.

Mrs Paterson closed her eyes tightly as if to wrench the image from them. She balled her hand into a fist and rammed it into her mouth.

'Is that the body of your husband, Mrs Paterson?'

All the woman could do was nod. Carruthers saw fresh tears pricking the woman's eyes. He wondered how she'd cope having lost both her son and now her husband.

Carruthers put his arm round Mrs Paterson and the older woman allowed him to pull her into a gentle embrace.

25

'As you know, Jim, when a body drowns the lungs fill up with water and act like a sponge.'

Carruthers stood on the other side of the body to Dr Mackie. Both men wore lab coats and goggles while Mackie conducted the post-mortem.

'Is that what killed him? He drowned?' The police officer peered over the cadaver as he spoke.

Mackie frowned. 'Not so quick, laddie. I'll be able to tell you in a wee while. Hold your horses. As you know not everybody that's pulled from the water will have drowned. You know that as well as I do. During the post-mortem I'll also be looking for signs of ante-mortem injury as well as pathological evidence of natural disease.'

Carruthers immediately thought of the man's heart condition and the possibility that he might have been in a fight. 'He had heart disease. I visited his GP practice.' *Well, that much was true.*

Mackie turned to Carruthers pointedly. 'Do *you* want to conduct this post-mortem, laddie, or shall I?'

Carruthers stood red-faced for a few moments. 'Can you at

least tell how long he's been in the water?' *What I want to know is did he die around the time our warden was murdered?*

'Questions, questions. You know as well as I that it is notoriously difficult to determine how long a body has been in the water. Temperature is likely to be the most important factor governing decompositional changes.' He looked Carruthers squarely in the face. 'I've told you this before: patience is not one of your strong points. I'll repeat my question. Do you *want* me to conduct this post-mortem or not? If you're going to barrage me with questions, I'll insist that you wait outside.'

Carruthers fell silent. He had to remember that this was Dr Mackie's domain and he was a mere visitor. The man had his own procedure to follow and he needed to be respectful of that. And he certainly didn't want to be thrown out in the middle of the post-mortem.

He had to agree with the ageing pathologist, though, about his own lack of patience. Mind you, the older man had not been tasked with investigating two suspicious deaths. All Mackie had to do was conduct the post-mortem and write up his report. In that moment Carruthers almost envied John Mackie the simplicity of his job.

Mackie cleared his throat. 'I'm surprised he floated so quickly. In cold water like ours here in Scotland the bacterial action that causes a body to float with gas may be slowed down so that the body stays on the seabed. Cold water also encourages the formation of adipocere. This is a waxy, soapy substance to you, formed from the fat in the body that partially protects the body against decomposition.'

Carruthers felt a momentary stab of frustration. He just wanted to know what had killed the fisherman.

'Unfortunately, estimating time of death for a victim who has been pulled from the sea is notoriously difficult. All I can tell you at the moment is that it's less than a week. At the end of the first week detachment of skin becomes likely.' He held up one of the fisherman's hands. 'The skin is still on the digits.' He looked up once more at the policeman.

Well, that we already know. Paterson had been alive and well, on Monday. Perhaps not well but definitely very much alive.

Carruthers stared at the bearded face of the local fisherman and felt a great sadness in his heart.

When Mackie looked up at Carruthers there was compassion in his eyes. This time his voice was gentler. 'I hear you knew him?'

Carruthers nodded. 'He lived in Anstruther.'

'Yet found at Shell Bay. It's got an interesting history. In the 1940s there was a Polish Rifle Brigade sent there to defend the North-East Fife coastline.'

'I didn't know about that,' said Carruthers, wondering where Paterson's body could have gone overboard. How much had the boat drifted and how far had the tide taken the fisherman? These were important questions that needed answers.

Mackie leant over the corpse once again. 'Fishing is a dangerous job, Jim. As a pathologist I've sadly seen a fair few fishermen in my time. Do you remember a case a few years ago? Elderly fisherman fell overboard and got tangled in his own net? That was a case of drowning. One of mine. Desperately sad.'

Carruthers didn't remember it. It had most likely been before he had moved back to Scotland.

'No froth was present in the airways of your man here, unlike my previous fisherman. This one's got a lot of deep lacerations and a bash to the head. Of course it may have been done by the rocks. But as you know he's also got some discolouration to the face that I don't think has necessarily been caused by the body being in the water–' Mackie touched the side of the man's face gently.

Carruthers leaned further over the corpse. 'You mean the

bruising. You thought he may have been in a fight?' he asked, eagerly. 'Do you still think that?'

Mackie nodded. 'I think it's highly likely, Jim. I definitely think these wounds could be the hallmark of him having been in a fight. And a recent one at that.'

He needed to talk to Frank Dewar again. And urgently.

'Unless you want to stay for all the gory bits I suggest you go and get a strong cup of black coffee and come back in forty-five minutes. I'll have more information for you by then.' Mackie picked up a saw as Carruthers turned away.

Carruthers who didn't actually enjoy being present at a post-mortem, let alone the post-mortem of someone he knew, could never stay once the pathologist picked up the saw. He gratefully left the examination room and went and got himself a black coffee in the canteen. He sat at a table with his hands clasped round the cup blowing on it until it was cool enough to drink. There were a few tables occupied with staff members in small groups of two and three. Just as he put the cup to his lips the swing doors opened and in walked Jodie Pettigrew.

The dark-haired woman barely glanced at him as she walked up to the serving hatch. Carruthers wasn't sure if she had actually seen him but then a furtive glance over her shoulder told him she had. Carruthers watched her out of the corner of his eye as she bought a roll and a can of juice and swiftly about-turned and walked back out.

Her dark hair had grown since he had last seen her and it was swept over one shoulder. The bronze woollen dress she was wearing looked familiar. *She wore that for our date*, he thought miserably, although on that night if he remembered rightly she had teemed it up with black knee length boots. Today she wore flat shoes. She was looking good. Gone were her glasses. *She must be wearing contact lenses*. He wondered if she was still wearing the scent she had worn for their date. Unexpectedly an image came into his mind of their first tentative kiss down by Anstruther harbour to the noise of the moored boats bumping against each other as the wind picked up. He remembered trailing a lazy finger over her eyebrow. *Those dark eyebrows always did drive me wild.*

Carruthers sat cradling his coffee trying to push all thoughts of his short-lived relationship with Jodie out of his mind. He tipped the last few drops down his throat, glanced at his watch and stood up. As he walked out through the door of the canteen he breathed in the familiar citrussy smell of the pathology assistant. His mobile rang curtailing his current thoughts about another lost love. He took it out of his pocket. It was Mairi. Sighing, he rejected the call and switched the mobile to silent as he went to find Mackie.

The pathologist stepped away from the body and peeled off his gloves. 'Okay. Now I'm ready to talk, but you're not going to like what I've got to say.'

'Just give it to me straight.'

'This is a difficult one, Jim, and I'm afraid that the PM has proved inconclusive.'

Carruthers' heart sank. *Shit. Shit. Shit.*

'The good news, in so far as it is good news, is your laddie here didn't drown so at least that will further your investigation. He was likely dead before he hit the water. However, I can't definitively tell you what killed him.'

Carruthers looked up from the body. *He didn't drown.* They were definitely further forward but the fact the post-mortem was going to have to be recorded as inconclusive was very bad news.

Carruthers looked at the old pathologist to see him frowning.

'Now, to the question of whether he's been stabbed. That's not so easy, I'm afraid. These lacerations on him – I'm just not sure whether he has been stabbed by human hand. There is evidence he has been caught on rocks. However, unfortunately, it's not always possible to determine whether some or all of the injuries present are ante-, peri- or post-mortem in origin. Plus, unhappily, a number of sea creatures have had a nibble of him.'

McTavish isn't going to be happy.

'What else have you got for me that might help? I need to take something more definite back to Sandra.'

Mackie faced Carruthers as he spoke. 'Well, the other thing I need to tell you is that his heart was indeed in an advanced state of decay. He literally could have had a heart attack at any minute. One of the arteries was blocked. But you already knew that.'

Of course they already knew that from Carruthers' ferreting through the patient notes. 'So if he didn't drown, you think he may have died from a heart attack?' Carruthers remembered the words of Paterson's friend, Frank Dewar, that Paterson hadn't been a well man and this, of course, had now been confirmed by the reading of his medical notes. Not for the first time the policeman wondered if Paterson had decided to keep this information about his failing health to himself. His widow clearly hadn't known about it.

'It's possible he had a heart attack on the boat, bumped his head as he fell and then toppled overboard but I can't definitely say for sure. Of course, it's also possible he could have had a heart attack on entering the water. You've heard of cold shock response?'

Carruthers nodded. He thought of what Paterson's widow had said about his health. 'Apparently he was on blood thinners. Could that have made a difference?'

'Ah that's interesting. So if he had been in a fight and he's taking blood thinners he could have gone into hypovolemic shock, bleeding out, which could have led to a cardiac arrest.'

In answer to Carruthers' confused face he added, 'Hypovolemic shock is a condition in which severe blood or fluid loss makes the heart unable to pump enough blood to the body, laddie. This type of shock can cause many organs to stop working and can lead to cardiac arrest.'

Mackie stared Carruthers straight in the eye. 'I know you won't be happy to hear this but I'm going to have to record the PM as inconclusive.'

In other words, thought Carruthers, *the death is going to be recorded as unexplained. Bugger.* It wouldn't further their investigation that much, and it would be hard news for Robert Paterson's widow to bear. The only good thing he could think of was that they had at least recovered Paterson's body. Mrs Paterson wouldn't need to spend the next few months at the window wondering if her husband would ever walk back through that door like she had her father. She could get on with the business of grieving. But she'd had so much grief in her life. Would this latest tragedy be too much?

26

The incident room was abuzz with activity but there was no sign of McTavish. She was clearly running late. The brief had been due to start five minutes ago. Carruthers glanced around him to see Superintendent Bingham pointedly looking at his watch. The thin man with the pallid complexion drew himself up to his full height and clicked his heels together.

The DI could see that he wasn't happy. Carruthers wasn't particularly happy either. The man had been absent from every other team brief they had had. He wondered just how Bingham actually spent his time now and exactly how much guidance he really was giving Sandra McTavish.

He almost smiled remembering the run-ins he'd had with his superior. He admired DCI Sandra McTavish. She'd come through her baptism of fire and was proving to be an able adversary to Bingham. Carruthers only hoped her difficult home life wouldn't adversely affect her ability to lead the investigation.

The door opened and in she walked. Whatever was going on at home she looked immaculate as ever. Her black hair was swept up in a tidy chignon and she carried the dark grey suit she wore with elegance. Her tights were unwrinkled and her black court shoes looked shiny and new.

She didn't apologise for her late arrival. *Never admit to any weaknesses*, thought Carruthers admiringly, *especially in front of our superintendent.* He saw the older man frown. Carruthers studied him covertly. A telltale tic appeared on his gaunt face indicating that he was displeased. The man clearly felt an apology was needed from their DCI and should be directed at him. Carruthers knew that facial tic from old. He'd been on the receiving end of it many a time. Carruthers wondered if the man would pull the station's DCI up later on her tardiness. And would she care? After all, he was retiring. And knowing her the way he did, she would have a good reason for being late.

McTavish plonked her briefcase down on her chair and went straight to the incident board on which were pinned photographs of the two dead men.

'Tom Ramsey and Robert Paterson.' McTavish looked around the room expectantly. 'Ramsey was killed by a stab wound to the heart.' She looked at Carruthers. 'I'm afraid we have bad news on Paterson's post-mortem. Jim attended it. Jim, over to you.'

Carruthers, who had filled her in earlier, took a deep breath before he addressed the incident room. 'I'm afraid the post-mortem is inconclusive.' There were murmurs of disappointment. 'Mackie can't actually say definitively what killed him; although we now know the fisherman didn't drown. It's possible that he had a heart attack on the boat and as he fell, hit his head on the side of the boat before falling overboard–'

McTavish cut in. 'I find it deeply suspicious that there's the blood of two different people on Paterson's boat. I'm afraid I'm not buying him simply having a heart attack and falling in, although I suppose he could have had an altercation with a second person, then had a heart attack. Have we got the result in for the second sample? Do we know whose blood it is?'

Harris answered her question. 'No.'

'Well, chase it up, will you? We need to know.' She expelled a deep frustrated breath.

Harris scratched his armpit. 'I agree with Sandra. If Paterson had been involved in some sort of rammy just before his death it does look awfy suspicious.'

This time McTavish spun her engagement ring round on her finger so that the diamond was no longer underneath and cutting into her hand. Carruthers thought that the DCI was losing weight.

'I also want to know more about Paterson and Ramsey's relationship,' she said. 'I've said this before. The two men knew each other in passing, apparently. Dig deeper. I want to know exactly what their relationship was like and I also want to know what their movements were in the run-up to Ramsey being murdered. Where were they? Who did they meet? Had they had any run-ins with anyone?'

'No point in us asking if there's any strangers in town,' said Helen Lennox. 'Apart from the fact the East Neuk of Fife is a tourist hotspot 11,000 people visit the Isle of May every year. And given that the island is shut to visitors from October to April that's one helluva lot of people going over in just six months.'

'Good work, Helen. That's the sort of information we need.'

Lennox beamed at McTavish's unexpected compliment.

'That wee island will be a pure nightmare for the forensics boys,' added Harris.

There were nods of agreement.

'However, I don't think we'll be looking at a stranger having done this,' continued McTavish. 'Like most murders I think it's much closer to home. We need to remember just how frenzied Ramsey's murder was.'

There was more agreement. McTavish scratched her head. 'That is a crime of passion if ever I saw one. I mean, the man had thirteen knife wounds.'

'That's hatred,' said Harris.

'Or love,' put in Lennox.

McTavish looked thoughtful. 'Yes, but somehow I can't see the ex-girlfriend committing that crime.'

Harris spoke up. 'She could have paid some low-life to murder him. And that way she would still come up with an alibi.'

'But how would he have got across to the Isle of May?' Lennox asked.

Carruthers responded to Lennox's question. 'Apart from the independent businesses who run the *May Princess* and the RIB there aren't that many folk who take out private customers by boat. We know Angus McCrae took the volunteers over from the May. We're still checking to see who else could have done it.'

'We still have no local suspects.' McTavish let out a short, frustrated sigh. 'And no motive. I'm baffled. And usually if you pay a hitman it's a lot more clinical than the frenzied attack we've got.'

'Aye.' Harris looked around him as he spoke. 'Thirteen stab wounds is pure overload.'

'Where did we get with accessing Ramsey's mobile and computer?'

Harris waved a sheaf of what looked like computer printouts in the air. 'I was just about to come on to that. I got these from Speccie Tecchie this morning.' He was referencing John Forrest, their IT specialist. 'I've had a look at both the emails on Ramsey's computer and the text messages he sent and received.

Ellie Robertson had been in touch with him up until about six months ago. She sounds very bitter.'

'Any threats?'

'I'm still reading through them.' Harris scanned one of the sheets. 'No threats yet but she does sound very bossy and controlling. And then, like I said, the emails and texts suddenly stopped about six months ago.'

'Maybe she got fed up of sending them. Keep going. Bossy doesn't bother me. Controlling, however, is a different matter. Keep a look out for any threats.'

'Aye, will do.'

Lennox's mobile rang. She glanced at her phone then looked up at McTavish. 'Sorry, ma'am I'm going to have to take this. It's Bristol CID. About time.'

McTavish nodded and Lennox got up. The younger woman was already in quiet conversation with the caller before she'd left the room.

'If Paterson *was* murdered,' continued McTavish as Lennox shut the door, 'it's entirely possible that he may have been killed cos he witnessed Ramsey's murder. Could he have been fishing and witnessed it from his boat?'

'Aye, it's possible,' said Harris. 'But then anything's possible.'

'If Paterson was murdered how did the perp get close enough to kill him?' McTavish continued. 'Did he board the boat to kill him? If so, how? Or was the fisherman on the island at any point?'

The door reopened and Lennox emerged. She waved her mobile in the air. 'Ellie Robertson's come back clean. There's nothing on her at all. It also looks like she has an alibi.'

'Which is?'

'She was with her partner. They went out for an Indian meal, apparently.' Lennox retook her seat.

'Thanks Helen,' said McTavish.

'It's not a great alibi though, is it?' said Harris. 'She could have got her partner to lie for her or, as we already said, she could have paid someone else to do it. She didnae need to be there in person.'

'Except if you are talking about a hired killer why stab him so many times? We've said before it doesn't sound like a professional hit.'

'An amateur hit?' Harris offered.

'At the moment we have no motive other than the ex-girlfriend's and she has an alibi,' said McTavish. She let out another frustrated puff of air. 'We also need more forensics back. Until we get a breakthrough with either we're going to struggle to further the investigation, although I do concede, however unlikely, it is possible that Ellie Robertson paid someone to kill him.'

Fletcher, who had been quiet for a while, suddenly piped up. 'Somehow I get the feeling that the location of the Isle of May is central to the mystery.'

McTavish was beginning to look fatigued. Her hair had started to escape its chignon and there were smudges of tiredness under her eyes. 'If that's the case then we are back thinking Ramsey was the main target as he was killed on the island and Paterson's death is secondary or accidental. I now think, given what we know about Paterson's heart condition, there's a very real possibility that his death is accidental, except for one thing – the blood of that second person on his boat.' McTavish couldn't keep the frustration out of her voice. 'Oh, I just feel we're going round and round in circles. Let's focus on what we can control for now. We need to get another press statement together. With one murder and one suspicious death the natives are going to get restless.'

'You cannae blame them. They'll be wondering who's going

to be next.' Voices around the room agreed with Harris' statement. 'Apparently the press are already snooping around. They've been trying to talk to folk in Cellardyke. One of the members of my darts team lives there.'

Bingham, who had been listening quietly to the proceedings from the back of the room, spoke for the first time. 'We need to get on top of the press situation and quickly, Sandra. A further press statement has to be a priority.'

At the mention of the press, Carruthers' thoughts turned to the sharp-faced blonde reporter he had seen down at Shell Bay. She hadn't approached him but he wondered if she had been sniffing round the uniformed police for information and then disappeared when she'd seen the detectives. He still couldn't remember her name. However, he needed to tell the team. 'There was a reporter down at Shell Bay. I think she works for one of the local papers.'

McTavish plucked a stray hair off her jacket. 'That's not good news, especially if they start linking Paterson's death to Ramsey's. The super's right. We need to get a press statement out ASAP but with Gayle still off someone else will have to do it.'

'Have you heard from Gayle?' Fletcher asked. 'I thought she'd be back at work.'

'She's had to take some more time off. I'm sorry to have to tell you this but her sister tried to take her own life.'

There were sharp intakes of breath all round the incident room. They had all wondered how Watson's family were coping with the sudden death of their colleague's niece and why Watson wasn't back at work. Now they knew.

'I know it's dreadful. When I next speak to her I'll pass on your wishes.'

Carruthers noticed Helen Lennox in particular looked upset. He wondered if she'd experienced a suicide in her family.

'Will she pull through?'

'I think so, Helen, thank God. I'll be phoning Gayle later. In the meantime we had better get our minds back on the case, as difficult as that is. The question is where is the murderer now?'

Lennox said quietly, 'I reckon he or she'll be long gone.'

Carruthers noticed she seemed subdued.

'I'm not so sure,' put in Fletcher. 'If he or she is a local there's a good chance they're still very close at hand and as we all know often murderers stick around to admire their handiwork.'

As Fletcher said this Carruthers thought of the many murderers who had offered their help to the police in the search for missing people. He felt a chill course up his spine.

'Helen, I want you to make some enquiries and find out if anyone has suddenly up and left for no good reason. Anyone gone on a last-minute holiday or disappeared to visit a sick relative? Start with those living in Anstruther and then widen the net to the nearby villages.'

'That's a hell of a lot of work. I'm going to need some help.'

McTavish shot back a curt response. 'I never said you were going to have to do it all on your own. See me after about it.'

Carruthers caught himself shaking his head at Lennox's response. What did the woman want? Did she want to be given more responsibility or not? She couldn't have it both ways.

'Right,' McTavish looked around, her eyes fixing on Fletcher. 'We've all got our jobs. Helen, I want you to team up with Andie.'

Carruthers noticed neither women looked happy about the prospect. He'd assumed Fletcher hadn't had a word with Lennox yet.

'Jim.' Carruthers looked up. 'I want to task you with finding out about the finances of our two victims. Did they have money problems? I want to see bank statements. Go through everything. We have one very nasty murderer out there and I want them caught before...'

Before? Carruthers wondered.

'Before it escalates,' finished McTavish. 'Jim, I take it there's still no news from Gus and this drugs shipment?'

Carruthers shook his head.

'Give him a call and find out what's happening.'

27

Carruthers went back to his desk and phoned Gus at the National Crime Agency.

The man's voice sounded weary. 'Sorry, Jim, we've been flat out. You've saved me a call, though. We've got a bit of news. We've actually located the *Asante Sana*.'

Carruthers found his heart thumping. 'Where is it?'

Gus didn't answer. His mind was obviously already racing ahead. 'We're still plotting our interception but it's so much easier now we know their position.'

'Do you know when the interception will take place?'

'Not yet but we're getting close. If we knew who their contact is in Fife it would help. I need to go, Jim. I'm heading into a meeting. I'll be in touch.' The man cut the call.

As soon as Carruthers put the phone down it rang again.

'Jim, it's Antoinette here.'

Carruthers could picture the tall, fine-boned forensic scientist with the glorious mane of red hair. Carruthers held his breath. This was the call he had been waiting for. What had they found on the boat? 'Have you managed to analyse that second blood sample?' he asked eagerly. *Who else had been on Paterson's boat?*

'That's the reason I'm ringing, Jim.' Her voice was slow and measured. 'It's not good news. I'm sorry to have to tell you this, but we can't use that particular sample. It's been spoiled.'

'Spoiled? You've got to be kidding me. Please tell me you're joking. What the hell happened?'

'I only wish I knew but these things can happen.'

'God, Sandra's going to go spare.'

'We took other samples, Jim. But it will just take a bit longer, I'm afraid. I'll call you as soon as I've got any results.'

Carruthers finished the call then approached his old office. He'd need to bring McTavish up to speed on recent events and he would rather have a word in person. The door was ajar and Carruthers was just about to knock and walk in but something made him hold back. Through the crack he could just make out his boss. It was the way McTavish was sitting, head slumped as if she'd just received bad news that made him hesitate. She was bent over her desk and Carruthers was horrified to see she was crying. Great wracking sobs made her shoulders heave. He saw she was holding something to her chest, which her hands had closed protectively over. It was the family photograph of her, her husband and their two children.

Carruthers hesitated for a moment before he closed the door silently. He stood with his back to it for a moment. He couldn't face intruding on such an intimate moment of grief. He would give her a few minutes then phone her instead.

As he walked away from the DCI's office Helen Lennox approached him.

'Is Sandra in her office at the moment, Jim?'

'Yes she is but she's not to be disturbed.'

'She's not in a meeting though?' The younger woman swept past him and Carruthers silently cursed.

'This won't take long,' she called over her shoulder. 'She wanted to see me anyway and I want to ask her about my chances of becoming a detective sergeant.'

Carruthers caught her up and stood in front of her. 'It's not a good time, Helen. I've already told you she's not to be disturbed. Try again later. And phone her first. If you want my advice, I don't think she'll be too impressed that you're looking for career advice when we're right in the middle of what might be a double murder investigation.'

Lennox let out an impatient sigh. 'I know, but I'm getting frustrated. I just don't want to be passed by.'

The annoyance in Carruthers built. 'Well, put your ambition to good use, knuckle down, do some hard graft and help the team you're a member of find the killer of our victims. You need to prove yourself capable of doing the job of a DS. You haven't been at this station that long. You still have to prove yourself to Sandra.'

Quietly he was sceptical as to whether Lennox had what it took to be a DS. In fact he was surprised that she had made it as far as detective constable. Clearly she had drive and most likely resilience, but in his opinion, she lacked emotional awareness, one of the core competencies of CID. She still had to demonstrate her ability to listen to others, which was vital in any rank. Too many times she interrupted other detectives and talked over them.

But Helen Lennox wasn't prepared to let it go. 'But that's my whole point. I'm not being allowed to prove myself. I know I'm not the same rank as Gayle or Andie but I'm not being given enough responsibility for the rank of DC. It's not fair.'

Carruthers firmly steered her away from the DCI's office as he answered her. 'It's the same for all of us when we first start here. You know yourself there's a pecking order. It's just the way things are. Try not to get people's backs up, Helen, and I think you'll get on a lot better.'

Lennox swivelled round and held his gaze for a moment. 'When have I got anybody's back up?'

Irritation shot through Carruthers. 'That's an easy one to answer. Just a few minutes ago when you told McTavish how much work she'd just given you. You can't have it both ways. What do you actually want?'

The challenge and resentment were evident in Lennox's eyes before she strode off without a backward glance. As Carruthers stared at her back he was grateful that he'd intercepted her before she'd disturbed McTavish. However, he was left wondering about the truth of her words. Did she have a point? Was she deliberately being missed out from all the good jobs worthy of her rank because she rubbed her colleagues up the wrong way? He gave it a few minutes then phoned McTavish from the open-plan office.

As a weary Carruthers approached the Anstruther harbour several hours later he saw Frank Dewar walking towards him. *Good. Just the man I need to see. And he's come to find me.* He hazarded a guess that the old fisherman had been repairing his nets when he'd spotted the police officer. Dewar's shoulders were hunched and the old boy looked tired, but not as tired as Carruthers felt.

There were no pleasantries or even a nod of greeting from the fisherman. Dewar kept his hands firmly in his pocket. 'Is it true Robbie's been murdered?'

Who would have told him that? 'His body's been found–'

'I heard it was found at Shell Bay. Is that right?'

Carruthers nodded and speculated how the news had spread

so fast. 'Yes, but there's no firm evidence to suggest he's been murdered.'

'Well, that's not what I've heard. The news about him having been murdered is all over Anstruther. Is it true?'

Bugger. Once again Carruthers thought of that female reporter.

'I've been to his post-mortem, Frank. There's no evidence to suggest he's been murdered but he had been in a fight recently.' He searched the fisherman's face to see if his expression gave anything away. It didn't. *He would make a good poker player.* 'How did you say you came by that cut above your head?'

'I told you. I hit my head on the glass shelving in the bathroom.'

Carruthers wasn't sure that he believed Dewar. 'You didn't have a fight with Paterson?'

'No, I would have told you if I had.'

Would you, though?

Dewar was a friend of Paterson so it would be normal for the man to be concerned and asking questions but Carruthers wondered if there was more to the fisherman's enquiries. 'I can't tell you any more than that at this stage, Frank. There's an official procedure to follow.'

Carruthers tried to walk away. He was too tired to be drawn into a conversation, especially when he had no fresh news to give.

To Carruthers' surprise the man grabbed his arm. The grip was tight. *Feelings would be running high*, he reminded himself. Carruthers thought he saw tears clouding the man's eyes. 'Bollocks to official procedure. I heard he'd been knifed. Is it true?'

'Who told you that?'

'Some woman reporter that came sniffing around.'

Carruthers inwardly cursed. *No guessing who that had been then.* 'This woman reporter. Does she have a name?'

'I can't remember her full name. Elaine or something. She gave me her card but I don't have it on me.'

Carruthers wondered if he was talking about Elaine Morgan. He hadn't seen her for a while and had heard she'd moved to another newspaper. He tried to picture the sly reporter. A thin, angular woman with peroxide bleached hair who Harris had unkindly nicknamed 'The Bone', on account of, not only how she looked, but also of how she resembled a dog with a bone when she ferreted out information. She must be back working for the *East Neuk Mercury*. Had it been her down on the beach?

'He had a bad heart, Frank. It may have been a heart attack.' Carruthers made a mental note to ring McTavish at home to give her the latest heads-up on the reporter as soon as he extricated himself from the fisherman. All they needed was a nosy hack.

Carruthers felt exhausted. His shoulders slumped and his legs felt heavy. 'There'll be an official announcement as soon as we can make one but, like I said, there is no strong evidence to suggest Paterson's been murdered. I'm sorry but I can't tell you more than that.'

Carruthers shook the man's arm off and walked away, feeling the eyes of the fisherman boring into his back.

He still felt Dewar knew more than he was saying, now more so than ever, but he reminded himself that everyone would be a suspect until they were ruled out.

Sleep didn't come easy that night. Carruthers lay awake for a long time tossing and turning. He couldn't get the sight of the bloated body of the fisherman out of his mind. What the hell was the connection between the warden of the Isle of May and Robert Paterson? There must be one. He would much rather believe that the fisherman's death had been an accident but the truth of it was that he was starting to suspect quite strongly that the man had, in fact, been murdered.

In the early hours, still wide awake, he wearily got to his feet, walked downstairs and made himself a strong black coffee. He went through the case notes on the coffee table in his living room relieved that his brother was no longer staying with him and that he had the house back to himself. He dozed in his chair until the urge of sleep came over him and he dragged his tired body back up to his bedroom. As he switched off the light his bedside clock said 4am.

28

THURSDAY

As Carruthers locked up his cottage the following morning, and with the tide on the rise, the inspector heard the first of the creel boats of the day chug out of the harbour.

Gulls wheeled in a fresh salty breeze, their screaming competing with the noise of the boats. This was a far cry from his life down in London. He'd missed the bright lights of the capital when he'd first moved to Fife but he wouldn't choose to live anywhere else now.

He spotted Frank Dewar down by the harbour and walked towards him; his mind still on the man's facial injury.

Dewar looked up. 'Any further news?'

'Not yet, Frank, but we only spoke last night. I can't work miracles.'

'Do the police still think it could be a heart attack?'

'We have to keep an open mind. As you know an investigation like this takes time. And it's still early days.' But as he said this Carruthers knew that the early stages of an investigation, before forensic evidence was lost, were especially crucial.

'So it's not being treated as a suspicious death then?'

He was hardly likely to tell the fisherman that the PM had proved inconclusive but he did need to ask Dewar some further questions about Paterson. 'Are you sure there's nothing further you want to tell me?'

'Like what?'

'If I find you've been lying about how you came by that cut, there'll be hell to pay. You do know if you have lied to me you might well be charged with perverting the course of justice.'

'How can I admit to something that didn't happen?'

'Okay, Frank.' *He's sticking to the story, then*, thought Carruthers. 'I need to ask you something. Did you ever see Robert Paterson angry?'

The old fisherman scratched his chest through his cable knit sweater. 'You still think he has something to do with Tom Ramsey's death.'

You could equally have something to do with Robert Paterson's death. You have a bloody big cut just above your eye and I'm not buying where you're telling us you got it from. The problem is I have no evidence you're lying. But if he had killed the fisherman, had he also murdered Tom Ramsey? He was double the man's age. It worried him that Ramsey had so few defensive injuries. If he had twisted his ankle trying to get away from his killer then surely there would have been more defensive wounds?

It was a statement rather than a question. 'That's not what I'm saying. You know I have to ask these questions, Frank. Can you please just give me a straight answer.'

'He wasn't given to angry outbursts. I've rarely seen him lose his temper and I've known him fifty odd years.'

'Since school?'

'Aye.'

'Tell me about the times you saw him angry.'

'There was a run-in, long time ago now, with some of our boats and some Danish sand eel fishermen who just about hoovered up everything on the ocean floor. To this day Robert still blames them for the decline of fishing in the East Neuk of Fife.'

Carruthers looked thoughtful. 'How long ago was this?'

'Thirty odd years.'

Too long ago for it to have a bearing on his death, thought Carruthers. Might have been a different story if the warden had been Danish – but the man had been English.

Another thought crept into his head. *Had Robert Paterson's finances ever recovered from what must have been a devastating blow to the Fife fishing industry?*

'Can you still make a good living from fishing?'

'Aye, if you're prepared to put the time in.'

'And did Robbie?'

'We're no' twenty any more, Jim. We've got older and since we first started going to sea there's been some big changes in the fishing industry here.'

'What sort of changes?'

Dewar scratched the back of his hand.

Carruthers noticed for the first time that the knuckles were bruised. *The man's definitely been in a fight. And recently. Why didn't I notice this before?*

'When I started the industry was totally fish. Langoustine was thrown back in the water. No market for them. As I said, fish used to be plentiful here and then with every passing year we would have to take the boats further and further out. There's hardly any white fish left and there's no facilities for those boats now in the area. It's a different world now. Hardly any of the haul we catch gets served in local restaurants. It's all about the prawns, lobsters, crabs, and scallops. They get packed up and sent up mostly to Peterhead for processing and packing and off to Europe.'

Carruthers struggled to keep his mind on Dewar's words. All

he could think of was that he had been in a fight. And that in itself meant the man had lied.

'You asked whether fishing is still a viable job. As I said you need to put the time in and you also need to weigh up the risks and rewards.'

Where had he heard that before? Risks and rewards? It had been something Fletcher had said in a previous conversation. Carruthers suspected fishing was more a young man's game. After all, it was a physically demanding job and, as Dewar had mentioned, older fishermen generally had poorer health than the average. 'You said you'd only seen him angry twice. When was the other time?'

'When his son committed suicide.'

'Who was he angry at?'

'Himself mostly.'

In all likelihood Paterson had never got over his son's death. *If there hadn't been the blood of two different people on Paterson's boat I wouldn't rule out suicide.* Those cards Carruthers was keeping close to his chest. He certainly wasn't about to tell Dewar.

Carruthers had just sat down at his desk when his phone rang. He picked it up. He heard the voice of Angela Boag from Forensics. He pictured the striking, dark-haired woman with the clear complexion and infectious laugh. 'What have you got for me?'

'We've analysed the blood on the jacket of Tom Ramsey.'

'And? I take it you've found something?'

'We most certainly have. We've found the blood of at least two other people on it.'

'Two other people? *Two*? Are you *sure*?' Carruthers could feel the excitement mounting in his chest. This was a major breakthrough, especially if they could identify who the blood samples belonged to. What was the betting that at least one of the samples would be that of their murderer?

He searched his messy desk and picked up a ballpoint pen. 'Do you know who the other samples belong to?'

'So far only one match has come back but we've still got some tests to run on the third sample.'

He opened his notebook. 'Do you want me to start guessing or you gonna tell me?'

'Robert Paterson.'

Carruthers drew in a deep and very shocked breath. For some reason he hadn't expected that. But it did tell them one thing. Finally here was definite proof that the two cases were linked. But still he couldn't believe it.

'Let me get this right so there's absolutely no mistake. You're telling me Robert Paterson's blood has been found on the body of Tom Ramsey?'

Did that mean Paterson was Ramsey's murderer? And to whom did the third blood sample belong?

'That's right, Jim. We're still analysing the third blood sample. I'll call you as soon as I know anything more.'

Carruthers rocked back on his chair. What did this mean? Did Robert Paterson have a hand in Tom Ramsey's death after all? Had he been on the island with Ramsey? Is that why his empty boat had been found so close to the May? But then who was the third person whose blood had been found on Ramsey's body? Did it mean Paterson was stabbed by more than one person? So many questions. He jumped up, got his jacket and went in search of McTavish.

29

'Right, listen up people. The investigation's now starting to gather pace. Two big pieces of news to give you.' The speaker was DCI Sandra McTavish and they were back in the incident room. Carruthers was impressed that she wasn't letting her upset from the day before show. Nobody else would have known she had had a meltdown at work. She was firmly back in control. He, more than anyone, knew how hard it was to remain professional at work when going through a painful marriage break-up. How much worse when there were kids involved and you were heading up a murder investigation?

The dark-haired DCI turned to Carruthers. 'Jim's had two calls from forensics which is why we've called this impromptu but emergency brief. Jim, as you've got the details it's over to you.'

Carruthers ran a hand through his short grey hair and cleared his throat. He looked over the room at the eager faces, noticing that once again Superintendent Bingham was missing. Only one other person was absent: Gayle Watson.

'First, a bit of bad news, I'm afraid. The second blood sample taken from Paterson's boat has been spoiled which means they can't analyse it.'

There were various cries from those in the room.

'How did that happen?'

'Anyone told Bingham? He won't be pleased.'

Carruthers' voice cut through the dismayed noise. 'I know. It's bitterly disappointing but these things do happen and there are other samples they can analyse. The results will just take a bit longer, that's all.'

He took a deep breath and as he spoke he felt the excitement build. They were finally getting somewhere and he knew the room would erupt with the news he was about to impart.

'It's not all doom and gloom, though.' He looked over at McTavish who nodded at him to continue. 'Crucially, Angela Boag from Forensics rang me a few minutes ago with the results of the blood taken from Tom Ramsey's jacket. There's blood from three different people on that jacket.'

Several cries went up at once.

'What? Three?'

'Whose?'

'There's more than one murderer then? There must be.'

Carruthers put a hand up to quieten the lively room. 'It's fairly obvious one sample was going to be Ramsey's. The second's just been confirmed as that of Robert Paterson.'

Lennox in particular was animated. She turned round in her chair so that she was facing the whole room. 'Paterson killed Ramsey, got injured doing it and then had a heart attack trying to get away and fell overboard. It's the only explanation that makes sense. Open and shut.'

'Except it isn't,' said Fletcher. 'Remember, there's *three* people's blood on Ramsey's jacket.'

'Oh shit, yeah. So there is.' She looked crestfallen.

'Let's not be too hasty,' cried McTavish. 'I agree it's one possibility that Paterson killed Ramsey, but if so, what was his motive? He doesn't seem to have one. As far as we know he had minimal contact with Ramsey.'

The room fell silent.

'Who does the third blood sample belong to?' Fletcher's eyes were wide with excitement.

'We don't know yet,' said Carruthers. 'They're still running tests.'

Helen Lennox looked around the room as she spoke. 'Well if Paterson didn't kill Ramsey how did his blood get on Ramsey's jacket?'

'We all know how easy it is for DNA to be transferred between people.' Fletcher leant forward in her seat as she spoke. 'You can just brush up against someone to have their DNA on your clothes. There's another possibility: that the person who killed Paterson went on to kill Ramsey or vice versa. That way you could easily have two different people's blood on the body of the warden. In fact, as far as I'm concerned it's the only thing that makes sense.'

Carruthers thought about Dewar's bruised knuckles. 'Sandra, given the fact that Frank Dewar has clearly lied about being in a recent fight I'd like to bring him in.'

The DCI shook her head. 'We don't have enough on him. There's no evidence to indicate that he's been in a fight with Paterson and there is absolutely nothing linking Dewar to the murder of Ramsey.'

The frustration in Carruthers grew but he knew the link was, at best, tenuous. He was just clutching at straws.

'You know we need hard evidence, Jim.'

'I just feel we now have evidence that links Dewar to Ramsey. Paterson's blood is found on Ramsey's body and I am confident that Dewar's been in a fight with Paterson.'

'That's tenuous at best and you know it.'

Carruthers fell silent. In his heart he knew McTavish was right.

'There's also been news from Gus at the NCA,' continued McTavish. 'The *Asante Sana* has now been located and it's just a matter of time before it's intercepted. Keep your ears to the ground. The crew will be making contact with someone in the local area. We need to know who that person is.'

McTavish glanced at her watch. It had gone 9pm. 'Look, it's been a long day and I'm not expecting any more results in this evening,' the DCI said. 'You're all tired. Go home. Get some rest and see you in here at 7am sharp tomorrow.'

The brief broke up, and the officers all filed out, some still talking, animatedly, despite their tiredness. McTavish quickly disappeared back to her office. Carruthers took his jacket off the back of his chair and said goodnight to Fletcher and Lennox. His stomach rumbled, reminding him that it had been a long time since his last meal. The Anstruther Fish Bar was open until 10pm. He'd grab a takeaway and if it was warm enough sit and eat it down by the harbour.

He sat staring out to sea while he ate his chips. He looked at his watch and wondered if his boss was still in her office. It was now too late to call Gayle Watson. He wanted to check up on her and make sure that she was okay. They were all devastated that on top of losing her niece Gayle's sister had now tried to take her own life.

The gentle lap of the water against the harbour walls could be heard and the knocking sound of the bumping of boats almost lulled him to sleep. His head bent forward and the half empty package of chips started to slip from his lap. A loud shout from a nearby pub jolted him fully awake and as he picked up the half fallen takeaway he spied Frank Dewar staggering along the cobbled stones down by the car park. The man was clearly drunk, still clutching a half drunk pint of beer, which was tipped at a precarious angle. Carruthers was once again reminded of how harsh, lonely and dangerous the world of a fisherman was.

30

FRIDAY

McTavish took her jacket off, hooked it over the back of her chair and sat down at her desk. She opened the correspondence received from the local authority while she sipped her early morning coffee. Her eyes skimmed the lines, widening in surprise and anger as she got to the last line. 'Shit!'

They had been fighting a long-standing battle with the school and the local authority to get their son extra help since he had been diagnosed with autism. She scrunched the sheet of paper up in her hands, her eyes blinking in shock. Her heart sank to the pit of her stomach and she felt physically sick. Her son had been turned down for the extra help he so desperately needed.

She picked up the phone to make a call to the authority then replaced the handset when she realised the time. It was not yet 8am. There would be nobody in the office yet and there was no point in phoning her husband. He would be getting the kids' breakfasts ready. There was a knock on her door. Helen Lennox's outline was distinguishable through the frosted glass. McTavish wondered what she wanted at this time of the morning. The younger woman was biting her top lip.

'Sandra, can I have a word, please?'

McTavish stared at the scrunched-up sheet of paper, which she started to smooth out. She decided she needed to keep it after all to show her husband. For all his faults he was still a good father. 'Does it have to be right now, Helen?'

'It's important. I know you're busy. I've tried to talk to Jim but he's just fobbed me off. And he's manhandled me.'

The older woman sighed. 'You had better come in. When you say Jim manhandled you–?' She offered Lennox a seat and wondered what Carruthers had actually done. It didn't sound like him. The younger officer remained standing.

'What's this all about? Are you here to make a formal complaint against Jim?'

'No. I've really come to see you about my chance of promotion. I want to know what my chances are of being promoted to DS if I remain at this station.'

McTavish fought back her irritation. She took in a deep breath as she appraised the younger woman. 'You're not nearly ready to become a DS, Helen. You've still got a lot to learn. I would suggest you focus on being a good detective constable and we'll review your progress in another six months.'

'I don't think I'm being given enough opportunity to progress and I feel there are certain members of the team who are being... obstructive.'

'How long have you been at this station?'

'I–'

Just as Lennox was about to answer McTavish's mobile rang. She looked at the caller ID. It was her husband. She needed to take the call. 'I'm sorry, Helen I need to take this. Like I said, we'll review your progress in six months' time but at the moment you're not ready and that's an end to it.' McTavish lowered her head to accept the call.

'Well, in that case I want to put in for a transfer.'

McTavish looked up to see Lennox shutting the door behind her.

'*Shit.*' The word was said with feeling.

'What have I done now?' The voice was that of her husband's. He sounded none too pleased.

'Not you,' McTavish said crossly. It was already shaping up to be a hell of a morning. She dismissed Helen Lennox from her thoughts and turned her attention to the correspondence she held in her hand.

'Paul, I've just opened the letter from the local authority...'

McTavish slammed the phone down. It rang immediately. She picked it up.

'What?' She didn't mean to shout but she knew she had.

'Sorry, ma'am.' The voice was that of DC Willie Brown. If he was fazed by her bad temper he didn't show it. 'Thought you'd want to know as soon as possible. I've just taken a call from a lad in Bristol. Claims to be Ellie Robertson's ex. You'll definitely want the details.'

McTavish pounced on a pen and a piece of paper and took them down.

Carruthers tapped on McTavish's door, which was ajar. He put his head round. The DCI had her head down and was busy scribbling. She looked up. Carruthers had the distinct impression from one look at her strained face that she was already having a bad morning.

'Is this about Helen Lennox?' She spoke sharply.

'No. Why? Should it be?'

She put her pen down. 'She came to see me a bit earlier about the likelihood of promotion.'

Carruthers swore silently. Helen Lennox was clearly not one

for following orders. He had expressly told her not to bother McTavish about her chances of becoming a detective sergeant and she had ignored him. *But then I am a fine one to talk. I'm forever ignoring orders.*

'Come in,' urged McTavish. 'Talking about Lennox can wait. I need to tell you about something else first. There's been a development in the Ramsey case.'

Carruthers walked into the office, shutting the door behind him. He sat down on the seat the DCI offered him and waited patiently for her to speak.

'I've just had Willie Brown on the phone. He'd taken a call from a Miles Butcher.'

Carruthers looked blankly at his superior but he noticed her dogged expression. This must be something big, but the name meant nothing to him.

'Miles Butcher lives in Bristol. He claims to be an ex-boyfriend of Ellie Robertson. He heard about the death of Tom Ramsey. No doubt you've seen it's been one of the leading stories on the national news.'

Carruthers hadn't had a chance to put the TV on but it didn't surprise him. It was the sort of murder that would grip the British public.

'This Miles Butcher phoned to say that Ellie Robertson was violent with him during their time together.'

'She battered him?'

'That's what he's claiming, although it goes further than that. He claims she threatened him with a knife in their kitchen one day. Didn't cook her eggs the way she likes them, or something.'

'Jesus.'

'In the end he finished their relationship but she wouldn't let him go. He says she continued to stalk him. He had to change his phone number.'

'Why didn't he talk to the police? Take out a restraining order against her?'

'According to Willie he said he decided not to. He didn't want to further inflame the situation.'

'So that's why there's nothing on file against her then?'

McTavish nodded.

Carruthers looked deep in thought. 'She didn't have a strong alibi, did she? Claims she was with her current boyfriend?'

McTavish pursed her lips. 'I want the boyfriend interviewed and away from Robertson. If she is an abuser it's very likely there will be a pattern of abuse with both current and former partners and they might be too scared to speak out.'

'You think it likely she threatened him into lying for her? Persuaded him to give her a false alibi?'

'I don't know but it's certainly a possibility. And you know what this means, don't you?'

Carruthers nodded. 'Ellie Robertson has just become our number one suspect.'

'What we now need to establish is whether she had means, motive and opportunity. I want Fletcher and Lennox to meet Robertson in person and form their own opinions of her. I particularly want to know if Robertson has any links to Fife other than her ex-boyfriend.'

'You thinking she could have paid someone local to murder Ramsey?'

'Maybe.'

McTavish continued. 'I'm also thinking about giving Helen Lennox the lead down in Bristol.'

'You're kidding.' Carruthers was incredulous.

'She's not happy, Jim. She wants to be given more responsibility.'

'Well, I know she's fiercely ambitious. She was wanting to

talk to you a couple of days ago about her chances of promotion to DS.'

'You stopped her?'

'Let's just say I caught her coming to your office at a bad time. I, er, put my head round your door and could see you were busy.'

McTavish reddened slightly. Carruthers cursed inwardly. Now she would know that he had witnessed her meltdown. He tried to keep his voice normal. 'I sent her away and told her she would be better off getting on with her job right now, since we're in the middle of a murder investigation.'

McTavish looked satisfied. 'I know. She told me. She's accused you of fobbing her off and she said you manhandled her in the corridor. You didn't touch her, did you, Jim? You know better than anyone that could be construed as assault.'

'She's made a complaint about me?' Carruthers said in surprise.

'Not an official one, Jim, and not about the manhandling but, like I said, she's clearly not happy. She's also accused certain members of the team of deliberately making things difficult for her, although she's not named them. Anyway, the long and short of it is that I'm afraid it's escalated and she's requested a transfer.'

Carruthers' mouth fell open. 'You're kidding? In the middle of a murder investigation? If that's her attitude she'll never make DS.'

'I know. I'm going to have to talk to her again. An important part of being a DS is working as part of a team and I'm afraid I just don't see her as a team player.'

McTavish has just echoed my thoughts exactly. In that moment Carruthers doubted Lennox would ever make it to DS let alone DI.

'She has a long way to go before making DS. However,'

McTavish paused and looked at her DI intently, 'there might be some truth to the claim that she's not being given a chance to prove herself and if she was given a bit more responsibility maybe it will be the making of her.'

The DCI fell quiet, as she seemed to be mulling something over in her head. 'Tell her that I want her to accompany Fletcher to Bristol to interview Ellie Robertson and although Andie can still be lead I want her to allow Helen to ask some of the questions.'

'Andie won't like that.'

'I'm sure she won't but I've decided I want to give our newest recruit a chance to prove herself. And I don't want ructions in the team during a murder investigation. It's not good for morale. We all need to pull together.'

Carruthers felt like telling McTavish that she was giving into the younger woman's petulance; that if he had still been DCI he wouldn't have rewarded bad behaviour. But he kept silent.

McTavish searched her desk and picked up a file, which she opened. 'While you're here I want to know your thoughts on the forensics results we got in last night.'

'Well, I have to admit it was a surprising result. I never expected to be told Robert Paterson's blood had been found on the body of Tom Ramsey. Do you have any theories?'

'If we leave Ellie Robertson out of the equation for a moment the most obvious one, as Lennox said, is that Paterson killed Ramsey. But as we've also said, we also know how easy it is to transfer DNA.'

As he spoke Carruthers tried not to glance at the photographs of McTavish's husband and kids. 'There's also the possibility that Ramsey's murderer first killed Paterson before going on to kill Ramsey and that's how Paterson's DNA has been found on the body of the warden.'

'Indeed. All conjecture at this point of course but the mere fact Paterson's blood has been found on the body proves that the two cases are connected so at least we've made some inroad. However, it's deeply frustrating Paterson's PM is inconclusive.'

'Could we ask for another post-mortem?' Even as Carruthers said it he knew how upset John Mackie would be.

McTavish shook her head. 'I don't think there's much point. Mackie's one of the best in the country. Doubtless the results would be the same.'

Carruthers continued talking. 'I'm getting that third set of results run through our database. See if we can find a match for them but like I said I have no idea where Ellie Robertson might fit into all this.'

'And yet she's the only suspect we've got who has motive. Pity her DNA isn't on the database. Keep me posted.'

'I still think Dewar is a serious person of interest. I'm convinced that he's lied about where he got the cut on his forehead. He told me he'd hit it on a bathroom shelf but I've seen the man's knuckles. They're bruised. He's definitely been in a fight and my betting is that it was with Paterson.'

'I know, but like I said earlier there's not enough to bring him in. I'm happy, however, if you want to do some further digging on Dewar.' She shut her file. 'Why did you want to see me?'

'Can you spare me for a few hours?'

'What do you need to do?'

'I want to go back to the Isle of May on my own. I just feel there's something we're missing.'

'And you think you'll find the answer on the island?'

'Yes, I do.'

McTavish frowned. Carruthers could see she had something else on her mind. His heart sank. 'By the way Jim, what were you doing going to see Paterson's GP without informing me?'

Carruthers reddened.

'I'm surprised that his GP was so open to you about his patient.'

Carruthers looked at his feet.

McTavish exploded. 'Fuck. He didn't give you any information, did he? How the hell did you find out the man had a heart condition?'

'I–'

McTavish's desk phone rang. She pointed an accusing finger at Carruthers. 'Bingham warned me about you but I told him I make up my own mind about members of my team. He said you were trouble. Don't prove him right.' She picked the phone up, unsmiling. 'Make sure Fletcher knows that I want both her and Lennox to conduct the interview in Bristol.'

Carruthers nodded and left his boss's office. After he had called Scott Gardner and arranged a passage over to the island he ran into Fletcher.

'You okay, Andie? How's the neck?'

'Easing up, thanks. But what's wrong with Lennox? She's got a face like thunder on her.'

He kept his voice low. There was no sign of Lennox. Perhaps she had disappeared to the canteen. 'Let's just say she's not very happy at the station. She's also made a complaint about me to Sandra.'

'What?'

'Yep, she's accused me of being unsupportive and she's told Sandra that certain members of the team are standing in the way of her promotion to DS.'

'Oh my God, you've got to be kidding? What the hell's wrong with the woman? We're right in the middle of a murder investigation. And when you say she's not very happy at the station she's put in for a transfer, hasn't she? Wow, I bet she's popular. Not.'

Honestly, there's just no getting anything past Fletcher. 'She's not flavour of the month with Sandra at the moment.' *And she's not the only one*, he thought. 'However, by the same token Sandra does think that perhaps Helen hasn't been given the breaks that she should have been given.'

'Do you think Sandra will accept the transfer request?'

'No idea. It's not the best time to lose a member of staff. Look, Andie, keep this to yourself, will you? I wasn't meant to have told anyone.'

'To be fair you didn't tell me. I guessed. All you said was that she was unhappy.'

God, I'm becoming just as much an office gossip as Fletcher and Brown, thought Carruthers. *When did this happen?*

Carruthers prepared himself to tell Fletcher something he knew would be deeply unpopular. 'Sandra wants you to take Helen with you when you interview Ellie Robertson and she wants you to let Helen ask her own questions.'

Fletcher exploded. 'You have to be kidding? With her track record of rubbing everyone up the wrong way?'

'That's what she's said. I think she wants to give her a crack at the whip and see how she responds. You'll still take the lead though.'

'She's obviously wanting to invest in Lennox cos this could be a really important interview. Well, she'll have to get a move on. I'm leaving within the hour. Doubt she'll have time to get herself organised.'

Fletcher drew in a short burst of air through her nose and Carruthers could tell she was furious. Without a further word she did an about-turn and walked towards McTavish's door. For the first time Carruthers was mightily relieved he wasn't DCI on the case. Murder he could cope with. Navigating the treacherous waters of complicated colleague relationships wasn't his strong point. As his colleague walked away Carruthers remembered he still hadn't phoned his ex-wife back.

31

'This could be the last crossing for a while. Weather's due to set in and we're expecting a strong north-easterly.' As he spoke the skipper pulled out of the harbour with practised ease and the inspector watched as the colourful little houses with their crow-step gables and red pantiled roofs receded into the background.

The day was changeable with hard shining sun one minute giving way to sudden showers of rain but there was no warning of the storm ahead. *Typical Scottish weather*, thought Carruthers. He was glad he was wearing his sky-blue waterproof jacket. When they got into the open sea Gardner put a spurt on and the engine chugged into life. As the boat dipped and his stomach lurched Carruthers zipped the jacket up to his neck and pulled the collar up as far as it would go. He was surprised at the speed of the boat and hoped he wouldn't be seasick.

'There's a fair bit of a swell already,' shouted Gardner, 'so if you're feeling seasick just keep looking at the horizon.'

Carruthers nodded and tried not to feel alarm. If truth be told he wasn't much of a sailor. The two men lapsed once more into silence.

Halfway over they met the RIB coming the other way. As the two skippers waved at each other Carruthers recognised the passengers as the scene of crime officers. They clearly weren't taking any chances of being stranded on the island.

What am I doing? he thought. *What if I get stranded? McTavish will go ballistic.*

To keep the waves of nausea at bay he went over the details of the case in his head. He kept coming back to the same question. What was the connection between Ramsey and Paterson?

At last the island came into view. Gardner cut the engine and Carruthers heard seawater slapping against the sides of the boat. The raucous calls of the birds filled his senses. He followed Gardner's gaze and couldn't help but smile. There, frolicking in the water, was a dolphin.

'It never looks the same, the island,' Gardner said. 'It's dark in the morning light but now look at it. It's like a chameleon. In winter she can look like an iceberg. Wind's picking up some more. I'm going to have to land at Altarstanes. This is just too dangerous.' He turned to Carruthers. 'I have to tell you, Jim, you're taking a risk. I'm hoping it will blow over but if it gets much worse, I can't come back for you.'

'I'll take my chances.' He didn't feel as confident as he sounded. Carruthers had also noticed the wind picking up again. It was tugging at his jacket, making his eyes smart. He looked up at the island. It was shining in the sun. Despite the blustery wind visibility was good and he took in the lighthouse on the island's highest point. To the right of it he could see the deep canyon, which seemed to split the island. He marvelled that much of the cliff appeared white due to the seabird droppings. Once again he thought what a strange existence it must be for those living on the nature reserve. Although only a short distance from the mainland it had a feeling of total isolation. A perfect spiritual sanctuary for those of a religious persuasion.

He looked over at Gardner who was still watching the dolphin as he navigated around the island.

'Do you know much about the history of the island?' Carruthers asked.

'Aye, a bit. There used to be an annual trip for the poor of the East Neuk back in the 1800s but it was stopped after a terrible tragedy.'

Another tragedy, thought Carruthers. 'What happened?'

'There was an accident. Five boats set off in calm weather apparently. Nobody really knows what happened but one of the boats struck a rock as it was entering Kirkhaven harbour. The passengers panicked rushing to the side and the boat capsized throwing all the holiday makers into the water.'

'God, how awful.'

'Thirteen lives were lost. After that the annual outings were stopped.'

Carruthers couldn't imagine the collective grieving that would have gone on in a wee village he now called home. Everyone would have lost someone or known somebody who had lost their life. The boat bobbed, frothy water crashing around them. Carruthers was aware that the wind had picked up further in the last few minutes. His stomach was starting to feel queasy again. He wondered if he had been foolhardy to attempt the crossing.

'There is a chance the storm may miss us and if the wind dies down enough I'll pick you up at Kirkhaven. I'll send you a text.'

'That's okay.' *I want to cover every inch of the island anyway*, he thought. *If I start out at Altarstanes I can end up over at Kirkhaven so it doesn't much matter to me where we dock; but I do quite fancy getting off this boat.*

'As a fisherman how close *can* you get to the Isle of May? I was surprised to hear there were no fishing restrictions. And do any of the fishermen ever hire their boats out or take private individuals to the island?'

'I like to think the fishermen are respectful of the fact this is a nature reserve with nesting seabirds. And to answer your second question I've heard there's been one or two taking folk over to the May, like Angus McCrae, but he does it more as a favour. If you want to know who else takes folk over you'd be better off asking local fishermen. Look up there. Quite a sight, eh?'

Carruthers followed Gardner's gaze and stared at the teeming birds all crammed on the narrow ledges.

'Did you ever see Robbie Paterson fish close to the island?'

Gardner shook his head. 'Never saw his boat that close, at least not within thirty metres.'

'But you did see his boat out when you made a crossing?'

'Aye, sometimes, from a distance.'

Gardner once again skilfully manoeuvred the boat towards the second harbour at Altarstanes. Carruthers wondered how many shipwrecks there had been over the centuries and once again thought of the ill-fated crossing of Fife's poor. Once they got to the island Carruthers gratefully disembarked.

'How long do you need?'

It took him a few moments to get his land legs. 'Can you give me a couple of hours?' As soon as he said this he debated as to whether he would need more time. However, he was also needed back at the station. And there was always the possibility that the storm could close in leaving him stranded. Dark brooding clouds appeared on the horizon.

With a wave of the hand Scott Gardner set off again into the Firth of Forth. The policeman spent no time at all watching the boat as it disappeared from view. Every moment was vital, but where to start? That was the question. The island might only be two kilometres long and less than half a kilometre wide but with so many cliff faces, beaches and caves, not to mention buildings, it was going to be like looking for a needle in a haystack. He doubted he would find the murder weapon, which had been used to kill the warden. In all likelihood the knife had been thrown into the sea.

Carruthers scrambled up the steep path and with long strides walked to Burnett's Leap. It had been named after the assistant keeper who had fallen onto the rocks in 1889. When he got to the low wall on the north of the High Road, he chose the lower of the paths, which took him to Low Light. The building had originally been a lighthouse but that had long since been abandoned and it was, Carruthers knew, now a bird observatory. He walked up to the front door and tried to open it, but the building was locked. There was a strange sense of abandonment about the place.

Carruthers thought of the men and women who had come to this incredible place of pilgrimage for over a thousand years but there was only one traveller he was interested in. The man or woman who had most recently come to the island and who had murdered the warden. The problem was they still didn't know why he had been killed. Why would a hard-working warden on an uninhabited island be murdered? Somehow he didn't buy the idea that Ramsey had been killed by his ex, however controlling she sounded.

He once again got the map of the island out and studied it. He reread the last paragraph of the information he had got off the internet.

The land tilts from here down to the eastern shore, which is mostly rocky with three small beaches: Pilgrim's Haven, Kirkhaven and Silver Sands. There is a peninsula in the north, known as Rona, which is almost a separate island, being cut off from the main island at high tide.

As he studied the map and reread the last line a thought hit him. He hadn't checked to see if anyone had got to Rona, the northernmost part of the Isle of May where many of the grey seals bred. Or had it been high tide and cut off from the main island? If this had been the case the SOCOs may have assumed it was itself an island. He whipped out his mobile; grateful to see he at least had a signal. He put a call through to Fletcher.

'Andie, it's Jim. Can you find something out for me? Did any of the SOCOs conduct a search on the peninsula on the Isle of May? Apparently the peninsula's called Rona?'

'Where are you, Jim?'

'I'm on the island at the moment. It's low tide just now and Rona is accessible. I don't know how long for, though.'

'I don't know and I'm actually at the airport.'

'Shit. I'd forgotten. Look, don't worry about it. I'll call the station and get someone there to check it.' Carruthers cut the call and phoned the station with his request. He wondered how long he'd have before the tide turned again and the peninsula would be cut off. Rather than waste time he decided to start his search on Rona.

He walked over to the peninsula and looked around him, getting his bearings. It was starting to spit with rain.

His mobile rang. It was Dougie Harris. 'No. Apparently it was cut off and the SOCOs didnae search it.'

'Okay, that's great, Dougie. Anything going on at the station I should know about?'

'It's surprisingly quiet but I'll let you know if anything changes.'

'Thanks. Keep me posted, will you? Did Lennox pass the information over to you about Ramsey's previous jobs?'

'Aye, I have it here. I'm just about to look at it.'

Carruthers thanked Harris and slipped his mobile back into the pocket of his jacket.

The murder was still a mystery.

He started his search of Rona. There were no buildings on the peninsula and no ruins. He stared hopelessly around him, searching behind the dark grey and green basalt rocks for a sign of a weapon or anything else untoward but there was nothing but a family of rabbits.

He glanced at his watch. He only had twenty minutes before he had to board Scott Gardner's boat. Where had the time gone? He looked at the sky. The dark clouds were gathering but the wind hadn't got any worse. With a bit of luck they would be fortunate and the storm would blow over or hit further out to sea. He left Rona and took long strides up to the murder site. As he walked he felt the heat in his cheeks from the exertion and tasted the sweat on his top lip.

Tom Ramsey had been out logging birds when he had been killed. Carruthers reminded himself that the warden had been found with his notebook and binoculars. He stared out at the rocks teeming with birds. He brought out his own binoculars and trained them on the rocks. He then did a sweep of the headland and horizon with them. Out of the corner of his eye something caught his gaze in the water. It was a frolicking seal. A half-formed thought lay unbidden. He lowered his binoculars and thought for a few minutes biting his bottom lip. What was he missing?

His mobile phone pinged. His hands were so cold he struggled to get the phone out of his pocket. The earlier wind had now dropped but it felt as if the temperature had also dropped a few degrees. It was a message from Gardner to say the storm had been downgraded and the skipper would try to land at Kirkhaven after all.

He sighed with relief as he scrambled back to the visitor's centre. Out of breath he gazed out to sea. Sure enough he could see Gardner's boat. He stood upright, breathing in the salty sea air as the boat drew closer. Gardner wasn't alone on the deck.

Carruthers could make out two figures on board. He walked towards the cliff edge and looked through his binoculars as he waved to the skipper. Gardener didn't see him, as he was too busy throwing mock punches at the younger man on board. Carruthers had a clear view through the binoculars of the second man. It was Gardner's son.

The boat was coming in a direction that would bring it close to where Paterson's boat had been spotted. And then it hit him full in the solar plexus what might have happened.

Ramsey had been out using his binoculars to log birds in the exact same place that Carruthers was now standing and had spotted Paterson in his boat. *And as they now knew Paterson hadn't been alone.* And this had been borne out by the blood of a second person on the fisherman's boat. *Who?*

The more Carruthers thought about it the more he now believed Ramsey had witnessed Paterson's murder and the murderer had seen Ramsey and come after him.

Carruthers felt his excitement rising. *And that's how Robbie Paterson's blood is on the body of Ramsey*, he thought. It was trans-ferred by their killer. All they needed to do now was to identify *whose* blood it was. But something troubled him. Why the excess force? Excess force smacked of a cry of passion; of someone losing all control and it was at odds with the calculated actions of the person who had murder in mind. Unless – unless it had been a ploy. A ploy to make the police believe they were looking for a frenzied killer.

Carruthers whipped out his mobile and rang Fletcher. She was best placed to find out if Ellie Robertson knew how to sail. The likelihood was, though, that she would now have her phone turned off for the flight. Predictably it went to voicemail. He then phoned Harris.

'Dougie, do me a favour. Make some enquiries, will you, and find out if Ellie Robertson knows how to sail a boat.'

'How in the hell am I supposed to get that sort of information?'

'Use your initiative. And if that fails get Fletcher to ask Robertson during the interview.' Carruthers spoke curtly before swearing away from the phone and then cutting the call. Honestly, Harris could be so lazy sometimes. He pocketed the mobile, got down on his haunches and started a fingertip search of the ground. After five minutes he found what he was looking for. Evidence that this had been the exact spot Ramsey stood when he had seen Paterson's boat. Half hidden in a puffin burrow was a ballpoint pen. Carruthers slipped on his nitrile gloves and bagged the pen. What's the betting Ramsey's DNA would be found on it? He even spotted a hole in the ground, most likely a rabbit warren where Ramsey could have twisted his ankle. He'd fled the scene, perhaps to ring the police. After all, his mobile had been found back at his accommodation, but he had never made it. The murderer had caught up with him by the visitor centre.

Carruthers was starting to feel a lot clearer as to what might have happened here but there were still two nagging thoughts in his head. The burning question was, who was it that Ramsey had identified, and with Paterson's boat found bobbing off the island, how had the perp made his getaway? Most likely in Ramsey's boat. But where was the boat now?

32

Carruthers stepped gratefully back onto the mainland, thanked Gardner for taking him over to the Isle of May then made his way to his car. Halfway over he stopped, did an about-turn and walked in a totally different direction. He knew he should really go straight back to the station but he wanted to go to Frank Dewar's house and have a nose about. He could go on the pretext of wanting to know who the reporter was that had given Dewar her business card. That was as good a reason as any to pitch up at his house.

Dewar's home was part of a row of quaint fishermen's cottages in Cellardyke. This was unusual. Carruthers knew that often these old cottages had been bought by those seeking second homes. For the most part in a lot of seaside villages the fishermen now lived in more modern buildings further back from the seafront. Carruthers rapped on the door. An elderly lady pushing a Zimmer frame finally answered. Carruthers knew that Dewar's wife was much older than him so he supposed this was her.

'Good afternoon. Is Frank home?' He flashed his warrant card.

'No, he's taken his boat out. I should imagine he'll be back soon though. The weather's poor.'

Good that he's not at home. They hadn't come across his boat, the *Ivy Rose*, so he obviously hadn't been anywhere near the May.

The older woman peered at Carruthers. 'Can I give him a message? I take it this is about the current goings on?'

Current goings on? Well that is one way of putting it, thought Carruthers. 'I'm investigating the murder of Tom Ramsey and the unexplained death of Robbie Paterson. I'm wondering if Frank ever mentioned a reporter to you?'

Dewar's wife shook her head as she leant heavily on her frame. 'A reporter?'

'Frank was given her business card. I'm trying to track down who she is and which paper she works for.'

A little white lie never hurt anyone.

Mrs Dewar shook her head. 'I don't remember seeing a business card. Most likely place I can think that he would keep it though is in his wallet. That's here in the living room. He doesn't take it out with him when he's fishing. I've seen his wallet this morning. Is it important?'

'It could be. Yes.'

'Well, you had better come away in then.' She opened the door wider and Carruthers stepped into the narrow hall.

He followed her through the hall, noting the stairlift, and into the living room. The chocolate brown leather three-piece suite looked new and there was a fifty-inch TV on the wall.

The tattered black wallet was lying on a coffee table. As Mrs Dewar picked it up a phone rang. She handed the wallet to Carruthers. 'Can you take a look? I need to get that call. My sister's been in hospital. Having tests.' Distractedly she turned away from Carruthers and, with the help of the frame, walked painfully out back into the hall.

Carruthers opened the wallet. Out dropped a business card onto the cream carpet. He stooped to pick it up. It was the business card of a journalist. One Elaine Morgan. The *East Neuk Mercury.*

He could hear Mrs Dewar's voice on the phone. She finished the call and came slowly back into the living room.

'Thank God, looks like my sister is okay. Just a benign cyst. I see you found the card.' She jerked her head towards the hand holding Elaine Morgan's card. 'Terrible business about that warden. And is it true Robbie was murdered?'

'We're treating his death as unexplained at the moment, Mrs Dewar.' Carruthers had a sudden thought. 'I'm so sorry to bother you but may I use your bathroom before I go back to the station?'

If Mrs Dewar was surprised she didn't show it. 'It's up the stairs and first on the left.'

Carruthers took the steep old creaky stairs quickly and opened the door to the bathroom. He walked in and took a good look around him. The bath had been replaced by a stylish wet room. He opened and shut a few cupboard doors quietly, flushed the toilet, then went downstairs again.

'Thank you. Sorry about that. Too many cups of tea at the station.' As he was leaving he turned to the old woman. 'Do you have a second bathroom or an en suite?'

At this the woman looked puzzled. 'No. Just the one.'

'Do you know where your husband got that nasty cut on his forehead?'

'Oh that.' She laughed. 'He had a bit of an accident. Tripped on the pavement. He likes a wee drink.' She looked rueful.

Well that was certainly true. An image came into Carruthers' mind of the old fisherman staggering out of the pub. However, what concerned Carruthers most was the two different stories: one for his wife, one for the police. 'Thank you, Mrs Dewar.

You've been most helpful.' *You certainly have*, thought Carruthers. *I now know Dewar was lying about how he came by the cut above his eye.* There had been no glass shelving in the bathroom.

~

Carruthers stood in McTavish's office. 'I want to bring Frank Dewar in for questioning.'

'He knows more than he's saying, Jim, that's for sure.'

'Well, he's lied to the police. He told me he got his cut from the glass shelf in his bathroom but I've been in his bathroom and there is no glass shelf.'

McTavish pursed her lips.

'Also his wife said something different. He told her he'd tripped up on the pavement. When I asked her how he came by his cut she alluded to the fact he's a drinker.'

'So you think he was in a fight with Paterson?'

'It's possible, although it's true he certainly likes his drink so he could have tripped but that doesn't explain the bruised knuckles.'

'I agree with you that he's not telling us everything, but I've said before we don't have enough to bring him in.'

'We've got to do something, Sandra. We can't just let it go. Our two main suspects are Ellie Robertson and Frank Dewar but I'm not convinced it's Robertson. Paterson was killed by someone he knew. Trust me on this one.'

McTavish thought this over. After a few moments she spoke. 'Fletcher and Lennox are going to be interviewing this Miles Butcher and I'm interested to see what comes of that interview. Both their interviews with Robertson and Butcher are going to be crucial. Certainly, while there is no evidence against Robertson her behaviour towards her ex is very damning, but I take on board what you've said and this is what I want you to do. I want you to go and talk to Dewar and ask him if he's willing to provide us with a DNA sample. He may not realise that we still have his DNA on our database. You could tell him we think the murders have been committed by someone local and we're going to be asking all local men to volunteer to give us a sample.'

'And if he refuses?'

McTavish smiled. 'Then we'll know he has something to hide and we'll use that and anything else we can find on him to apply for a search warrant.'

Carruthers went back to his desk and brought out the card Mrs Dewar had given him. *Elaine Morgan.* He keyed in the telephone number and set up a meeting with the journalist. She sounded most accommodating, almost gushing and was prepared to meet him in twenty minutes. *I bet she is.* His thoughts turned to Fletcher; he idly wondered if Lennox had made the flight to Bristol and what they would get out of the interview.

Within half an hour the policeman was sitting opposite the blonde middle-aged journalist in a quaint 1920s-style café in Anstruther. Ordinarily he would have thought that this must be a slow day at the paper for the woman to have dropped everything to meet him at such short notice, but the bloody murder of the warden of the nature reserve was probably the biggest scoop of her career. Or so she was hoping.

'What have you got for me?' Morgan's eyes lit up as she stirred her latte. She wore a brown tweed skirt and a white blouse. Her blonde hair was loose around her pinched face.

The teashop was empty except for the two members of staff. The older lady was busy stacking cups and saucers behind the counter and the teenage server was cleaning each table with a cloth. From time to time she looked at the smartphone she was carrying. Neither of them paid any attention at all to their two guests.

Carruthers stopped staring at the paper doily on the table and looked up into the reporter's eyes. 'I'm here to ask you to stop spreading rumours which may hinder the investigation.'

'What rumours?' But even as she said it a guarded look came into her eyes.

He took a measured sip of his black coffee and placed the small patterned cup back in its saucer. They looked vintage. 'You know very well what rumours. The rumour that Robert Paterson has been murdered. The post-mortem was inconclusive and it's entirely possible the fisherman had a heart attack and fell overboard.'

She was looking at him shrewdly. 'You don't really believe that, do you?'

'Yes,' said Carruthers. *May God strike me down for lying.*

She dived into her handbag and brought out a notebook and pen. 'Let's just say I might be in possession of some facts that could help your investigation.' As she emphasised the word 'facts' her right eyebrow rose.

The policeman and journalist observed each other in silence for a few moments. Carruthers was curious as to what 'facts' the journalist thought she was in possession of. He decided to feign disinterest and play it cool.

It was Morgan who spoke first. She replaced her coffee cup and leant into the table. 'If I help you by telling you what I know, what will you give me in return?'

I won't have you charged for hindering a police investigation for starters, is what Carruthers wanted to say but he kept quiet and just continued to assess the local reporter through narrowed eyes. Carruthers had got wise to a certain type of pushy reporter a long time ago and he was mindful of the rules governing inter-action between police officers and journalists – most notably that off-the-record 'conversations' should only happen in 'exceptional circumstances'.

Most likely he was putting his career on the line by even being with this woman and if DCI Sandra McTavish found out the very least he would get would be a sky-high bollocking.

He voiced his thoughts. 'You know as well as I do what the rules are. Everything needs to go through the press office.' A number of police officers had been sacked and even arrested after giving unauthorised information to journalists. But she had got him interested.

'And yet here you are.'

Carruthers felt himself colouring. 'Okay then, what could you possibly give me?'

The woman lowered her voice so she was talking in hushed tones. 'What would you say if I told you I'm close to finding out who killed Ramsey and Paterson and why.'

Interesting that she also thinks they have both been murdered, and by the same person.

'Who?'

She laughed. 'Oh no. I'm not just going to hand over what I've got just like that.'

'Do you have evidence that the police could use?'

'Not yet but what I will say is that my informants tell me it's to do with a huge shipment of drugs coming in to Fife.'

Carruthers felt the hair on his neck prick up. *How did she know about the shipment? And who were her informants?* Was he about to sell his soul to the devil to find out?

'Your informants?'

'That's right.'

'You're telling me the deaths of both a local fisherman and the warden of the Isle of May are connected to drug dealing?'

She nodded.

Carruthers scratched his stubbly chin. *They hadn't seriously considered drugs might be the cause of both men's deaths.* There had been no evidence to suggest a link with drugs. And if she was right it would let Ellie Robertson off the hook. However, he thought about the new TV and three-piece suite in Frank Dewar's home. *Was he involved in drug dealing? It seemed so unlikely. But then why do I think it unlikely? Because I know him?*

Morgan laughed. 'Well, like I said, you don't seriously think I'm just going to hand it to you on a plate? And I've told you more than enough for now.'

Carruthers continued to sip his coffee wondering what he could give her in return that wouldn't compromise his position but he drew a blank. His eyes never left the pinched face of the journalist. He wasn't giving anything away. But then again, what did he actually know that he was prepared to tell?

'If you have leads why haven't you been to the police?'

She dropped her voice further. 'Because I value my life, that's why.'

'But you're here now so what's changed?' Carruthers was beginning to feel he was playing a game of tennis with this woman. The ball was constantly being batted to and fro.

She expelled the air from her lungs and sat back in her seat watching him. Carruthers could see that she was trying to decide just how much to tell him. 'I'm being forced out of the newspaper by my boss.' She scowled. 'Ageist bastards. Thirty years' experience and I'm now being given all the menial jobs. But I reckon if I could give them something big they wouldn't be able to let me go. That's where you come in. I want sole access to whatever you discover and in exchange I'll tell you what I know.'

Carruthers decided he had to play by the rules. Had he really thought she would just hand over everything she knew? She was far too canny for that. 'We don't work like that in Eden-side. This isn't the 1970s anymore. You know I can't just release information. It has to go through the right channels nowadays.

And if I did tell you what you want to know, that is, if I know anything that could be useful, I could be sacked or even arrested.'

'And yet, as I said, you are here.' She stood up abruptly.

He grabbed her sleeve. 'Okay, tell me what you want.'

Morgan sat down again. 'The first thing I want to do is to go to the Isle of May and get some photos of the crime scene. Can you help arrange that for me?'

Carruthers shook his head. 'No way. You can't get over to the island at the moment, Ms Morgan. It's still an active crime scene. No press allowed.' *I'm not going to tell her that the island is currently deserted as the SOCOs have all left fearing a severe storm. She doesn't need to know that.*

She stared at him. 'I need to get to the island. I also want exclusive access to everything you find out.'

'As I said, the first is a "no" and as to the second I can't give that assurance without first talking to my boss.'

She stood up before speaking. 'Your loss.' She walked away leaving her half-drunk latte.

Carruthers swore; slapped down a ten-pound note on the table, took up his jacket and went after her. The two members of staff stopped what they were doing and looked up, startled. Ignoring the front door that had just swung in his face he caught up with the reporter.

He knew she now thought she had the upper hand. 'Like I said I need to talk to my boss. I can't make any promises,' he said.

She kept walking away from him as she spoke. 'DCI Sandra McTavish or Superintendent Bingham?'

'You're well informed.'

She turned to face him. 'I make it my business to be well informed. I'm a journalist, remember?'

'You said you knew who'd killed Tom Ramsey and Robert Paterson. Do you have names?'

'Not yet. But I'm working on it.' She leant into him. 'Look, I won't deny I'm ambitious and I don't want to be forced out of the paper, but there is something else.' Carruthers looked into the reporter's eyes and for the first time saw another emotion other than naked ambition. He saw concern and something else. An emotion he couldn't identify. 'I want these people caught. We're actually on the same side, you and I. We both have a duty of care to the public. I'm doing my job and I want you to do yours. Catch these bastards.' And with that she turned on her heel and walked away. Carruthers watched her go then whipped out his mobile and punched in the number for Gus at the National Crime Agency.

33

Lennox's non-stop chat all the way to Bristol annoyed the hell out of Fletcher, who rubbed the back of her neck from time to time. She had popped a couple of painkillers before the flight just to be on the safe side but she could still feel twinges. She glanced over at her colleague who was still talking excitedly.

'Haven't you got a book to read or something?' *Anything to stop your inane babble.* Fletcher knew she was being impolite but she couldn't help herself. 'Or you could just go over the notes on the case.'

Lennox grinned. 'I've already done it. In fact I'm ready to take the lead if you want me to.'

Bloody hell.

'We need to be discreet if we're interviewing her at her place of work.' Lennox looked serious for a moment. 'After all, we don't want her to think she's a suspect, even if she is one, and for her to get all defensive.'

Fletcher was surprised. This was the first time her colleague had showed any sensitivity. Perhaps she had been too quick to make her mind up about her. She was starting to wonder if the woman's irritating manner had clouded her judgement about her aptitude as a detective.

'Pity we couldn't interview her at home away from the prying eyes of her colleagues but you never know if someone's going straight out after work. We might miss her. And what with needing to interview Miles Butcher and her current boyfriend too, it's going to be pretty tight to get that flight back.'

Fletcher thought about Lennox's words. If Bristol was anything like London most folk went straight out after work. With the time it took to get around the capital it wasn't worth going home first. But then again Bristol was much smaller than London.

'Shame we can't stay overnight.' Lennox sighed. 'I love Bristol. It's a great city.'

An hour later they were in a taxi on their way to the firm of property developers in Clifton where Ellie Robertson worked as a legal secretary. As Lennox reread her notes making adjustments or comments with her black ballpoint pen here and there Fletcher leaned back in the leather seats and admired the grand Georgian townhouses that lined this leafy, affluent part of Bristol.

Twenty minutes later they were sitting in a private office of a bright, modern building they had commandeered for their interview with Robertson.

'I don't really understand what this has got to do with me. I haven't seen Tom for a long time,' Robertson said finally.

Fletcher assessed the woman who sat opposite them. She was striking rather than pretty, her thick dark hair cascading down her back. *Robertson's confidence is reflected in how she dresses*, thought Fletcher. *The navy and ivory print jersey dress really suits her. She's taking the fact she's being interviewed at work really well. I thought she'd kick off.*

'This is just standard procedure, Ms Robertson,' said Lennox. 'We're talking to anyone who knew Tom Ramsey well and we're asking everyone the same questions.'

'I understand you used to date him. When did you last see him?' Fletcher asked.

'Look, I would never wish anyone dead but you might as well know our relationship didn't end well.'

'I believe you accused him of having an affair?' Fletcher waited with bated breath for an answer to her question.

'You've done your homework. He *did* have an affair. With my mother.'

Lennox's mouth dropped open. 'He had an affair with your *mother?*'

Fletcher flinched at Lennox's knee-jerk response but it seemed to work in the police officer's favour. Her response seemed to put Ellie Robertson at ease. Her body language visibly relaxed. Her shoulders dropped and her face lost some of its previous tension. She started to open up. 'It went on for six months. From what I can gather mostly dirty chat down the phone. We were due to move in together. Of course that never happened. I ended the relationship when I found out. My father went to see him. I'm afraid he punched him. Broke his nose. Nothing short of what he deserved of course.'

If this was true Fletcher wondered what her relationship was now like with her mother. And if she even had a relationship.

'I take it Tom didn't press charges?'

Robertson shook her head. 'No, within a week he had packed up and left. None of us have heard from him since. I had no idea he was in Scotland. First I heard of it was when I saw his murder on the news. I was shocked. I had wondered if he'd done the same thing up there.'

'Did he have a track record for having affairs with married women?' asked Lennox.

'Apparently wherever he went he left a string of broken hearts. I must admit I knew one of his ex-girlfriends.' She bit her lip.

Fletcher wondered what she was going to say next.

'Actually, I started seeing him when he was still seeing her. I guess the best you can say is that his private life was always a bit of a mess.'

Fletcher had been listening very closely to this. If Ellie was telling the truth, perhaps this was the reason Tom Ramsey never managed to stay living in the same place or doing the same job for long, although it seemed he'd had no love interest while on the Isle of May. She wanted to ask Ellie whether she'd ever seen Tom do drugs but before she had a chance to open her mouth Lennox asked her next question.

'Ellie, when you were with Tom was he ever a drug user?'

The girl looked surprised. 'Do you think he was killed over drugs, then?'

'It's a line, among several, that we're pursuing,' said Fletcher. 'Did you ever see him take drugs?'

'No, never. And my father would never have stood for it.'

'Your father?'

'Didn't I say? He's in the police force.'

The two detectives exchanged looks. 'Is he... does your father live locally?' *We need to interview him*, thought Fletcher. *We might just have found a new suspect.*

'Yes, just round the corner from me, actually but he's not in Bristol at the moment. He's in Antigua with mum. They decided to patch things up and in the end they stayed together. He must really love her.'

'How long has he been in Antigua?'

'Just short of a week. He's due to fly back tomorrow.'

Ellie Robertson's father had an alibi, although it would need to be checked. *But did Ellie?* 'Can I ask you where you were on Monday morning?'

'You don't *seriously* think I would kill Tom?'

Lennox glanced up from her notebook. 'Like we said we're asking everyone who knew Tom the same questions.'

'I've already been interviewed by Bristol CID. I'm going to tell you what I told them. I was here in Bristol. On the Sunday night I went for an Indian meal with my boyfriend, then on Monday morning I was in work.'

'I'll need to get the restaurant details from you and we will need to check,' said Lennox.

'If that's what you need to do...' She shrugged.

Fletcher made some notes in her black notebook. They already knew her alibi checked out, and, on the face of it, it seemed to her there was no viable way Ellie Robertson could have murdered her ex-boyfriend. However, as alibis went it was still a weak one as it had been her current boyfriend who had provided it. And even if Robertson had been in Bristol she could still have paid someone to kill Ramsey. Her current boyfriend had already been interviewed by Bristol CID but Fletcher was keen to speak to him herself. And what might be most revealing was what he didn't, rather than what he did, say.

'Just out of interest can I ask you if you know how to sail a boat?' Fletcher asked.

'What an odd question, unless you think – you think I sailed to the Isle of May and killed my former boyfriend!' She laughed.

Fletcher was starting to feel impatient. 'Can you just answer the question please?'

'Oh my God you are serious. No, I don't know how to sail a boat and I wasn't anywhere near the Isle of May when Tom was killed.'

Helen Lennox took a sip of water from the small bottle she

had brought with her before speaking. 'We've spoken about Tom's ex-girlfriends; what about your ex-partners?'

Fletcher watched Ellie Robertson closely for her reaction. It didn't disappoint. The younger woman looked uncomfortable. 'Why are they relevant?'

Lennox flicked over the page of her little black notebook. 'Miles Butcher?'

'What about him?' Robertson glanced at her watch. She stood up. 'Look, I really need to be getting back to work.'

'I'm afraid we're not done yet,' said Fletcher. 'Please sit down.'

Robertson reluctantly took her seat again.

Fletcher continued with her questions, noting how uncomfortable Ellie Robertson had become when Butcher's name was mentioned. They said nothing about the fact that they were going to be shooting off straight after this interview to talk to him. Noting how evasive Robertson was being about Butcher Fletcher wondered if, perhaps, they were on to something. 'Were you ever physically violent towards Mr Butcher?'

Robertson looked from one officer to the other. 'Who told you that? Was it Miles?'

'I'm afraid we're not at liberty to say, Ms Robertson,' put in Lennox. 'Please just answer the question.'

'It was a... volatile relationship. We've both got a temper. There were occasions where we both hit each other.'

'So you do admit to being physically violent towards your partner?' urged Lennox.

'I've already said I did hit him. Once or twice.'

'Did you ever seriously injure him?'

Ellie Robertson shook her head vehemently.

Lennox referred to her notebook before her next question. 'He said you pulled a knife on him once.'

'I didn't "pull a knife". We had an argument in the kitchen

when I was chopping veg. I just happened to be holding a knife at the time. God, he always did exaggerate. That's one of the reasons I left him.'

'*You* left *him*?'

'That's right. Why? What's he been saying?'

'Well, that was interesting,' said Fletcher, thirty minutes later as they left the building where Miles Butcher lived. She put up her hand for a taxi.

Lennox looked up from checking her mobile as a taxi stopped in front of them. She sighed. 'I didn't believe a word that man said. Did you?'

'If it went to court you certainly couldn't convict just Robertson on a charge of assault.'

'What do you make of the interview with Robertson?'

Fletcher leant into the taxi driver. 'Gloucester Road, please.' She sat back in her seat and buckled up. 'I dunno. She's admitted to being violent towards Butcher so she's certainly not the innocent in all this. Let's see what her current boyfriend has to say about her. After all, he's the one who provided her with an alibi.'

34

'Gus, it's Jim here.' Carruthers didn't give the officer a chance to speak. He just powered on with what he needed to say. 'Look, I've just spoken to a local journalist, an Elaine Morgan from the *East Neuk Mercury*. She knows about the drugs shipment. Is there any way the press could have got wind of this?'

Gus's voice was sharp. 'Not from us but there's clearly been a leak somewhere. This could compromise the whole operation.'

He heard Gus talk urgently away from the phone before he was back on the line. 'Could it have come from your end – the leak?'

It would have to have come from a member of their own CID. Carruthers couldn't face even thinking about that. And he couldn't imagine any of their team leaking the information to a member of the press.

The two men talked for a bit then Carruthers finished the call. Of course he would have to tell McTavish. He wondered how she would take the news. He sat and ate his cold bacon roll at his desk while he thought about what he would say. Instead of wolfing it down he took slow, deliberate bites. He thought back

to his meeting with Elaine Morgan. It had broken up in stale-
mate and he still felt frustrated by it. He'd put his career on the
line by having a private meeting with a journalist and for what?
But he was still surprised by the human side she had shown
towards the end. Had her life too been touched by drugs?

His thoughts then drifted to his phone conversation with
Fletcher who had filled him in with their interviews down in
Bristol. Disappointingly, they had got nothing out of the current
boyfriend. He was insisting they had eaten a meal in the *Urban
Tandoor* on Small Street. He had the credit card receipt to prove
it and the waiters had remembered Ellie as she had compli-
mented them on the food they had served.

His phone rang. He had to shift various buff files before he
even found it.

His DCI's voice brought him back to the present. 'Jim, I've
just taken a call. A Scott Gardner. I'm not sure why he came
through on my line. He rang to find out when he can start the
boat trips back to the Isle of May.'

Carruthers wondered why McTavish would mention this
to him.

'Apparently some journalist is hassling him, insisting
someone take her over to the island. I want her stopped.'

'Who?' But he had already guessed without McTavish telling
him.

'Elaine Morgan.'

He couldn't help but feel concerned. If Morgan was going
round asking the wrong sort of questions to the wrong people
she might be in danger. The net was starting to close in on the
murderer and as much as he disliked Morgan he didn't want her
right in the line of fire. He stood up abruptly, knocking a couple
of files off the corner of his desk. They hit the floor with a thud.

He thought back to his conversation with the reporter. 'I
knew she wanted to go over to the Isle of May.'

'How do you know that? I hope you haven't had any private meetings with her, Jim. You know the rules.'

Carruthers sighed.

'Do you think she might be in danger?' McTavish asked.

She's obviously decided to let that one go. Thank God. But she's picked up the concern in my voice.

'When I spoke to her she seemed to know more about the cases than us.'

'How so?'

'She told me she thought both the deaths of Ramsey and Paterson were drug-related. She seemed to know about the drugs coming into Fife.'

'Why didn't you tell me about this conversation, Jim?'

'I didn't really have anything concrete to go on.' But even as he said it he knew he had made a mistake.

McTavish's voice was frosty. 'If a local journalist has got wind of the drugs haul that's on its way into Fife then I need to know about it. Understood? If word has got out it might compromise the entire operation.'

'Yes, Sandra.'

'And you need to inform the NCA. Immediately.'

Carruthers didn't tell her that he had already phoned them. She wouldn't be pleased that he had told the NCA ahead of her. And why hadn't he told her? Perhaps because he would then have to admit to meeting the journalist. He was no longer a DCI but that didn't stop him wanting to stay one step ahead of everyone else involved in the case. But he hung his head. He had made a mistake.

'We need to find that journalist. I don't want her to compromise the investigation but more than that I'm concerned for her safety.'

'Leave it to me, Sandra. I'll find her.' He cut the call before his boss had a chance to reply, put on his jacket and left the station. He drove the six miles over to Anstruther and as luck would have it found Scott Gardner in his hut down by the harbour. Carruthers put his head round the wooden door.

'Scott, have you got a sec? It's important.'

Gardner put down the handful of receipts he held. 'What's up?'

'I hear you've had a journalist, an Elaine Morgan, asking to be taken over to the Isle of May?'

He put down the pen he was holding. 'Aye, she came to see me earlier. Sorry, I'm a wee bit distracted. As you can see, I'm busy issuing refunds to everyone who booked to go over in the last few days.'

Carruthers had been so caught up with the murder investigation he hadn't had time to think about how the recent tragic events had impacted on Scott Gardner's business.

'I told her I couldnae take her over. Once we've been given the green light to start our day trips up again we're going to be booked solid. And the weather's no' great today. That storm warning's back in place. For that reason we wouldnae be taking the boat out even if we had paying passengers.'

Gardner looked worried. 'By the way, do you know how long the island's going to be out of bounds for? I don't know what to tell my customers. The phone's not stopped ringing. People want to know when they can rebook.' As if right on cue Gardner's phone rang. He ignored it.

Carruthers shook his head. 'I don't know how long the SOCOs will be on the island. Is there anyone else she could get a passage over with?'

'Well, I told her the May was still out of bounds due to it being a crime scene but she was adamant that she was going.'

I'm right, thought Carruthers. *Elaine Morgan's on the Isle of May.*

'Angus McCrae does the occasional run and I found out that

there's a couple of fishermen that have started running private trips over. Course they'd want to keep it quiet from me. After all, they're taking my customers.'

No doubt supplementing their fishing income.

'Anyone in particular?'

'Alex Mitchell. He's got the last property in Dreelside.'

Carruthers thanked Gardner and raced off. He found Mitchell's terraced house but it took an age to get anyone to come to the door. Finally a rather harassed dark-haired woman opened the door. Her hands were covered in flour.

'Mrs Mitchell, is Alex home?'

Carruthers fully expected Mrs Mitchell to tell him that her husband was currently on the Isle of May but she nodded and pointed up the stairs. 'He's no' well. Come down with a summer virus. Nothing ever floors him but he's flattened with it.'

'Can I see him?'

'He's a popular man. He's already had one visitor today. Honestly. *That woman.*'

'Which woman?'

'Journalist woman. I can't mind the paper she works for. Wanted a passage over to the May. Told her he was ill. Next thing I know she's taking the stairs two at a time.'

'Do you know where she went after she left here?'

'I think my husband organised for someone else to take her over.'

Carruthers was already walking past the woman. 'It's urgent I speak with Alex.'

'Well, since it's the police... He's awake. I've just taken him a wee cup of tea. First room on your left at the top of the stairs.'

Carruthers thanked her and legged it up the stairs. He hesitated and knocked briefly on the door of the bedroom. He didn't wait for an answer but put his head round to see Alex sitting propped up in bed putting his cup back on its saucer.

The man's moon-shaped face was pale except for his bulbous nose, which was red. His dark uncombed hair was sticking up at all angles.

'Sorry for this intrusion, Alex.' Carruthers got out his warrant card.

'I am popular today.'

'It's about your earlier visitor. I understand Elaine Morgan wanted to be taken over to the May. I also believe you organised for someone to take her there?'

'She wouldn't take no for an answer. Annoying besom.'

That sounds like her.

'Can I ask who took her instead of you?'

'Aye, the only other person I know doing trips to the May is Bill Suttie. I phoned him and he was going to meet her down by the harbour.'

Carruthers was out the room and on the first step before he heard Alex calling him back.

'I don't know what this is about, Jim but I thought you should know Bill Suttie didn't take her in the end. Frank Dewar stepped in.'

35

Carruthers thought once more of the fifty-inch flat-screen TV and expensive brown leather three-piece suite in Dewar's home, not to mention the wet room and stair lift. He wondered how the fisherman had been able to afford them. He was starting to feel a bit sick. 'Did Elaine know this when she left here that she would be taken over by Dewar?' *How would she react if she did, especially if she thought he was the murderer? And had she worked it out?*

'No, she thought she was meeting Bill.'

Shit.

Carruthers took the stairs and barrelled past a puzzled Mrs Mitchell and out of the front door before he wondered if he'd remembered to thank Alex.

As he headed back to the harbour his mobile rang. It was a breathless DCI Sandra McTavish. 'Jim, I thought you'd want to know as soon as possible. The third blood sample that was found on the body of Tom Ramsey has just come back from the lab and we have a match on the database.'

'It's Frank Dewar.'

'Yes it is. How did you know?'

'I've just worked it out myself.'

'We're going to bring him in.'

He thought quickly. 'No point in sending anyone to his home address. I think he's taken that journalist, Elaine Morgan, over to the May.'

'Good God. Where are you now?'

'Anstruther.' Carruthers had just walked past the Scottish Fisheries Museum.

'If Dewar's the murderer and he thinks Morgan's on to him she may have walked straight into a trap.'

Or he's just got lucky, thought Carruthers.

But if she had already worked out who the murderer was, as she had claimed, what was she doing getting on a boat with him? Unless it was under duress and Morgan was going to go the same way as Paterson. Would they even make it to the Isle of May?

'We need to get over to the island as soon as possible... For God's sake, Jim, make sure you take backup. I don't want you to go over on your own.'

Carruthers agreed, broke the call and put his phone away. He popped his head back round the hut by the car park. It was Scott's wife, Margo, behind the desk.

'I'm sorry, Margo. Is Scott around? I need to know if the RIB is available for use? It's an emergency. I need to get over to the May ASAP.'

'He's just popped out for a few minutes.' She frowned. 'I thought there was nobody going over to the island at the moment except the police?'

'There shouldn't be. Is Scott insured to skipper it? Don't worry. We'll pay you for his time but this is urgent. A woman's life might be in danger.'

'You're not talking about that journalist woman, are you?

Scott told me she was looking to go to the island. Funny thing is–'

'What?'

'I saw her not half an hour since getting into the *Ivy Rose*. She didn't look happy.'

Ivy Rose. Frank Dewar's boat.

'How did Dewar seem?'

'I don't know. I felt something was off but I couldn't put my finger on it.'

'Did you get the feeling she was getting on to Dewar's boat under duress?'

'Well, not at the time but thinking about it now I'm not so sure. I just felt something was a bit off... Jim, what's going on?'

'I'm afraid I can't tell you.'

Thirty minutes later Carruthers, Scott Gardner, Harris, Brown and a handful of uniformed officers were sitting in the RIB. They left Anstruther harbour and once they were in the open water the inflatable picked up speed.

'Can this thing not go any faster?' shouted Carruthers. As it was he was gripping the side of the RIB for dear life. Every time they hit a wave the force almost took him out of his seat. *After twenty minutes of this, my arse is going to be fair sore*, he thought glumly. His face was wet, the tips of his ears were ice cold and his hands were already numb. He hadn't thought about bringing gloves with him. *Just as well I'm wearing waterproofs*, he thought, although he had begrudged the few minutes it had taken to put them on. *Thank God Fletcher's not on here with her bad neck. I don't think she would survive.*

'If we go any faster we'll take off,' remarked Brown.

He stole a sideways glance at a wet Harris who nodded at

him. Rivulets of sea spray were running down the older man's waterproofs but it was his face that interested Carruthers. It was set like a steel trap. They were all thinking the same thing. If Frank Dewar was the killer, would they be in time to save Elaine Morgan? If the man had already killed two people, he wouldn't think twice about killing a third.

'I dinnae see the boat, Jim,' shouted Harris, wiping spray from his face. 'Those fishing boats can go a fair speed and they have at least forty-five minutes on us. It's unlikely we'll catch him. And who's to say he willnae chuck her overboard? He may not even be taking her to the island.'

Cheery thought. Is that what happened to Paterson? Carruthers wondered. *Had he tussled with Frank Dewar and been thrown overboard?* Likelihood was that they would never know what really happened to Paterson unless the killer was prepared to talk.

Carruthers thought about Morgan's chances of still being alive. Surely Dewar would want to know who else Morgan had spoken to. He may even have found out about the meeting with Carruthers. Gossip tended to travel fast in small communities. It might however, work in her favour. Dewar wouldn't kill Morgan until he was satisfied he had found out what she knew and, more importantly, who she'd told. At the very least it might buy her some time. And she was nothing if not astute.

At last the island came into view; the whiteness of the seabird droppings on the impenetrable cliffs looked like ash from a volcanic explosion. All Carruthers could think of was where was the boat? Where was the *Ivy Rose?* Had it even gone to the Isle of May? Maybe it had gone in a totally different direction.

'We haven't passed her. She may have moored the other side of the island.'

If she's there at all.

'There she is!'

The shout went up from Harris. Carruthers' followed the line of the stocky man's arm and right enough there in the sheltered harbour, was the *Ivy Rose* bobbing up and down. Carruthers strained to see if there was any sign of Dewar or Morgan but as they drew closer they saw the boat was empty.

'They could be anywhere on the island.' Being the senior officer Carruthers took charge. 'Right, Harris, I want you and a couple of uniform to go over towards the priory and Pilgrim's Haven. Brown, take a couple of officers and head towards Bishop's Cove.' He turned and addressed his comments to the fit ex-army officer with the head like a bullet. 'Mikey, you come with me. I want to go to the spot where Ramsey was killed. If they're not there we'll make our way to his accommodation.'

Carruthers knew that Morgan wanted to get photos of the crime scene but did she know where on the island the warden had been found dead? He tried to remember the details of their conversation. And where was Frank Dewar likely to take her?

He walked up the jetty away from the boat, being careful not to slip on the wet stone and kept walking towards the visitor centre. Out of the corner of his eye he could see the others fan out silently among the rugged bleakness of the island. They walked for a few minutes. The headwind was in their faces now making conversation difficult and the cries of the seabirds didn't help. Mikey turned round to say something to him but Carruthers shushed him. He had heard another noise. It sounded like the terrified shriek of a woman, but it was hard to tell over the screaming of the birds. Carruthers edged round the side of the wooden hut, finger to lips. There by the edge of the cliffs 200 feet away stood Frank Dewar. He was struggling with Elaine Morgan, whose feet were perilously close to the cliff edge. The wind buffeted her and her blonde hair whipped her face.

Carruthers covered the distance between them. 'Let her go, Frank.'

Elaine Morgan let out another shriek. She dug her heels into the earth and fought Dewar with all her strength. He was sporting a bleeding cut to his cheek where her nails had dug in.

Carruthers moved forward until he was no more than twenty feet away. He could see the terror in the reporter's wide, glassy eyes. 'Step away from the cliff, Frank. Game's up.' There was a glint of steel in Dewar's hand. Carruthers stopped advancing as soon as he saw the knife. The knife that most likely had killed two other people. There was a beep of an incoming text off a mobile. With one hand now clamped round Morgan's throat Dewar struggled to get the phone out of his pocket with the hand that held the knife.

Whatever that text is it's important, thought Carruthers.

There was a shout from Dewar as Morgan struggled free and bit him. He dropped the phone and knife to the ground and, cursing, grabbed Morgan with both hands.

'Ease up, Frank, ease up,' called Carruthers. 'Why did you kill them? Answer me that.' As he spoke he noticed Mikey retreating behind him. No doubt he would be trying to find another way to approach Dewar. A splat of cold rain landed on his head as he tried to edge slowly forwards. 'Paterson was your friend. As you told me yourself, you'd known him for fifty odd years.'

Dewar glanced down at the knife on the ground.

Splat. Another drop of rain. Carruthers looked at the stain on the ground. *I've got to find a way to stop him picking up that knife.* He edged forward a few more steps.

The fisherman was still wrestling with the journalist. 'I didn't want to kill him.'

'He found out how you were making the extra money. It was drugs, wasn't it?'

As he talked Carruthers edged still closer to Dewar. *I have to save Morgan.* A powerful flashback came into his head of the last time he had been in this position. He had been standing in his ex-wife's house and Mairi had been in the grip of the frenzied serial killer, knife at her throat. Morgan was no Mairi and the knife was now on the ground, but even so, Carruthers broke out into a cold sweat.

'Keep back,' shouted Dewar. He advanced a few inches closer to the edge of the dizzying cliff. The drops of rain had now become heavier, darkening the ground.

Morgan had been right all along. It had been drugs-related. If only she had gone to the police rather than take matters into her own hands.

36

A shout went up a bit further away and Dewar was momentarily distracted. Mikey took a run at the fisherman, but not before Dewar stooped down and grabbed his knife, momentarily letting go of Morgan. *For an older boy he's certainly still quick with his reflexes*, thought Carruthers. The journalist took her chance and gave Dewar an almighty shove, but the action somehow unbalanced her and she staggered and tripped on a small rock. All Carruthers could do was watch in horror as, with a scream, she fell over the side of the cliff.

Dewar was now wielding the knife like a madman. Carruthers was desperate to get to the cliff edge to see if anything could be done for Morgan, but he stood his ground. The fisherman appeared to be a man possessed, but Carruthers knew it was a case of self-preservation. Dewar brought the knife down on Mikey, who took a slash to the arm. But the younger, fitter officer wrestled the knife out of the fisherman's hand and pinned him to the ground, his face in the dirt. Dewar's mobile phone beeped again where it lay on the ground. Even from his prostrate position the fisherman tried to grab his phone. Mikey brought his foot down on Dewar's hand, crushing a couple of fingers. Dewar cried out in pain.

Carruthers rushed to the edge of the cliff, as close as he dared go, and leant over. He scanned the rocks and ledges that teemed with seabirds as his eyes desperately sought any signs of Elaine Morgan. His eyes widened as his gaze eventually fell on the lifeless body of the journalist about thirty feet below. She was lying flat on her back on a ledge; her brown tweed skirt had ridden up her legs to expose her thighs. Around her head was a pool of blood and the unnatural angle of her neck confirmed that it was broken. There was nothing anyone could do for her now. The disturbed birds around her squawked and screamed and Carruthers tore his eyes away from the pitiful sight of a mother gull whose babies lay crushed underneath Morgan's body.

Feeling sick he turned his attention back to his fellow officer. 'Mikey, you okay?'

'Just a scratch.'

Carruthers looked over at Mikey whose arm was bleeding heavily. It was a lot more than a scratch but the man would survive. Other officers, alerted by the scream, ran towards them. Carruthers' mobile rang. It was McTavish.

'Jim, what's happening?'

'We've got him, Sandra, but Morgan didn't make it. She's dead.' His words came out in one long gasp.

'Damn.' There was a momentary pause from the DCI. 'Are you okay?'

'Yep. Don't worry about me. I'm fine. Mikey Denning's been injured but it's not life-threatening.'

'Get back to the mainland as soon as you can. Have you got anything out of Dewar yet? Do you think it's drugs? Just to let you know I've had a call from Gus Kerr at the NCA.'

Carruthers was surprised. He thought Kerr would have his hands full plotting the interception of the drugs boat.

'Sources think that the crew of the drugs boat have been in contact with someone local in the Fife area and that they will be trying to set up the location of the drugs drop.'

Carruthers looked down at Dewar who was still on the ground. All the fight seemed to have gone out of the fisherman. He thought about how desperate the man had been to answer his mobile.

'I think the contact could be Frank Dewar.'

'I was just about to say the same. We've already sent officers round to Dewar's house and they've got into his computer. They've recovered what they think is a coded satellite phone email message from the vessel. Get him back into the custody suite as soon as possible. And confiscate his mobile.'

'There's already been one text that's come in on Dewar's mobile in the last few minutes.'

'Any idea who it's from? Is it them?'

'Hang on a sec.' Carruthers stretched across and picked the mobile up from the ground. He wiped it dry on his jacket sleeve. His hands stiff and clumsy with the cold. 'What's your password?'

Dewar remained silent.

'It will be much better for you if you co-operate with the police.' Carruthers thought of the stairlift that the man had organised for his wife. For all his failings he clearly loved her. 'Think of your wife.'

Dewar mumbled the password without looking at the officer.

Carruthers put in the password and scrolled to the last text. 'It's a non-UK number,' he said to McTavish.

'Why would Dewar be receiving a text from outside the UK? That could be the text we're waiting for.'

Suddenly Dewar found his voice. 'I need to answer that text. These people don't mess about. Please.' There was a wheedling note to his voice. 'And they know where I live. They'll go after my wife.'

'Then you had better co-operate with us, hadn't you?' said Carruthers. He read the text. It was a list of co-ordinates and a time. Meaningless unless you knew what you were looking for. He knew what he was reading was the co-ordinates for a location in the North Sea and the time for the pickup. He repeated them to McTavish.

Carruthers listened to McTavish's words. 'That sounds like the co-ordinates we're waiting for. We need to act fast, Jim. If he doesn't answer that message they'll know the game's up and the boat will turn round and go back.'

'Surely they can still be intercepted?'

'I think the NCA wants to intercept the smugglers while they're ditching the drugs in the sea for pickup. And with their AIS navigational beacon switched off... If Dewar wasn't up on a murder charge we'd be looking to offer him a deal. We need the names of the people he's been in contact with.'

Carruthers turned his back to the wind that was starting to pick up again and lowered his voice out of Dewar's hearing as he spoke. The rain was now coming down in sheets. 'He knows he's going to prison for a long time. His biggest worry is what will happen to his wife.'

'She's disabled, isn't she?'

'She's older than him and has mobility problems.'

'Does he have any family as far as you know?'

'No kids. Not sure of nieces or nephews.' At the mention of nieces his thoughts went to Gayle Watson's niece. He hadn't even asked how Watson's sister was doing.

The hard rain bounced off the ground. Carruthers could

hear the excitement in his boss's voice. 'He's got an Achilles heel,' she said. 'Good. We have something to bargain with after all, then. Perhaps we can tell him his wife will be looked after while he's in prison if he gives us what we want.'

37

Two hours later they were back at the station. Carruthers had followed McTavish's instructions and insisted Dewar answer the text message to the drug runners. The police now knew what time the boat was due to arrive at its drop-off point in the North Sea. Unsurprisingly it was the middle of the night. The details had been passed to the NCA.

Carruthers put his head round McTavish's office door. 'His solicitor's arrived. He's in with him now.'

The DCI picked up her notes and they walked together, in silence, to the interview room. McTavish took her seat next to Carruthers. Dewar's shoulders were hunched and his body language told the inspector he knew he was beaten.

Dewar's solicitor was a poker-faced man in his late forties who glanced nervously at his client. As well he might for the evidence against the fisherman was not just overwhelming; the police had already got a confession out of him. Here was a man who was going to go to prison for a very long time, lesser sentence or no lesser sentence. Carruthers looked at the man who, in all likelihood, would die behind bars. He leant over and switched the tape on.

'5pm and present are DCI Sandra McTavish, DI Jim Carruthers, Frank Dewar and his solicitor, Bruce Murray.'

McTavish had made it clear that she wanted to take the lead. *She's more like me than I want to admit.*

'How did you get involved with drugs in the first place?' McTavish asked.

Dewar raised his head. 'The usual way. I got approached in a pub. It started by my just being asked to provide a safe house for the drugs. It was a way of making a bit of extra money. Paterson found out. But by then I was in deeper. I think he already knew that.'

'How did he find out?' Carruthers knew that Robbie Paterson, who had lost his only son to a drug-related suicide, would not turn a blind eye to his friend's involvement.

Dewar glanced at his solicitor who whispered something in his ear. 'He saw me out one night picking up the drugs in the Firth of Forth. They'd been thrown overboard and were attached to a buoy. He'd just started taking his boat out for prawn. I guess what I was doing must have looked suspicious. He confronted me when we were both back on land. He wanted me to turn myself in. I couldn't do that. I knew I'd get a prison sentence. Who would look after my wife?'

McTavish looked over the top of her glasses. 'So what happened?'

'We argued.'

'That's how you got that cut above your eye?' She looked up from her note taking.

Dewar touched it ruefully. 'That happened later. We were on his boat. He got a punch in. But the next punch he threw I dodged and he overbalanced and toppled over.'

'So you're saying his ending up in the water was an accident?'

'Yes, of course. I never set out to kill him. He was my friend.'

So it had been an accident after all. 'How did you get to be on Paterson's boat in the first place?'

Carruthers sat quietly taking notes and let McTavish ask the questions. He watched Dewar carefully.

'He said that he was going to go to the police after his fishing trip that night. I told him I needed to speak with him. I met him down at the harbour. I suggested I get on the boat and go with him. I was going to try to get him to change his mind. But then when we got close to the May we argued.'

'And then it turned physical.' It wasn't a question. It was a statement.

Carruthers looked up from his note taking before he spoke. 'You thought the island was empty; that everyone was on the mainland; that there would be no witnesses,' he said.

Dewar was defensive. 'I never set out to kill him.'

Carruthers glanced at McTavish who gave him the nod to continue. 'You didn't know Ramsey had decided to stay behind, did you? Or that you had been seen as you fought with Paterson?'

'After Paterson fell overboard I glanced up and saw Ramsey looking through his binoculars. Must have seen them in the glint of the sun. I knew he'd witnessed the fight and seen Paterson falling overboard.'

You knew he could identify you, thought Carruthers.

Falling overboard or being pushed overboard? We'll never know now. Dewar was clearly going to stick to his story of it being an accident and the only witness to the skirmish was now dead.

'Let's take a coffee break. We'll continue the interview in thirty minutes.' McTavish leant over and switched the tape off.

McTavish took up the reins once more. 'Frank, you've told us in your own words what happened the day Robbie Paterson died.'

Dewar kept his head down and mumbled a response.

'Please speak clearly for the benefit of the tape.'

'I didn't set out to kill Robbie. I've already said that.'

'We know that. But the warden of the Isle of May was stabbed thirteen times in what can only be described as a frenzied attack. Yet you hardly knew him?'

Bruce Murray leant over and whispered something else in his client's ear. Dewar remained silent with his head bent.

'Tom Ramsey's family have a right to know what happened to him.' McTavish's voice was like steel. 'Not only do they have a right to know; they need to know so they can move forward with their lives.'

Murray shot a warning glance at Dewar but Dewar shook his head at his solicitor. 'I want to talk.' He looked up at the officers. 'You're right. I hardly knew Ramsey but he'd seen the fight.'

'Is this the fight on board the *Maid of the Mist*?'

'That's right.'

'And you knew he could identify you?'

'I thought there was a good chance. Yes.'

'But you had nothing against him?'

'No.'

So his murder wasn't personal, thought Carruthers. *Ramsey was just in the wrong place at the wrong time.* Hadn't Ramsey's parents said the same thing – that their son had been in the wrong place at the wrong time?

Dewar looked from his solicitor to the two detectives. 'I couldn't afford for him to identify me. And I knew I had to go through with the pickup.'

'This is the pickup from the *Asante Sana*?' McTavish referred to her own notebook as she spoke.

Dewar nodded.

'Please answer yes or no for the purposes of the tape, Frank.'

'Yes. I couldn't let Ramsey live. Surely you can see that?'

'You say that you had to go through with the pickup?' McTavish looked at Dewar through narrowed eyes. 'What would have happened if you hadn't?'

'These aren't people you say "no" to. They would have killed me,' he said simply.

'You still haven't explained why you stabbed Ramsey thirteen times?'

'I had to make it look like a frenzied attack from some nutter.'

It was all about self-preservation, thought Carruthers, disgusted. He was feeling sick to the pit of his stomach. They had been wrong about Ramsey's murder. It hadn't been a crime of passion at all. The murder had been cold and calculating. And now Dewar had confessed perhaps he felt he was safer in prison, although even that wasn't a certainty.

A thought crept into Carruthers' head. 'Did you smash the webcams on the island?'

Dewar nodded. 'I wanted to throw you off the scent. Confuse you.'

He'd done that, thought Carruthers. The smashed webcams had made it look as if the murder had been carefully premeditated yet the frenzied nature of the attack smacked of the perpetrator losing all semblance of control.

'Once Paterson found out about your involvement he was always going to try to stop you, wasn't he? He lost his own son through drug-taking.'

'His son committed suicide.'

'We've spoken with Mary Paterson,' said Carruthers. 'Her son's suicide happened after his life spiralled into addiction. He was a happy boy until he got mixed up in drugs. According to Mrs Paterson heroin changed him from an outgoing boy to someone withdrawn and unhappy. Did you know that repeated heroin abuse changes the brain? And that there is a strong relationship between addiction and suicide? Criminals like you are responsible for the death of countless people.'

A flicker of emotion crossed Dewar's face. The fisherman clearly didn't want to be forced to think through the consequences of his actions, but Carruthers wanted him to face what he had done.

'One of our officers has just lost a niece to drugs. Heroin.' He pushed the words out, although it was difficult. 'Her niece was seventeen years old and about to go to beauty school. Seventeen. How does her family come to terms with that young woman's death?'

There was no answer from Frank Dewar. Instead he looked down at his feet.

38

'Are you going to the brief? It's about to start.'

Carruthers' eyes widened. 'Brief?' He looked up from his desk to see Fletcher staring down at him.

'Didn't you get the memo?'

Carruthers quickly skimmed his emails on his open computer. 'It's not there.'

'I did hear there have been IT problems this morning. Apparently not all the emails are getting through.'

Thank God for that. I'm not as spaced out as I thought. Having been up most of the night waiting on McTavish's call about the interception, he was exhausted. However, despite his fatigue and the fact it was Saturday, he, like the rest of the team didn't want to miss seeing the results of their investigation.

He hurriedly stood up, took up a notepad and pen and followed Fletcher out of the office. The incident room was already full but Carruthers was surprised to notice that Helen Lennox was missing. He squeezed into a seat at the back near Superintendent Bingham. The man managed a nod in his direction. Having heard about his decision to retire later that year

Carruthers was treating him as if he had gone already. And to be fair, Bingham was taking even more of a back seat than usual. Carruthers felt he was dumping far too much on McTavish's shoulders. He slapped the notebook down on the table in front of him and watched as their DCI walked up to the front of the incident room and started the brief.

'We're going to start the brief with some good news.' There was a sparkle in McTavish's eyes as she spoke. 'We had word at 4am this morning that Border Force intercepted and arrested the drug smugglers on the *Asante Sana* just after they dumped a massive haul of heroin in the North Sea.'

A huge cheer went up and Harris, who had just appeared in the room with a coffee, clapped Brown on his back before taking his seat. He mouthed a sorry to McTavish. She smiled at him. Any other time she would have given him a ticking off for his tardiness but today everyone was in a good mood.

Carruthers could only imagine what a huge international operation this had been involving not just Police Scotland but also Border Force and the Royal Navy. He was only sorry he hadn't been able to participate in it.

'What sort of amount are we talking about?' Brown asked.

McTavish's smile was nothing short of Cheshire cat. 'One of the largest amounts in UK history. Fifty-five million. In fact it might be the biggest.'

There were whistles all round. Carruthers knew that the amount was bigger even than the haul from the *MV Hamal*.

'Apparently the heroin was in blocks weighing 2.2lbs. They were sealed in containers and dumped in the sea attached to buoys.'

'Think of all the lives that have been saved,' said Harris. There were smiles and whoops but Carruthers knew that they were all thinking of at least one life that nobody had been able to save – that of Gayle Watson's niece.

'Do we know how Gayle's sister is doing?' Fletcher asked.

'She's still in hospital but much better. She's going to pull through. And Gayle will be back at work tomorrow.'

There were sighs of relief all round.

'I do have a bit more bad news to give you, unfortunately,' McTavish continued. 'You'll have noticed that Helen Lennox isn't with us for the debrief. The reporter who was killed, Elaine Morgan, was her cousin so she's understandably upset.'

Carruthers' eyes widened in surprise. He had had no idea. Another thought entered his head. Could it have been Lennox who had leaked the information about the drugs haul to Morgan? It had to be. He bit his lip.

'She'll be in work later this morning. I've got a meeting set up with her but I thought it only fair to warn you so you don't put your foot in it.'

Carruthers was so busy thinking about Lennox he struggled to process the rest of the debrief. He just caught snatches. They had their man on the ground safely in custody. In a bid for a lighter sentence Frank Dewar had agreed to co-operate fully with the police and had given them the names of everyone he had been communicating with. It had included a couple of locals.

'I still can't believe Dewar would get into drug smuggling when his oldest friend had lost a son to suicide through his drug addiction,' he heard Fletcher say.

'He got greedy,' said Carruthers. 'He wanted to make easy money. In the end it was anything but easy. He got in way over his head and once these people have you in their clutches they won't let go.'

McTavish looked up from her notes. 'And the final piece of news to give you is that Tom Ramsey's boat has been found over at Ruby Bay by a member of the public. I believe the woman who called it in was out having a picnic with her daughter.'

Carruthers pictured Ruby Bay near the village of Elie, so named due to a ship from the Spanish Armada having run off course and capsized there. Its spilled cargo had been rubies. Or so the story went. *So the boat has been found nine miles away from the Isle of May.*

39

The brief broke up. Fletcher stood up, gathered her paperwork and walked back to the open-plan office. She sat at her desk looking at her phone before picking it up and calling Lennox on her mobile.

Fletcher was nervous. She hated giving apologies but it had to be done. She had behaved badly. The younger officer answered her mobile almost immediately. She sounded subdued. Fletcher ploughed on. 'Helen, we've just had our debrief and Sandra told me about Elaine Morgan being your cousin. I'm so sorry for your loss.'

Lennox mumbled a response. 'Thank you. I've actually just arrived at the car park. I'll see you in a few minutes.' She cut the call.

Fletcher waited for Lennox to walk into the office. She took in the younger woman's blotchy face and knew she had had a good cry on her way to work. She really didn't know how to start such a difficult conversation. In the end she just jumped in. 'Look, I know you're dealing with a bereavement so sorry if this is bad timing but I'll come straight to the point. I hear you've put in for a transfer.'

Lennox nodded.

'I have a big apology to make to you, Helen. I wasn't fair on you.' Fletcher pushed on. 'You're right in that you weren't given a fair opportunity to shine. And it's not Sandra McTavish's fault. It's mine. I'm going to take full responsibility for it.' Fletcher swallowed the lump down in her throat. She hated to admit to any sort of failing but felt what she said next was important. 'I felt threatened by you.'

Lennox's mouth dropped open. Whatever she had been expecting Fletcher to say, it clearly wasn't this. '*You* felt threatened by *me*? But we're a different rank.'

'Yes, I did. I was the same when Gayle Watson arrived at the station.'

Lennox looked doubtful.

'Seriously, I was. Just ask her. I made her life hell.'

Lennox managed a half smile.

'What I'm trying to say is I think you should stay here. You're part of the team and we'll all help you towards becoming a DS if that's what you want.'

Lennox's face finally visibly relaxed. 'It is.'

'Look, I was really impressed by your interviewing skills down in Bristol. It made me realise that we never really gave you a chance. In fact, it was Jim who told me what my behaviour towards you was like. So if you want to thank anyone, thank him.'

'I know I can sometimes be annoying.' Lennox's voice was quiet. 'My own family tell me. I do have a habit of interrupting. I'm going to try to work on that.'

'I think we all have annoying habits,' said Fletcher, smiling. 'I happen to be too nosy for my own good.' As she said that she wondered if Carruthers had set up another meeting with his ex-wife. *Well,* she thought, *at least Lennox has some self-aware-ness after all.* Perhaps things would improve but in order for them to do so they all had to play their part. It wasn't just up to Lennox. She left her junior colleague and went to find Carruthers.

She spotted him coming out of McTavish's office. 'Jim, look, I just wanted you to know I've made my peace with Helen.' She hesitated for a moment. 'I know it's none of my business but I just wondered, now all this is over, if you were going to catch up with your ex-wife?'

Carruthers thought about this for a moment. He placed a hand on Fletcher's shoulder. 'Actually, no. She hasn't been back in touch and I've decided to let sleeping dogs lie. If it's important she'll get back to me.'

With his hand still on Fletcher's shoulder he steered her towards their open-plan office. 'Now stop looking for things to gossip about and go and do some work.'

The look Fletcher threw him over her shoulder was one of amusement.

Though he had told Fletcher he wasn't going to contact Mairi, he had actually decided to find a quiet place and give her a ring after all. Now the investigation was over he was curious to know why she had been trying to contact him. And as for Fletcher, from now on he would tell her things on a need-to-know basis – and she really didn't need to know whether he was going to contact his ex.

Carruthers caught up with Lennox. 'Helen, can I have a word before you go in to see Sandra?' He knew it wasn't his place to ask her about her cousin but he couldn't help himself. He lowered his voice. 'I need to know something. Did you tip Elaine Morgan off about the drugs shipment coming into Fife on the *Asante Sana*?'

Lennox looked at him sadly. 'I wouldn't do that... although–'

'What?'

'I took my police notebook home with me and my mum had

Elaine over for dinner. I'm wondering if she sneaked a peek when I was doing the washing up.'

As she spoke Lennox looked both troubled and upset.

For some reason Carruthers believed her. He wondered if she still lived with her family. It wasn't uncommon these days due to the housing shortage.

'Why didn't you tell us your cousin was a reporter?'

Lennox bit her lip. 'Look, I knew how important getting a scoop was for Elaine. I also knew how the paper were treating her... She's done a lot for me and my family – financially I mean.' Tears shone in her eyes. 'But that doesn't mean I would jeopardise the operation. I've worked really hard to become a detective.'

Carruthers didn't doubt Lennox had worked hard but he wondered how McTavish would see it.

'There's something else,' Lennox continued. 'The last station I was at, I told my colleagues about having a crime reporter as a cousin and it was a big mistake. Two of them started to bully me and in the end it became so unbearable I had to leave.'

That went some way to explaining why Lennox was so prickly. And why she hadn't said anything.

Carruthers was starting to feel sorry for the younger detective. It sounded like she had been seriously conflicted and life clearly hadn't been easy at her last place of work. He wondered how much pressure Morgan had put on her for information.

He knew the relationship between the police and crime reporters had definitely become a strained one since the Leveson enquiry, the judicial public enquiry which, in part, had examined the relationship between the police and newspapers following the phone hacking scandal. The change in police practice had resulted in crime reporters often accusing the police of giving them very little and police officers being nervous about making contact with journalists.

However, whichever way you looked at it Lennox was in trouble. He knew that unless she could convince the DCI she hadn't tipped her cousin off there would be a huge cloud hanging over her head, and not just for her future at Edenside CID but also her future in Police Scotland.

'Try not to worry, Helen. I believe you.'

'Thank you. That means a lot.'

Carruthers left an emotional looking Helen Lennox and walked back to the office. He decided he would put in a good word for her. After all, God knows, he'd made enough mistakes in his career. He hesitated for a fraction of a second. As he opened the door he heard the raucous noise of celebration and a cork pop.

THE END

ACKNOWLEDGEMENTS

There are many people I would like to thank who have helped make this book possible. First, as ever, my thanks go to my publisher, Bloodhound Books, for offering me a second book deal. Thanks also to my editor, Clare Law, and publicist, Heather Fitt.

I knew very little about the Scottish fishing industry when I started writing the storyline and, like all my books, I spent a great deal of time doing research for it. I had invaluable help from one of the crew of the *May Princess*, Scott Gardner. He went above and beyond and I'm most grateful. By way of thanks, I make him a character in the book. Roy Giles, who skippers the RIB (rigidly inflatable boat), was really helpful in answering my questions on the boat over to the May and my thanks also go to several fishermen whom I accosted with my friend Caroline Young in a pub in Anstruther! We also popped into the Scottish Fisheries Museum and they too were most helpful and informative. If there are any factual inaccuracies, I hope you can overlook them for the sake of the story! Finally, a big thank you to our wonderful East Neuk of Fife fish merchant, John Kerr, who pops over to Edinburgh to sell his mouth-watering fish. Another gent I accosted with my questions.

Huge thanks to the warden of the Isle of May, David Steel, who was brilliant in answering my questions and allowed me to look round his accommodation on the island so I could better describe it. I must make it clear that the character in the book in no way resembles him. All my characters are purely fictitious.

I can't even begin to thank all our wonderful book bloggers. Special thanks go to Dee Groocock, Craig Gillan, Livia Sbarbaro, Alfred Nobile, Lynsey Adams and Kelly Lacey. I'm also not sure where I would be without the help from my first readers: Alison Baillie, Sarah Torr, Jackie McLean, Simon Clarke, Helen Barrow, Neet Neilson and Craig Gillan. They sacrificed their time in order to read and comment on the book and it can be a huge undertaking. Also thanks go to my partner, Ian Brown, for his suggestions and plot ideas!

Can I also say a big 'thank you' to you, my readers, for investing in the series. If you have enjoyed this book, please consider leaving a brief review on Amazon or Goodreads. Reviews and sales ensure continuation of a series and are vitally important.

If you would like to know more about me or my books, I have a website at tanacollins.com and can be found on Twitter @TanaCollins7